JUNIOR CYCLE FIRST YEAR ENGLIS

FIRE AND ICE

1

PAULINE KELLY • DEIRDRE MURPHY

TOMÁS SEALE • MARY-ELAINE TYNAN

GILL EDUCATION

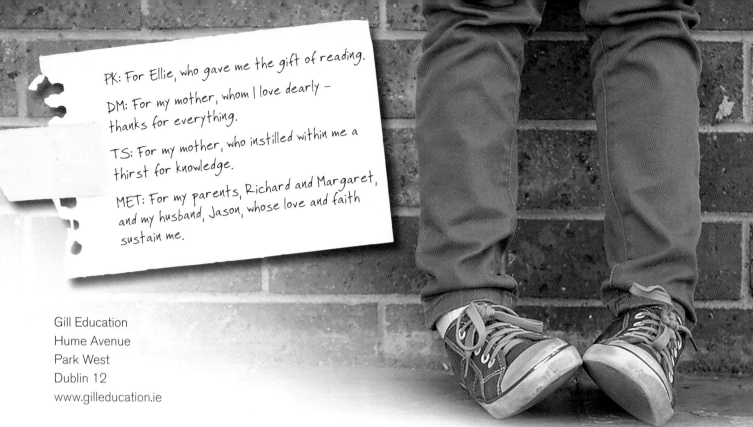

PK: For Ellie, who gave me the gift of reading.

DM: For my mother, whom I love dearly – thanks for everything.

TS: For my mother, who instilled within me a thirst for knowledge.

MET: For my parents, Richard and Margaret, and my husband, Jason, whose love and faith sustain me.

Gill Education
Hume Avenue
Park West
Dublin 12
www.gilleducation.ie

Gill Education is an imprint of M.H. Gill & Co.

© Pauline Kelly, Deirdre Murphy, Tomás Seale and Mary-Elaine Tynan 2016

ISBN: 978-0-7171-69580

Design and layout: Anú Design (www.anu-design.ie)
Cover design: Martin O'Brien
Illustrations: Derry Dillon and Brian Fitzgerald
Audio recording: Millbrook Studios

At the time of going to press, all web addresses were active and contained information relevant to the topics in this book. Gill Education does not, however, accept responsibility for the content or views contained on these websites. Content, views and addresses may change beyond the publisher or author's control. Students should always be supervised when reviewing websites.

The paper used in this book is made from the wood pulp of managed forests.
For every tree felled, at least one tree is planted, thereby renewing natural resources.

Contents

Introduction

Fire and Ice 1 is a first-year textbook designed to meet all the requirements of the new **Junior Cycle English Specification**. There are thirty-nine learning outcomes in the Specification across the three strands: **Oral Language (OL)**, **Reading (R)**, and **Writing (W)**. A subset of twenty-two learning outcomes for First Year has been highlighted to take account of and to provide for continuity with learning in primary education.

In line with the Specification, *Fire and Ice, Books 1* and *2* ensure that over the three years of Junior Cycle, students have a wide and varied experience of texts that **stimulate, engage, inspire and challenge**. Each chapter, or 'collection', is **based around a theme**: a variety of texts is given for each theme, allowing for a contextual approach to teaching and learning.

Engagement with texts is central to the development of language and literacy. The *Fire and Ice* series uses a wide variety of texts — **oral, aural, written, visual, digital, multi-modal** – in the lessons.

With the new emphasis on the development of oral language, the *Fire and Ice* series places a strong focus on **oral proficiency**, including the vital importance of learning through oral language.

Using this Book

The **learning outcomes** are referenced for the teacher at the beginning of each collection. These have been translated into easy-to-follow **spidergrams** for the student. All twenty-two learning outcomes for first year are taught (several times) in the book.

SHOW WHAT YOU KNOW
The skills you learn in this collection will enable you to **show what you know** in your final tasks at the end of this collection.

For my portfolio task I will:
Write an informal letter/email to a new friend

For oral communication I will:
Speak for one minute to introduce myself

Students are then shown the **summative written task and oral communication** that they are working towards in the collection. The learning in each collection has been carefully designed to scaffold the students toward these tasks to ensure the greatest chance of success.

What I will learn:

to use adjectives and verbs; to state and explain my opinion about my experience in a new school; to use the five senses to describe something

Every lesson has a strong AfL focus, beginning with a student-friendly skills-based learning intention, **'What I will learn'** to involve the learner in the whole process of learning and assessment.

SHOW WHAT YOU KNOW

Each collection culminates in **written tasks and oral communication** that prepares the student for assessment.

These activities are scaffolded with clear **success criteria** to prompt the student to fully address the task and to encourage self- and peer-assessment and assist students in their reflection notes.

SUCCESS CRITERIA

I must
- Write a draft of what I'm going to say, using paragraphs (around four), with one main point per paragraph
- Consider my audience – make it interesting but not too serious
- Include basic information about myself (name, age, family and hobbies)
- Describe myself (my personality)
- Practise reading it aloud and ensure it lasts for around one minute

I should
- Tell them a little-known fact about myself
- Tell them about my dreams or hopes for the future
- Include some powerful verbs and interesting adjectives
- Use the speaking tips from p. 2

I could
- Tell them an anecdote (true story) about myself to give them an insight into my personality
- Use humour
- Tell them what other people would say about me

Throughout the book you will see various easy-to-follow symbols:

Other features to help the student in Fire and Ice 1*:*

Prepare

This section precedes texts, using AfL strategies to encourage students to explore their prior knowledge and to predict before they read/listen/watch.

Mind Your Language

These sections concentrate on the nuts and bolts of language – grammar, punctuation, spelling, etc.

Remember

Something the student has come across before in the book that will help here.

PIE

The **PIE** symbol appears wherever this strategy will help the student to answer a question, prompting them to fully develop their points by illustrating and explaining them.

The 5Ws

Reminds the student to ask 'who', 'what', 'where', 'when' and 'why' when reading an article or watching a news clip.

Research Zone

Students are prompted to go beyond the textbook to research a topic or theme.

Additional ideas for teachers:

Audio Available

When the aural symbol appears without the word 'Listen', it indicates that the poem or piece of prose is available to listen to in the ebook (and on www.gillexplore.ie for teachers), though it's not integral to a lesson.

Groupwork/Pairwork

These symbols appear within any of the other sections as a methodology within them.

Think Pair Share

This activity encourages higher-order thinking that involves students thinking individually, then pairing with a partner, then sharing ideas with the wider group.

Worksheet

This symbol appears where there is a suitable (photocopiable) worksheet for the lesson.

Note on film/video: Wherever possible, film/video has been embedded within the ebook for offline use. This is indicated by the 👁 and 🎧 icons. Where permission was unavailable, or where there is audio/digital material that will be of further interest to students, we have directed you to a source on **You Tube**. Students will need to be online to play YouTube clips. A full listing of all YouTube clips and links is available on GillExplore.ie.

New Beginnings

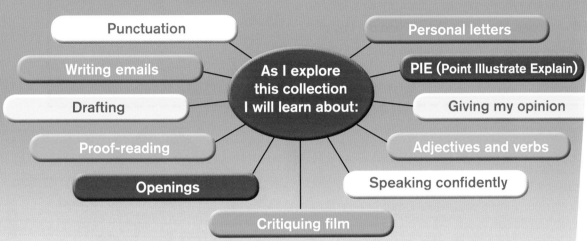

As I explore this collection I will learn about:

- Punctuation
- Writing emails
- Drafting
- Proof-reading
- Openings
- Critiquing film
- Personal letters
- PIE (Point Illustrate Explain)
- Giving my opinion
- Adjectives and verbs
- Speaking confidently

SHOW WHAT YOU KNOW

The skills you learn in this collection will enable you to **show what you know** in your final tasks at the end of this collection.

For my portfolio task I will:
Write an informal letter/email to a new friend

For oral communication I will:
Speak for one minute to introduce myself

WELCOME TO FIRST YEAR ENGLISH!

This is the beginning of your time as a secondary school English student, so welcome! For most students it is both exciting and daunting. It always takes time to settle into a new place, especially if you've come from a small primary school and your new secondary school is huge by comparison. Even if you *are* used to lots of other pupils, it takes time to adjust to a new place with new teachers, new schoolmates, new classrooms, new subjects – new **everything**!

Before we set off on our journey into English, it is a good idea to think about your strengths and weaknesses in the subject. Write down what you like about English, what you find difficult about it and what you want to learn. Put this into your **portfolio**. You can look at it again in a few months to see how you have progressed. Here's an example:

In English, I really like	I find it difficult to	I really want to
reading	understand punctuation	be able to write an exciting story

Learning Outcomes
OL1, OL2, R3, R10, R13, W4, W5, W11

Exploring the Theme – New Beginnings

Two Truths and a Lie

As you may not know everybody in your class very well, let's do an **'ICE-BREAKER'** exercise. Hopefully you will find out lots of things about the other students in your English class, so you will all get to know each other a little better.

Write down **three statements** about yourself. Two must be **true** and one must be **false**. You don't need to say anything too private, but make your statements as interesting as possible. For example:

* ✻ I can speak four languages.
* ✻ I am a vegetarian.
* ✻ I have represented my country in fencing.

Working with someone you don't know very well, look at each other's statements. Guess which two are true and which one is false.

Tell each other the truth and elaborate (explain) a little on what you have written. Write down the two facts and the one lie about your partner and then double-check that you have it right.

Each pair will now stand up and take it in turns to introduce their partner to the class by reading out the three statements, indicating which two are true and which one is a fib.

Speaking Tips

* Try not to read your speech straight off the page – just glance at your **key words** (your most important words) and then look back up toward your audience.

* You don't need to look directly at your audience – find something in front of you that is at eye-level and look at that.

* Speak slowly and clearly.

* Smile – it gives a more positive impression and makes the audience want to smile back at you!

Hi, my name is Eoin, and this is Halina. She can speak four languages: English, Irish, Polish and French. Her name means 'light'. She has never represented her country in fencing – that was a lie!

Hello. I'm Halina and this is Eoin. I've learned that Eoin has six pets and that he broke his leg skiing last year. He also told me that he is a vegetarian but this wasn't true – he loves hamburgers too much!

WRITE

Working in pairs again, you have **five minutes** to write down as many facts as you can remember about as many students in the class as possible. You get **two points** for every correct fact. See who gets the most points!

A Poem

What I will learn:

to use adjectives and verbs; to state and explain my opinion about my experience in a new school; to use the five senses to describe something

PREPARE

Now that you know a little more about your classmates, it is time to think about the differences between your old primary school and your new secondary school.

For most students, the first few months of first year is a daunting time because of all the changes involved: lots of unfamiliar teachers; many new subjects; heavier books; and, of course, different faces.

Working with another partner (somebody else you don't know very well), discuss your old school and new school. When you are describing it, try to use at least two **adjectives** in your description.

Adjectives *n.*

Definition: a describing word, telling us more about a noun, e.g. the teachers who are *unfamiliar*, the subjects that are *new*, the books that are *heavier*, and the faces that are *different*

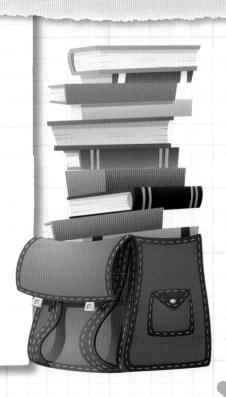

Compare and Contrast using a Venn Diagram

Now show the similarities and differences (also known as to **compare** and **contrast**) between your old school and your new one using a Venn diagram. A Venn diagram is usually used in Maths and is a really easy way to show things in common and differences. Unique features of your old school go into the left circle, unique features of your new school go into the right circle, and the things they have in common go into the centre, where the two circles overlap.

VENN DIAGRAM

Old School

New School

Things in common

Think about your first day in your new school and make a list of the things you noticed: what you saw, heard, smelled, tasted and touched. Do you recognise that list? It is the **five senses** – sight, sound, smell, taste and touch. Make a note of all these experiences.

Now that you have thought about your own experience in a new school, here's another 'school' of thought on the subject (did you get the play on words – that's called a **pun**). The poem you will now read, by John Walsh, describes a young boy's experience on his first day in a new school, and is written from his perspective.

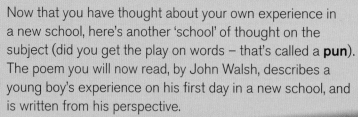

The New Boy

by John Walsh

The door swung inward. I stood and breathed
The new-school atmosphere.
The smell of polish and disinfectant,
And the flavour of my own fear.

I followed into the cloakroom; the walls
Rang to the shattering noise
Of boys who barged and boys who banged;
Boys and still more boys!

A boot flew by me. Its angry owner
Pursued with force and yell;
Somewhere a man snapped orders; somewhere
There clanged a warning bell.

And there I hung with my new school mates;
They pushing and shoving me; I
Unknown, unwanted, pinned to the wall;
On the verge of ready-to-cry.

Then from the doorway a boy called out:
'Hey, you over there! You're new!
Don't just stand there propping the wall up!
I'll look after you!'

I turned; I timidly raised my eyes;
He stood and grinned meanwhile;
And my fear died, and my lips answered
Smile for his smile.

He showed me the basins, the rows of pegs;
He hung my cap at the end;
He led me away to my new classroom ...
And now that boy's my friend.

1. Write a summary of this poem in thirty words or fewer starting with, 'This is a poem about …'

2. You will notice there is a rhyming scheme in the poem, because the last words of the second and fourth lines in each stanza rhyme. Make a list of all the rhyming words.

Stanza n.
Definition: a group of lines in a poem, usually separated from other stanzas by a space; similar to verses in a song. Stanzas sometimes have the same rhyming scheme.

3. In the second and third stanzas, the poet describes the noise of the school. Choose three words which, in your opinion, convey the noise most powerfully.

4. The poem describes how this experience impacted on the new boy's senses. Make a list of the things the boy saw, heard, smelled, touched and tasted.

5. Compare and contrast your first day in school with the new boy's experiences. You can do this by using a Venn diagram.

The poet uses powerful imagery to convey the boy's feelings. Choose one image that you liked and draw it, labelling it with quotes from the poem.

Working in pairs, continue the conversation from the poem by doing a role play. Imagine that one of you is the new boy in the poem and one is his new friend (or alternatively the new girl and her new friend). Spend one minute planning and then do an **improvised dialogue** between you. The dialogue should last between one and two minutes. The dialogue will start with these lines from the poem but it doesn't need to rhyme.

TOP TIP

A dialogue is a conversation between two or more people (usually as featured in a book, play or film). An improvised dialogue is one which is spontaneous and unscripted – you just make it up on the spot.

Hey, you over there! You're new!/ Don't just stand there propping the wall up!/ I'll look after you! …

VERBS

Strong verbs and adjectives help you to create powerful images. An image is a description which appeals to the reader's senses (sight, hearing, touch, taste and smell). You have already learned how to use adjectives. In primary school you learned about verbs – do you remember what they are?

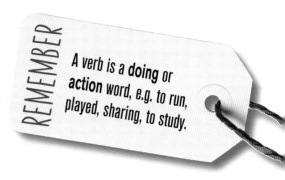

REMEMBER

A verb is a *doing* or *action* word, e.g. to run, played, sharing, to study.

How do we make verbs work harder? By choosing the most accurate verb. Identify the verbs in these sentences.

The tractor drove down the road		The tractor bounced down the road
He kicked the ball into the net		He smashed the ball into the net
The cat drank its milk		The cat lapped up its milk

Now, do you see a difference between these three sentences? By using a specific verb you can paint a much clearer picture for the reader. For example, you can really 'see' a big old tractor bouncing down a country road!

Now in your copy, rewrite the following sentences by replacing the highlighted verbs with more powerful or specific verbs.

1. The dog **ran** down the road behind the car.
2. Ms O'Reilly **looked** at Andrejz.
3. John **ate** his dinner before training.
4. As Mr McDonagh **spoke** to the class, Oisín **played** with his phone under the desk.
5. Marcus **looked** at his watch, **put** his laptop into the bag and left the room.

Working with another student, identify the most powerful verbs and adjectives in this description.

❛ He slumped heavily against the crumbling stone wall and gulped a salty tear while she marched away without a backward glance. ❜

Imagine what happened immediately before and after the moment described.

AS EASY AS PIE!

What I will learn:

to express and support my opinions using PIE

When we read a poem or a book, when we see a play or a film, when we listen to a song or radio programme, we often want to talk to other people about it and tell them what we think. We might have varying opinions about the experience, but if you want to express an opinion, it is always best to be able to back up your point with an example or even a quote and to explain yourself properly.

Sometimes it can be difficult to know how to explain yourself clearly, so it is useful to have a trick to remind yourself how to do this. The PIE acronym is a good one to use because, well, it's as easy as pie (and who doesn't like pie?).

Acronym *n.*

Definition: an abbreviation formed from the first letter of other words and pronounced as a word, e.g. PIE!

The acronym **PIE** stands for **Point-Illustrate-Explain**

When you use **PIE**, you:

1. Make your **POINT**

2. **ILLUSTRATE** your point (give an example), e.g. by using a quote

3. **EXPLAIN** the relationship between your point and the example, and how you feel about it

  in Action

Question: Do you think that the poem, 'The New Boy', is easy to understand?

Answer: Yes, I found 'The New Boy' very easy to understand **because the poet uses clear and effective phrases like 'I stood and breathed/The new school atmosphere'.** This simple language paints a very clear image of the poet's experience as he enters the front door. I was surprised by this because I always thought that poetry was difficult to understand.

Now try it out yourself. Name one thing you liked or didn't like about the poem 'The New Boy'. Explain your answer using PIE.

I liked/didn't like the poem, 'The New Boy', **because** ... For example, this is highlighted in the poem when the poet says ... I think that ...

P   POINT

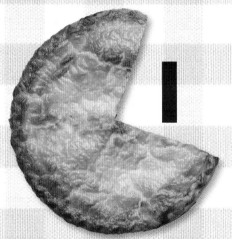

I   ILLUSTRATE

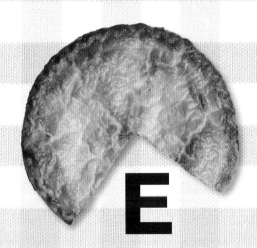

E   EXPLAIN

Every time you see [P I E] next to a question, remember that you need to make your **Point**, give an **Illustration** (example) of your point, and **Explain** the relationship between your point and the example you've chosen.

Emails and Personal Letters

What I will learn:

the structure of a personal (informal) letter and an email

'The New Boy' described one young person's feelings about their first day in a new school. There are many other ways the writer could have expressed his feelings. For example, he could have written in his journal, or perhaps written a short story, or maybe penned a letter or typed an email to a friend.

 READ

Read this email from an Irish boy, James, to his friend, Conor, describing his first day in secondary school. Pay attention to the different elements of an email, and as you read it, think about how James's experience in his new school differs from or is similar to your own.

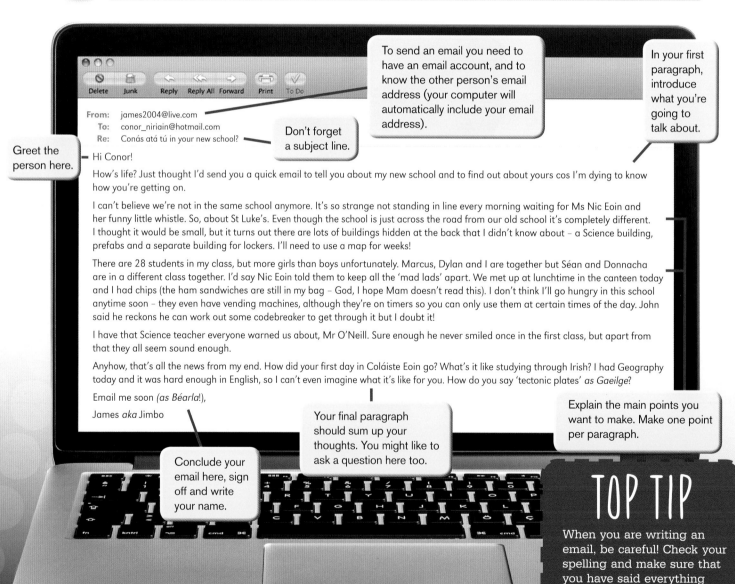

To send an email you need to have an email account, and to know the other person's email address (your computer will automatically include your email address).

In your first paragraph, introduce what you're going to talk about.

Don't forget a subject line.

Greet the person here.

From: james2004@live.com
To: conor_niriain@hotmail.com
Re: Conás atá tú in your new school?

Hi Conor!

How's life? Just thought I'd send you a quick email to tell you about my new school and to find out about yours cos I'm dying to know how you're getting on.

I can't believe we're not in the same school anymore. It's so strange not standing in line every morning waiting for Ms Nic Eoin and her funny little whistle. So, about St Luke's. Even though the school is just across the road from our old school it's completely different. I thought it would be small, but it turns out there are lots of buildings hidden at the back that I didn't know about – a Science building, prefabs and a separate building for lockers. I'll need to use a map for weeks!

There are 28 students in my class, but more girls than boys unfortunately. Marcus, Dylan and I are together but Séan and Donnacha are in a different class together. I'd say Nic Eoin told them to keep all the 'mad lads' apart. We met up at lunchtime in the canteen today and I had chips (the ham sandwiches are still in my bag – God, I hope Mam doesn't read this). I don't think I'll go hungry in this school anytime soon – they even have vending machines, although they're on timers so you can only use them at certain times of the day. John said he reckons he can work out some codebreaker to get through it but I doubt it!

I have that Science teacher everyone warned us about, Mr O'Neill. Sure enough he never smiled once in the first class, but apart from that they all seem sound enough.

Anyhow, that's all the news from my end. How did your first day in Coláiste Eoin go? What's it like studying through Irish? I had Geography today and it was hard enough in English, so I can't even imagine what it's like for you. How do you say 'tectonic plates' *as Gaeilge*?

Email me soon *(as Béarla!)*,

James *aka* Jimbo

Your final paragraph should sum up your thoughts. You might like to ask a question here too.

Explain the main points you want to make. Make one point per paragraph.

Conclude your email here, sign off and write your name.

TOP TIP

When you are writing an email, be careful! Check your spelling and make sure that you have said everything you want to say and nothing you don't! Once you press 'Send,' you can't take it back. As the saying goes, 'Act in haste, repent at leisure'.

44 Main Street
Birr
Co Offaly
29 August 2016

Your address here

Date here

Greeting here and the name of the person you're writing to

Hiya Jimbo,

Quick introduction (thank them for their letter or refer to the reason that you're writing)

Thanks for the email yesterday. Apologies for the snail mail reply (you're probably rolling on the floor in shock) but I've been banned from using the computer for a week (more on that later). I was dying to tell you all about my new school so I thought I'd write you a letter and get my mam to drop it down on her way to yoga tonight. I'd come down myself but I'm grounded as well as being banned from the computer.

Main purpose of the letter or the bulk of the information goes here

So what happened for my social life to come to such a grinding halt? Two words – my sister! Today was my first day in school and even though we're completely banned from speaking English in every class (except English), everybody says a few words at break-time when the teachers aren't around to hear us. Even though I really didn't mean to, I didn't know what to do when Mícheál O'Riain spoke to me in English in the queue for the tuck shop. I was in such shock that a third year knew my name (he said I should definitely make the Minor team) so I just answered him in English. Just as I say something, who creeps up but Saoirse. In her sickly sweet voice and perfect Irish she whispered, 'I'm telling Mam – you promised her you wouldn't speak English all day and it's only break-time!' Before I could even say anything she put her arm around me, hugged me like she was the best sister and sauntered off, smiling at Mícheál!

I was disgusted because I knew she'd tell on me, and sure enough she texted home to tell Mam, and by the time I got home I was grounded. Turns out Saoirse is too, as she was texting during school when we're meant to have our phones switched off. Karma, baby, karma!

So that's all my bad news. On the upside, school is great craic. The school isn't as big as yours by the sounds of it, and we don't have a canteen, but we've Spar next door. We're allowed out at lunchtime as we have an hour. Everyone just stands at the shop talking for a while and then we go and kick a ball around.

See you soon (I hope). Cross your fingers that I'll be allowed to go to training on Thursday night, but if I'm not there you'll know why. No point arguing with the boss woman! In the meantime, write back by snail mail – if I can do it, so can you!

Sign-off here

Your (grounded) friend,

Your name here

Conor

PS Since when did you start calling yourself Jimbo? You sound like a cartoon character!

EXPLORE Based on what you learned in primary school about the layout of personal letters, pick out the similarities and differences between the layout of an email and a personal letter.

SPELLING

Remember the Safe Cross Code for crossing the road? Well, learning spellings is similar except that you use the **Safe Spelling Code**. So when you're trying to learn a spelling, here's what you do:

Look
Cover
Write
Check

Look at the word and memorise the spelling; **cover** it so that you can't see it; try to **write** it out; then **check** to make sure you spelled it correctly. If you don't get the spelling right the first time, go through the process again until you know it.

Now learn how to spell the following ten words, which featured in the two letters.

separate
completely
tectonic
disgusted
sandwiches
sauntered
apologies
definitely
arguing
unfortunately

CREATE

Write the text message that you imagine Saoirse (Conor's sister) wrote to their mother (in English) and then the one that their mother sent back to her.

SPEAK

In groups of three, write or act out the conversation between Conor and Saoirse that took place at home that evening, with one person acting the part of Conor and Saoirse's mum or dad. Make a general plan for the conversation by writing down a bullet point list of what each character would say. Use those bullet points to guide the conversation and improvise the rest. Make it clear who is speaking in your script.

Extract from a Novel

What I will learn:

to write a letter in response to a character in an extract; to use PIE when stating and explaining my opinions; to revise basic punctuation

In this extract, from the novel *See if I Care*, Luke, an Irish boy, and Elma, an English girl, reluctantly write letters to one another when their teachers set up a pen-pal scheme between their two schools. Life isn't going well for either Luke or Elma, so both invent new, more glamorous lives in their letters, but little do they know how similar their lives actually are.

Extract from *See if I Care*

by Judi Curtin and Roisin Meaney

It was the first letter he'd ever written in his life, apart from the ones he'd sent to Santa when he was small, and they didn't really count, according to his teacher.

Mrs Hutchinson said letter writing was becoming a lost art. 'Put up your hand if you've never written a letter, apart from Santa ones,' she said, and hands went up all over the class.

'When I was your age,' Mrs Hutchinson told them, 'everybody wrote letters. There was no email, or text and certainly no mobile phones. We wrote to our friends and posted the letters, and I remember how excited I'd get when I saw an envelope with my name on it coming through the letter-box.'

Mrs Hutchinson was somewhere between twenty-five and sixty. Luke wasn't very good at guessing people's ages. Her hair was bright red, but that could have been fake – maybe it was snow white underneath. And when she pressed her mouth together, a row of lines appeared above her top lip, like the folds of an accordion. She was probably quite old, at least thirty.

'Why do we need to write letters now, when we have all the other stuff that you said?' Luke asked her.

Mrs Hutchinson sighed and pushed her glasses higher on her nose.

'Because writing letters is an exercise in patience,' she said. 'Because people nowadays have forgotten what it feels like to have to wait for something. And because maybe, just maybe, it'll help your spelling and grammar too. Oh, and no typing – I want you to practice your handwriting, so stay away from those computers.'

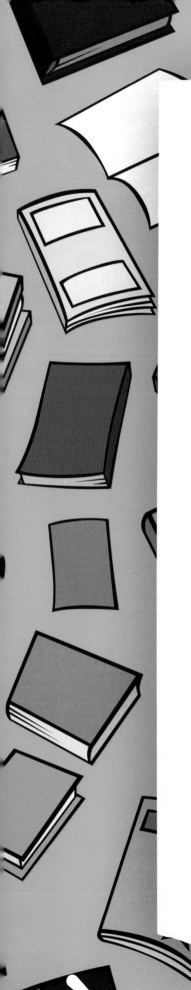

She had a friend, she told them, who was a teacher in England. 'In a school in Manchester, and they're all dying for Irish penfriends.'

Yeah right, Luke thought, just as much as we're all dying for English ones.

'Can we choose a boy or a girl' one of the girls asked, and everyone groaned when Mrs Hutchinson shook her head.

'They're going to pull your envelopes out of a hat. There are more girls than boys in that class, so it's the only fair way to do it. You take whoever you get.'

She handed out the empty envelopes and got them to copy the address of the English school from the blackboard. 'Bring them back with a stamp on, and your letter inside, before Friday.'

'Will you be reading the letters?' a boy asked.

Mrs Hutchinson considered. 'Not unless you want me to – letters should be private. Just make sure they're interesting and polite, and watch your spelling. Use a dictionary to spell words you're not sure of.'

Now, as he wondered what on earth to write, Luke chewed on the end of his biro and hoped like mad that a boy pulled his envelope out. It was bad enough having to write to anyone, but if he got a girl, it would be an utter disaster.

What did girls talk about? He had no idea, even with two sisters in the house. Anne was still such a baby, and Helen hadn't said a word to him in well over a year, unless you counted 'Pass the salt', or 'Shut up, you'.

He picked up the stamp he'd bought on the way home. It had a picture of a man's head on it. The man had long curly hair and looked like a right dork. Luke read Patrick Sarsfield 1650–1693 underneath the picture. He licked the back of the stamp and stuck it upside down in the corner of the envelope.

'It's good to stand on your head,' he told Patrick Sarsfield. 'It sends blood to your brain.'

Then he turned to the first page of the notebook he'd bought on his way home from school. What on earth could he say? Not the truth anyway – no way could he write the truth. Nobody would want to hear that. After a few minutes he took the biro out from between his teeth and began.

Dear Penfriend,

My name is Luke Mitchell. I'm eleven years and eight months old, and one hundred and fifty-three centimetres tall, and I have jet black hair with electric blue tips, and my nose and left eyebrow are pierced. I have a tattoo of a unicorn on my shoulder, and I'm a genius on the computer.

My older sister is a model and is often on the cover of magazines. My father is an astronaut and is training to be the first Irishman in space. We live in a big house out the country, with a lake in the back garden, and we own three racehorses. Their names are Thunder, Rocket and Diamond. Last year Rocket won a race in Leopardstown, which is a big famous racecourse in Dublin, and we got €10,000. My father bought me a new laptop computer, the latest model.

In my spare time I like mountain climbing, and white water rafting. I've climbed Carrauntuohill, Ireland's highest mountain, three times, and last summer I went white water rafting in Turkey. What are your hobbies?

Must go now —I have tons of homework.

Yours sincerely,

Luke Mitchell

1. Based on what you have read, what do you think of Luke? In your answer, use at least two adjectives to describe him. You will need to use the **PIE** formula to write your answer. For example:

I think that Luke is an unusual character **because he sticks the stamp on the letter upside down saying, 'It's good to stand on your head … It sends blood to your brain'.** This is a strange thing to do and makes me think that he is an interesting person. It also makes me want to read on so I can learn more about him and perhaps understand him better.

2. Make a list of all the information that Luke gives about himself and decide which information you believe is true and which has been made up.

3. Rewrite the letter from Luke to Elma correctly, laying it out like a personal letter. You will need to include a date and address (you can make one up). You must also write the envelope to accompany this letter.

4. Would you like to have Luke as a penpal? Explain your answer.

CREATE

W1.7

Imagine you have received Luke's letter and must now reply. Write a letter in response to introduce yourself. You should include some 'tall tales' (fibs) while still remaining credible (believable).

RESEARCH ZONE

W1.8

Research either of the authors of this book, Roisin Meaney or Judi Curtin, and do an author profile on them. Include biographical details about them: where they live, when they were born, other works they have written, the genre of books they write (horror, young adult fiction, etc.), the name and website address of their publishers, etc. You could even include a photo if you can find one online.

MIND YOUR LANGUAGE

CAPITAL LETTERS AND FULL STOPS

At the beginning of each sentence we use a **capital letter** and at the end we use a **full stop**.

Genre *n.*

Definition: a style or category of art, music or literature

Synonyms: class, group, list

Working with a partner, make a list of other occasions when you would use a capital letter and a full stop.

When is a capital letter used?

* For the **pronoun I**: 'Did you know that I am half-Lithuanian and half-Irish?'
* Names of **people** and **places**: Jason, Cork, J. F. Kennedy (all of these are also called *proper nouns*)
* **Days** of the week and **months** of the year: Sunday, February

* **Book** and **film titles**: *Wuthering Heights, Macbeth.* Some longer titles have some lowercase letters, e.g. *A Portrait of the Artist as a Young Man*
* **Brand names:** Kerrygold, Amnesty International, Benefit, Superdry

When is a full stop used?

* At the **end of each sentence**: 'The dog gobbled down its dinner.'
* **After initials:** J. K. Rowling, Michael D. Higgins, M. Leavy
* For **abbreviations**: Ms. (Miss) Jones, Dr. (Doctor) Robert Scanlon, Hill St. (Street), St. (Saint) John (though some people prefer to leave them out when the last letter of the abbreviation is the last letter of the word)
* To indicate the **end of speech** in dialogue: 'Stop.'
* In **price numbers**: €14.95

Abbreviation *n.*

Definition: a shortened form of a word or phrase

K k M m?? full stop.

In your copy, rewrite the following sentences correctly by uppercasing or lowercasing letters as appropriate and inserting full stops where necessary.

1. last monday morning julia's Mother wrote a letter to her teacher, ms de burgh, because julia's new adidas top was stolen from her Bag julia was very angry because she had saved For months to buy it – it had cost €5995

2. the population of lithuania was Almost 3 million in 2013 according To figures released in october

3. in 2009 world-famous barcelona striker thierry henri was accused of handball in a world cup play-off match between ireland and france disappointed irish Fans watched on in disbelief as the referee Failed to penalise the french team for this clear breach of the rules

4. for christmas Efe aked for a new iphone and was disappointed when she received a samsung galaxy

5. this morning booker award winner emma donoghue signed copies of her novel room in easons on o'connell Street dublin

A Poem

to read texts to understand and appreciate language; to use punctuation to improve meaning and presentation; to structure sentences correctly; to draft and proof-read my work

whatspunctuation
by John Foster

whatspunctuationweallneed
itsothatwecanread
whatotherswritewithoutitwed
besoconfusedwewouldnotknow
ifweshouldstoporgo
onreadingwewouldlosetheflow
ofwhatthewritermeanttosay
yeswedallloseourway
sopunctuationsheretostay

If you want your writing to be properly understood, even if all the words are right and you have used the correct spellings, capital letters and full stops, there is something else very important that you must use. Do you know what it is? It is a word beginning with *p* …

Write down all the types of punctuation you can think of in one minute (e.g. a full stop, a comma). Now compare your list with a partner's and see who found the most examples.

If you don't really believe that punctuation is important or you think that it is only for people who are really good at English, this poem may help to change your mind.

Working in pairs, try to read the poem aloud exactly as it is written (pausing only at the end of each line). Next, see if you can make sense of it by saying it again, this time adding in pauses between words.

Rewrite the poem with the necessary spaces between each word. You should also add capital letters, full stops and any other relevant punctuation.

THE PROOF-READING WHEEL

Writing Drafts

Nearly all writers, whether they are novelists or journalists, sports writers, poets, songwriters or blog writers, famous and otherwise, write many drafts of their work before they are happy with it. A draft is simply a rough version of your writing work. When you 'redraft', you re-write your work to improve it. We need to write drafts because our writing is rarely perfect the first time.

What is Proof-Reading?

When you are writing, after you have done the first draft, you should check over your work, looking for mistakes or areas that need to be clearer or improved. This process is called 'proof-reading' and the second version is called the 'redrafted' version.

This **Proof-Reading Wheel** will help you check over your work. (You may already know some of these points from primary school.)

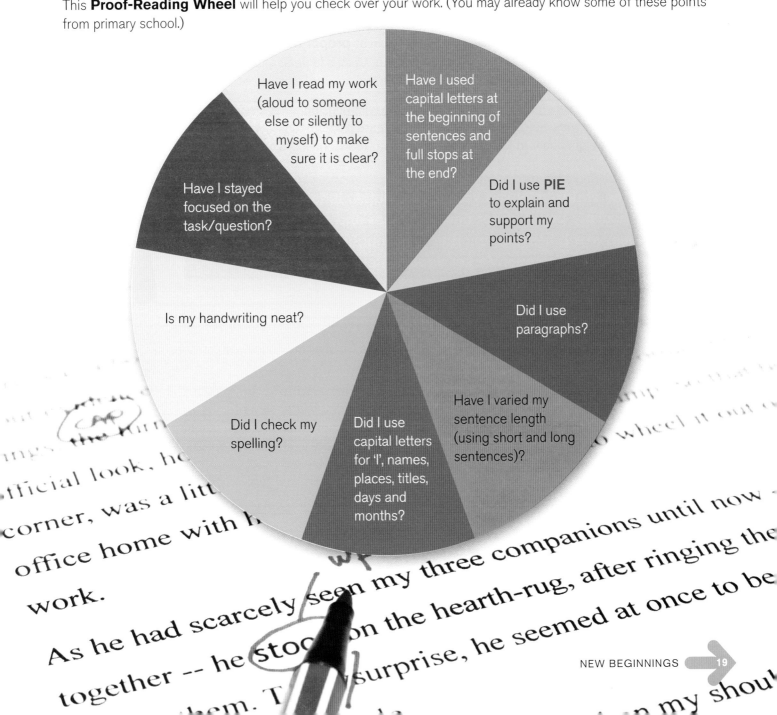

Using a piece of cardboard (maybe the back of an old cereal box or art paper), make your own Proof-Reading Wheel. Decorate it or use different colours like we have – something that will make each part stand out. Put it somewhere you will see it regularly (like inside your homework journal). Check it whenever you write a sentence and you'll find that your writing improves quickly.

NOUNS

A **noun** is a naming word: of a person (*boy*), place (*city*), creature (*fox*), thing (*chair*) or idea (*a joke*).

Not all nouns have a capital letter (unless they are at the beginning of a sentence): these are known as **common nouns**.

Nouns which take capital letters are known as **proper nouns** and they are more specific than common nouns, e.g. *Marcus* (a person), *Donegal*, *Kay's Café* (places), *the River Lee* (a thing).

Make a list of all the nouns you find in the following sentence. Decide which ones are common nouns and which are proper nouns. (*Hint:* There are eight nouns in total. The first noun is 'children', and it is a common noun.)

> All the **children** looked very smart, but Aoibheann was particularly proud of her new red dress and matching shiny shoes, which her grandmother had bought for her in Shaw's Department Store in Market Square, Roscrea.

Look around the room that you are in and make a list of all the nouns you can see.

Rules
- All nouns must be visible from the room you are in.
- You must spell them correctly and use capital letters, where relevant.

When the minute is up, compare your work with a partner's and give each other a mark for each correct noun. If necessary, use a **dictionary** to check their spellings.

Now make a list of as many nouns as you can think of beginning with the letter P, e.g. Peppa Pig, potatoes, pineapple, Poland, pride …

Rules
- All nouns must begin with the letter P.
- You must spell them correctly and use a capital letter, where relevant.

When the two minutes are up, compare your work with a partner's and give each other a mark for each correct one. If necessary, use a **dictionary** to check their spellings.

Novel Extracts

What I will learn:

to consider how an interesting opening for a short story or novel is written

According to some research, we judge people within around seven seconds of meeting them. First impressions, it seems, count! Similarly, if a book, film or documentary doesn't grab our attention quickly, we are less likely to continue reading or watching it. That means that the beginning of a story must be *compelling* – you must feel almost forced to read on because you want to know what happens.

Here are the opening lines of some popular novels.

'It was the day my grandmother exploded.'

The Crow Road by Iain M. Banks

'I write this sitting in the kitchen sink.'

I Capture the Castle by Dodie Smith

'"She's so ugly," whispered Roger. Scott and Randy laughed. David laughed too, even though he didn't think it was funny. Mrs Bayfield wasn't ugly. She was just a lonely old lady who dressed kind of weird …'

The Boy Who Lost His Face by Louis Sachar

'They've gone now, and I'm alone at last. I have the whole night ahead of me, and I won't waste a single moment of it. I shan't sleep it away. I won't dream it away either. I mustn't, because every moment will be far too precious.'

Private Peaceful by Michael Morpurgo

'Gordon Edgley's sudden death came as a shock to everyone – not least himself.'

Skulduggery Pleasant by Derek Landy

'I've always been fascinated by spiders. I used to collect them when I was younger. I'd spend hours rooting through the dusty old shed at the bottom of our garden, hunting the cobwebs for lurking eight-legged predators. When I found one, I'd bring it in and let it loose in my bedroom.'

Cirque du Freak by Darren Shan

'It is a truth universally acknowledged that a single man in possession of a good fortune must be in want of a wife.'

Pride and Prejudice by Jane Austen

'It was a bright cold day in April, and the clocks were striking thirteen.'

1984 by George Orwell

? **EXPLORE**

1. Which of these books would you most like to read, based on their opening lines? Explain your answer using **P I E**

2. Which book does not appeal to you? Give one reason using **P I E**

3. Now working in pairs, imagine the possible opening sentence for two of the following short story ideas:

✱ Two friends go on a camping trip which goes hilariously wrong.

✱ A boy finds himself attracted to a girl who would never usually be his type.

✱ A girl moves to a new city and encounters a bully in her new school.

✱ A boy loses a precious souvenir and must find it before an important family event.

A Short Film

*to predict, critique and understand
the content of a short film*

In recent years, Ireland has become home to many thousands of people not born
here, but who have travelled here for a new start, a new beginning, a new life.

Yu Ming is Anim Dom (Daniel O'Hara, dir.)

Before You Watch

The name of the short film you are about to watch is
Yu Ming is Anim Dom. What do you think it is about?
Think about this and then share your
ideas with another student.

WHILE YOU WATCH

Now watch the film, looking out for the answers to these questions.

1. During the film, Yu Ming experiences different emotions. Make a list of three of the emotions
   that you think he feels (e.g. frustrated) and explain why you think he feels that way.

2. In the film, we see Yu Ming shaving in the mirror and asking, '*An bhfuil tusa ag caint liomsa?*'
   ('Are you talking to me?'). He is copying a scene from a famous film called *Taxi Driver*. Later
   we see him ask a statue of Patrick Kavanagh the same question. What change can you see
   between the first time he asks this question and the second time?

AFTER YOU WATCH

1. Working in pairs, discuss what sort of film you think this is: happy, sad, funny, scary, worrying? Explain
   and justify your answer to another pair of students.

2. Now discuss what you think of the way that Yu Ming makes his decision about which country to move
   to. Together, make a list of the advantages and disadvantages of this method of decision-making.

3. Imagine you made lots of decisions based on the toss of a coin or the roll of a dice. Join up with
   another pair of students, and working in a group of four, imagine the decisions you might make based
   on such a method of decision-making.

SHOW WHAT YOU KNOW

You have learned many writing and speaking skills in this collection of texts. Now it's time to *Show What You Know*!

My Portfolio Task

You made a new friend while on your summer holidays. Before you went home, you exchanged home or email addresses and agreed to write to one another. Write this letter or email to your new friend.

SUCCESS CRITERIA

I must

- Use the correct layout, including an (email) address, date, greeting and sign-off
- Describe my new school (e.g. teachers, new friends, subjects)
- Talk about a new hobby
- Say what I intend to do during the mid-term break
- Use the Proof-Reading Wheel to check my work
- Use a **dictionary** to check any spellings I'm not sure of

I should

- Be creative (invent some details to make the letter interesting)

I could

- Make a confession about a fib I told them on holiday
- Tell them lots of fibs in this letter/email about my school life

Self-Assessment

Re-read what you have written and then write down two things you think you did well and one thing you could improve on.

Redrafting

Reviewing the success criteria again to make sure you have met all the requirements, and taking into account your own self-assessment notes, you can now revise your letter/email to create a second draft. When you are happy with it, you can put it in your **portfolio**.

Reflection Question

How did the email/letters you read in this collection help you to write your own email/letter for the portfolio task?

Oral Communication

Speak for **one minute** to introduce yourself to a small group of other students who you haven't worked with yet.

SUCCESS CRITERIA

I must

- Write a draft of what I'm going to say, using paragraphs (around four), with one main point per paragraph
- Consider my audience – make it interesting but not too serious
- Include basic information about myself (name, age, family and hobbies)
- Describe myself (my personality)
- Practise reading it aloud and ensure it lasts for around one minute

I should

- Tell them a little-known fact about myself
- Tell them about my dreams or hopes for the future
- Include some powerful verbs and interesting adjectives
- Use the speaking tips from p. 2

I could

- Tell them an anecdote (true story) about myself to give them an insight into my personality
- Use humour
- Tell them what other people would say about me

Peer Assessment

Reflect on your classmate's oral communication task and then write down two things you think they did well and one thing they could improve on.

Sample Introductory Speech

Hello everybody, my name is Luke Ryan. I'm twelve and I was born in London on 22nd January 2004. My mum was born in Reading in England and my dad is from Kilkenny. We moved back to Ireland when I was three and after living in Dublin and Cork, we settled in Kilkenny and we've lived here ever since.

I have one brother and two sisters, and they're all younger than me. Sam is the youngest — he's five. It infuriates me when he barges into my room at seven o'clock in the morning and shrieks in my ear until I agree to entertain him. Even still, we all worship him because he's hilarious, though he often doesn't mean to be!

I would describe myself as an outgoing sports fanatic. My sisters think that I'm as stubborn as a mule because once I make my mind up about something, I won't back down. They're probably right, though I'd never admit that to them!

On Christmas Eve when I was seven I broke my leg when I fell off a wall at the back of our house, so I was in hospital for Christmas Day. On the plus side I met loads of famous people who came in to visit the ward. Even though it took a long while for my leg to mend and I hated not being able to play hurling, I didn't have to do any housework for months. Still, I wouldn't be too keen on doing it again! In a few years I really want to be on the county hurling team and eventually I want to be a fireman.

Changes

Planning and brainstorming

Tone

Acquiring new skills

Using the five senses to write powerful descriptions

As I explore this collection I will learn about:

Formal and informal language

Understanding and using descriptive language

Developing aural skills

Understanding poetic language

SHOW WHAT YOU KNOW

The skills you learn in this collection will enable you to **show what you know** in your final tasks at the end of this collection.

For my portfolio task I will:
Write a formal letter to my principal to request permission to hold an event

For oral communication I will:
Plan and read aloud an announcement for a group of first year students

Learning Outcomes
OL1, OL5, OL6, R8, R13, W12

Exploring the Theme – Changes

What changes have you experienced in your life? Have you ever moved house, suburb, city or country? Have you changed school? Do you have a new friend or hobby? Think about things that have changed for you. Then think back to how your life was five years ago and compare it to how it is today. Use the sentences below to help you.

Change n.

Definition: to make or become different

Synonyms: alter, adapt

Five years ago ...

I was living in

I was going to school in

My best friend was

My favourite band/book was

I loved to spend my free time

My biggest dream was

My biggest fear was

I would have described myself as

Today ...

I live in

I go to school in

My best friend is

My favourite band/book is

I love to spend my free time

My biggest dream is

My biggest fear is

I would describe myself as

The thing that has changed most is

Now imagine your life in ten years' time (be as creative and ambitious as you like).

In ten years' time ...

I will be living in/with

I will be studying/working/doing

I will spend my free time

My biggest dream will be

My biggest fear will be

I would describe myself as

The thing that will have changed most is

Poetry

What I will learn:

to understand and appreciate descriptive and poetic language in texts;
to refer to the five senses to write powerful and memorable descriptions

Many poets like to write about changes they witness in the natural world. Some are very influenced by the seasons of the year and how they appeal in different ways to the senses and the imagination.

Before we read some poems, think about and discuss these three questions with your partner:

1. How do you feel about poetry?

2. Do you find it easy or difficult to understand?

3. Is there any poem you know off-by-heart?

CREATE

Make a list of all the colours you associate with autumn. For each of the colours you choose, create an image, e.g. brown = brown, crunchy leaves. Now, using some of those words, see if you can write a short autumn poem of at least four lines (it doesn't have to rhyme).

READ

Read this short autumn poem by a famous Irish writer, Ulick O'Connor.

Suddenly Autumn
by Ulick O'Connor

It is heartening as the leaves brown,
To see the pert blackberry look down
Tart to the tongue with bright gleam.
But today fear crackled off the crop,
Time has telescoped to make it seem
A day since Fall last fired the trees' top.

1. Are there any words in this poem that you do not understand? Look them up in your **dictionary** and write down their definitions down in your copy.

2. What is the main message of the poem (what is the poet trying to tell us), in your opinion? Discuss what you think the meaning of the poem is with another student. Then, working on your own, write a brief summary of it in thirty words or fewer, starting with the line, 'This poem is about …'

Now read another poem about autumn. This poem was written by the late Seamus Heaney, one of Ireland's most famous poets. He was also a playwright, translator and lecturer, and won a Nobel Prize for Literature in 1995.

 If you look on YouTube, you will find a video of the poet reciting this poem.

 # Blackberry-Picking

by Seamus Heaney

Late August, given heavy rain and sun
For a full week, the blackberries would ripen.
At first, just one, a glossy purple clot
Among others, red, green, hard as a knot.
You ate that first one and its flesh was sweet
Like thickened wine: summer's blood was in it
Leaving stains upon the tongue and lust for
Picking. Then red ones inked up and that hunger
Sent us out with milk cans, pea tins, jam pots
Where briars scratched and wet grass bleached our boots.
Round hayfields, cornfields and potato drills
We trekked and picked until the cans were full,
Until the tinkling bottom had been covered
With green ones, and on top big dark blobs burned
Like a plate of eyes. Our hands were peppered
With thorn pricks, our palms sticky as Bluebeard's.

We hoarded the fresh berries in the byre
But when the bath was filled we found a fur,
A rat-grey fungus, glutting on our cache.
The juice was stinking too. Once off the bush
The fruit fermented, the sweet flesh would turn sour.
I always felt like crying. It wasn't fair
That all the lovely canfuls smelt of rot.
Each year I hoped they'd keep, knew they would not.

1. Who, do you think, is the 'we' in the poem that the poet refers to? Explain your answer.

2. The poet refers to all five senses. Find an example of each sense.

3. The poet conveys (shows) a number of emotions in the poem. Find three and explain how the poet conveys them.

4. Write a list of the colours mentioned and what each of them describes.

5. Now read the poem again and see if there are any colours implied (colours that aren't mentioned but you can imagine, e.g. sun = yellow/orange).

6. What are your favourite and least favourite images in the poem? Explain your answer.

7. What do you think of the final line in the poem? Choose two adjectives which best describe your thoughts about this line (e.g. sad, surprising).

RESEARCH ZONE

Do a poet profile on Seamus Heaney, Ulick O'Connor or another well-known Irish poet. You should include details such as their place and date of birth, their most important poems, the main ideas of their poetry and any other interesting facts you learn about them.

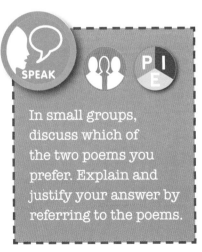

SPEAK

In small groups, discuss which of the two poems you prefer. Explain and justify your answer by referring to the poems.

Formal Language

What I will learn:

formal versus informal language;
formal speaking skills

The letters you read in the first collection were all personal, friendly letters – 'informal' letters. Informal letters tend to be between friends or for less formal occasions. They require a less formal *register* or *tone*. As you will remember from primary school, there are occasions when we need to change the type of language and format we use such as when we write formal letters. They have a more 'professional' register and more serious tone.

Register n.
Definition: the way that people communicate (write or speak) for different situations, including choice of words, grammar and pronunciation

Formal n.
Definition: done in accordance with established form or convention; suitable for an official or important occasion

What is Formal Language?

Do you know what formal language is? Discuss with another student what you think it is and when you think you might use it. Now, working alone, respond to the following statements by deciding whether they are **true** or **false**.

In pairs, you have one minute to write down the way that you would greet the following people:

- **Your principal**
- **Your brother/sister**
- **Your best friend**
- **Your best friend's mother**
- **Someone interviewing you for a job**

Statements

- ✱ I use formal language when I'm with my friends.
- ✱ Formal language is just for speaking.
- ✱ I would use formal language in a job application.
- ✱ A formal letter has a different layout to a personal letter.
- ✱ Formal language is only for old people.
- ✱ People tend to use more formal language when speaking to someone in authority.

TOP TIP

Writing in a formal manner is not about changing what you have to say, but how you say it, that is, the style and tone of your writing. To do this, you need to carefully select suitable words and phrases to communicate your point.

Formal versus Informal Language

Informal language	Formal language
Hi (speaking)	Good morning/afternoon/evening
Hello (writing)	Dear Sir/Madam/Mr/Mrs/Ms
Just wanted to let you know	I am writing to inform you
To start with	First
Can you tell me	Could you kindly
I want to	I wish to
Can I	May I
I'd be very grateful	I would really appreciate
Call me if you need anything	Please do not hesitate to contact me if you require any further information
Thanks	Thank you for taking the time to read this letter/listen to me
Hope to hear from you soon	I look forward to hearing from you at your earliest convenience
Bye/Best regards/Love	Yours sincerely, (if you know the name of the person you're writing to and their name is listed at the top of the letter)
	Yours faithfully, (if you don't know the name of the person you're writing to, or if you are writing to a group of people and their names are not listed individually)

Formal Verbs

You also need to consider the types of verbs that you use: they should be formal if the situation is formal. Working in pairs, match the casual expressions and verbs with their more formal counterparts. (Two have already been done for you.)

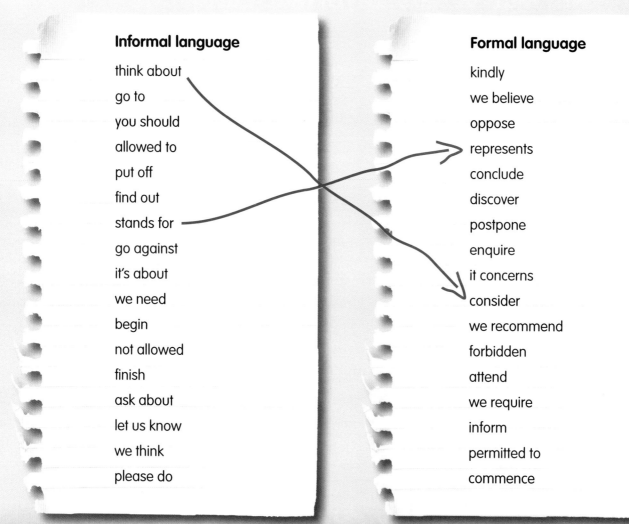

Informal language

think about
go to
you should
allowed to
put off
find out
stands for
go against
it's about
we need
begin
not allowed
finish
ask about
let us know
we think
please do

Formal language

kindly
we believe
oppose
represents
conclude
discover
postpone
enquire
it concerns
consider
we recommend
forbidden
attend
we require
inform
permitted to
commence

SPEAK 2 MIN

Using the formal language you have learned, work in pairs to do a two-minute role play of a job interview between a young person and the manager of a shop. One person will take the role of the interviewer and the other of the interviewee (the person applying for the job). Remember that you must use formal, polite language. The interviewer should ask questions and the interviewee should answer them. The interviewee may ask a couple of questions at the end.

Writing a Formal Letter

What I will learn:

how to format and write a formal letter

PREPARE

Make a list of the people/companies who might send formal letters to your home. When you have finished, compare your list to another student's list and see how many you had in common.

Sample Formal Letter

Sender's name and address

Sender's telephone/fax/email address and website

St Anthony's College Waterford
Embracing Equality in Education
Principal: Ms C. Fitzsimons
Roll No. 10209S

St Anthony's College
2 College Hill Road
Waterford City
Tel 051 12345   Fax: 051 56789
Email secretary@stanthonyscollege.ie
Website www.stanthonyscollege.ie

17th October 2016

Date

Sender's letterhead

Parent(s)/Guardian(s) of Dimitri Abakumov
25 Upper Green
Ballybricken
Waterford City

First paragraph introducing subject

Recipient's name and address

Re: Christmas Examinations 2016

Subject of letter

Dear Parent(s)/Guardian(s),

As this is your son's first year in our school, we are writing to explain the arrangements for the Christmas examinations. In our school, 40% of students' grades are allocated to their project work and homework (continuous assessment). The remaining 60% will be based on their performance in the terminal assessment (i.e. Christmas examinations).

The examinations will take place in our school assembly hall, commencing on Monday 28th November for first years. The exams will last for two weeks so we recommend that your son makes sure to get plenty of sleep, and fresh air whenever possible, as it can be quite a tiring time. During this time there will be no classes, so students will be permitted to leave the school premises when their examinations are finished each day. It is also advised that students come with a snack to eat at break time every day as our canteen will be closed during this time.

Main paragraphs giving details

Should you have any queries or concerns, please do not hesitate to contact our secretary between 10 a.m. and 2 p.m. Monday to Friday. We are always here to support your son and will do anything we can to make this period as easy as possible.

On behalf of my colleagues, we wish your son every success in his upcoming examinations.

Final paragraph to sum up

Yours sincerely,

Caitríona Fitzsimons

Sign-off (sign and type name)

Ms Caitríona Fitzsimons
Principal

CREATE

Make a list of any examples of formal language in this letter.

After studying this letter, write a formal letter to the parents/guardians of second year students in another school. The aim of the letter is to inform parents about an upcoming match.

Include the following information in your letter:

* There will be a match, which will start at 4 p.m. next Friday.

* All second year students are asked to go to the match.

* Students on detention this week are not allowed to go.

* There will be a coach to take students from school to the match, costing €2 per student.

* Students attending should bring a warm jacket and something to eat.

* The bus will return to the school at 7 p.m.

* Parents/guardians are to let the school know if their child is going (instructions should be given on how to reply, e.g. via telephone call, email, text message, reply slip, etc.).

The following words may help you in constructing your letter.

provided   to attend   **to transport**   **invite**   inform   **forbidden**

are advised   **commence**   **return**   **supporters**   **appreciate**   **kindly**

Letter from a Literary Legend

What I will learn:

*to appreciate formal language and understand its use in a letter;
to consider tone when writing a letter*

In the first collection you read a number of personal letters written by young people to other young people. Now read one which was sent by a famous author to a young person about the house he used to live in.

READ

In 1976, as part of a class project, a teacher in Dublin asked her class to find out who used to live in their families' houses. One student, twelve-year-old John Hughes, discovered that his house had once been the home of the famous Irish author (and Nobel Prize winner for Literature), Samuel Beckett, and so he wrote to him via Beckett's publisher. He must have been quite surprised when Beckett replied!

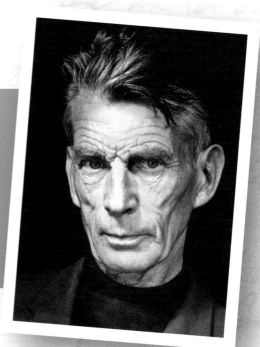

Perhaps you too
were born in
April,

Paris
28.10.76

SAMUEL BECKETT

Dear John Hughes

Thank you for your letter.
My schools were
1. Miss Elsner's Kindergarten on the Leopardstown crossroad between the old Leopardstown level crossing and the main Bray road. The house was then called Taunus.
2. Earlsford House School, Dublin, as a day boy.
3. Portora Royal School, Enniskillen, as a boarder.

As a boy I slept with my brother in the room at the top of the house next the ~~attic~~ attic where the water tank is – or was then. As an undergraduate, before I went to live in T.C.D., I slept in the tiny room, originally my father's dressing room, beside the big bedroom with the bay windows (where incidentally I was born).
If you ever meet my ghost in house or grounds, give it my regards. Wishing you happy years in that old home, I am
yours antiquatedly
Sam. Beckett.

Perhaps you too
were born in April

Paris
28.10.76

Dear John Hughes

Thank you for your letter. My schools were 1. Miss Elsner's Kindergarten on the Leopardstown crossroad between the old Leopardstown level crossing and the main Bray road. The house was then called Taurus. 2. Earlsford House School, Dublin, as a day boy. 3. Portora Royal School, Enniskillen, as a boarder. As a boy I slept with my brother in the room at the top of the house next [to] the attic where the water tank is – or was then. As an undergraduate, before I went to live in T.C.D. [Trinity College Dublin], I slept in the tiny room, originally my father's dressing room, beside the big bedroom with the bay windows (where incidentally I was born). If you ever meet my ghost in [the] house or grounds, give it my regards. Wishing you happy years in that old home, I am

Yours antiquatedly,
Sam. Beckett

1. When was this letter written?

2. If he was twelve when the letter was written, what age would John Hughes be now?

3. With whom did the writer share a room as a child?

4. Where was his next room located?

5. What does the writer tell John to do if he meets his ghost?

6. What does 'Yours antiquatedly' mean, and why do you think the writer chose to sign off in this way? (You might need to look it up your **dictionary** to figure it out.)

7. How would you describe the tone of the letter? Is it formal or informal? Explain your answer.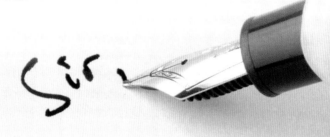

Imagine that you are twelve-year-old John. Write either:

* The initial (first) letter that you wrote to Samuel Beckett
  or
* The reply that you wrote to Samuel Beckett, to thank him and answer some of the points he raised.

Considering Tone

Consider the **tone** of your letter carefully. The tone of the first letter would need to be more polite (formal) than the second letter, which could have a more friendly (informal) tone. Tone is the general attitude of a piece of writing (or a way of speaking). It expresses a particular feeling or mood.

In speech, tone is shown in how a character delivers their line. For example, 'That's fantastic news' could express genuine excitement or sarcasm, depending on how it's delivered. In writing, it needs to be expressed more clearly: 'That's fantastic news,' she shrieked, hopping from one foot to the other. 'That's fantastic news,' he drawled, raising one eyebrow.

1. In small groups, discuss and each choose a famous person you would like to write to.

2. Now working alone, make a list of the points you would like to include in your letter.

3. Draft your letter, making sure to refer to the sample letter on p. 35 to ensure that you have included the correct information, such as your address, the date, an appropriate greeting and sign-off.

4. Show your letter to your partner. They will use the Peer Assessment Worksheet to check you have included everything.

5. Finally, when you are happy that you have included everything, show it to your teacher.

If you can find that person's address online, you might like to send your letter to them. You never know – they might reply!

FUN FACT

Many famous writers can be contacted through their agent or publisher. You can usually find this information under the **Contact** section of the writer's website.

An Autobiographical Extract

What I will learn:

to read texts to understand and appreciate language; to describe something new that I have learned; to understand the RAFT structure; to write plans and brainstorm

Just like the life of Jimbo (from the first collection) is changing, your life is also changing and you are always learning new things.

Write a list of things which you have learned to do since you were young (e.g. to walk, to ride a bike). Now focus on one particular thing you can remember learning.

Try to remember how you learned to do it. Did somebody help you? How did you feel while you were learning?

Can you remember that moment when you finally succeeded in doing it properly?

Choose one moment from your memories of learning this new skill and describe it in detail to a classmate. If you cannot remember a particular moment, use your imagination and make it up – as long as it's realistic, it's fine! Your description should be so good that your partner should be able to picture the scene. Here is a sample paragraph with words removed which may help you to describe this experience.

When I was _____ I learned _____. I learned from/was taught by _____. It was a very _____ experience. The thing which helped me to learn was _____. The most difficult part was _____. When I _____, it was like _____. I distinctly remember the smell/taste/feel/sound of _____. Afterwards I felt _____. The advice I would give to somebody learning _____ is _____. To become good at _____ _____ I think that you need to _____. In the future I would like to learn _____.

Here are some words that might help you to write your description.

Skills	Acquisition	Practising	Frustrating	Challenging	Exciting
Difficult	Emotional	Funny	Practice	Exhilarating	Rewarding
Empowered	Succeeded	Accomplished	Disappointed	Proud	Ecstatic
Persistent	Goals	Prepared	Focus	Experience	Enjoy

TOP TIP

There are lots of writing styles. The style you use will depend on what you are writing and who your audience is. The **RAFT** writing strategy (Role of the Writer, Audience, Format and Topic) is important when writing a story or examining a piece of writing. You'll learn more about **RAFT** in Collection 4.

READ

Now that you have reflected on your experience of learning a new skill, you might enjoy reading about how one of the world's most successful men, Richard Branson, learned some important lessons and skills and how his experiences might have changed him.

Extract from Richard Branson's autobiography

No. 1 International Bestseller

'Branson has a list of achievements unmatched by any other UK businessman. For anyone burning with entrepreneurial zeal, his reminiscences are akin to a sacred text' Mail on Sunday

Losing My Virginity

Richard Branson

The Autobiography

The must-read updated edition

My childhood is something of a blur to me now, but there are several episodes that stand out. I do remember that my parents **continually** set us challenges. My mother was determined to make us independent. When I was four years old, she stopped the car a few miles from our house and made me find my own way home across the fields. I got hopelessly lost. My youngest sister Vanessa's earliest memory is being woken up in the dark one January morning because Mum had decided I should cycle to Bournemouth that day. Mum packed some sandwiches and an apple and told me to find some water along the way.

Bournemouth was fifty miles away from our home in Shamley Green, Surrey. I was under twelve but Mum thought that it would teach me the importance of **stamina** and a sense of direction. I remember setting off in the dark, and I have a vague **recollection** of staying the night with a relative. I have no idea how I found their house, or how I got back to Shamley Green the next day, but I do remember finally walking into the kitchen like a **conquering** hero, feeling **tremendously** proud of my marathon bike ride and expecting a huge welcome.

'Well done, Ricky,' Mum greeted me in the kitchen, where she was chopping onions. 'Was that fun? Now, could you run along to the vicar's? He's got some logs he wants chopping and I told him that you'd be back any minute.'

Our challenges tended to be physical rather than **academic**, and soon we were setting them for ourselves. I have an early memory of learning how to swim. I was either four or five, and we had been on holiday in Devon with Dad's sisters, Auntie Joyce and Aunt Wendy, and Wendy's husband, Uncle Joe. I was particularly fond of Auntie Joyce, and at the beginning of the holiday she had bet me ten **shillings** that I couldn't learn to swim by the end of the fortnight. I spent hours in the sea trying to swim against the freezing-cold waves, but by the last day I still couldn't do it. I just splashed along with one foot hopping on the bottom. I'd **lunge** forward and crash beneath the waves before **spluttering** up to the surface trying not to swallow the seawater.

'Never mind, Ricky.' Auntie Joyce said. 'There's always next year.'

But I was determined not to wait that long. Auntie Joyce had made me a bet, and I doubted that she would remember it the next year. On our last day we got up early, packed the cars and set out on the twelve-hour journey home. The roads were narrow; the cars were slow; and it was a hot day. Everyone wanted to get home. As we drove along I saw a river.

'Daddy, can you stop the car, please?' I said.

The river was my last chance: I was sure that I could swim and win Auntie Joyce's ten shillings.

'Please stop!' I shouted.

Dad looked in the rear-view mirror, slowed down and pulled up on the grass **verge**.

'What's the matter?' Aunt Wendy asked as we all piled out of the car.

'Ricky's seen the river down there,' Mum said. 'He wants to have a final go at swimming.'

'Don't we want to get on and get home?' Aunt Wendy complained. 'It's such a long drive.'

'Come on Wendy. Let's give the lad a chance,' Auntie Joyce said. 'After all, it's my ten shillings.'

* STOP AND THINK *

How do you think Richard's parents will react? Discuss this in small groups. *Now read on …*

I pulled off my clothes and ran down to the riverbank in my underpants. I didn't dare stop in case anyone changed their mind. By the time I reached the water's edge I was rather frightened. Out in the middle of the river, the water was flowing fast with the stream of bubbles dancing over the boulders. I found a part of the bank that had been **trodden** down by some cows, and waded out into the current. The mud squeezed up between my toes. I looked back. Uncle Joe and Aunt Wendy and Auntie Joyce, my parents and my sister Lindi stood watching me, the ladies in **floral** dresses, the men in sports jackets and ties. Dad was lighting his pipe and looking utterly unconcerned; Mum was smiling her usual encouragement.

* STOP AND THINK *

Did they react the way you imagined? Were you correct? What do you think will happen next? *Now read on …*

I braced myself and jumped forward against the current, but I immediately felt myself sinking, my legs slicing uselessly through the water. The current pushed me around, tore at my underpants and dragged me downstream. I couldn't breathe and I swallowed water. I tried to reach up to the surface, but had nothing to push against. I kicked and **writhed** around but it was no help.

Then my foot found a stone and I pushed up hard. I came back above the surface and took a deep breath. The breath steadied me, and I relaxed. I had to win that ten shillings.

I kicked slowly, spread my arms, and found myself swimming across the surface. I was still bobbing up and down, but I suddenly felt released: I could swim. I didn't care that the river was pulling me downstream. I swam triumphantly out into the middle of the current. Above the roar and bubble of the water I heard my family clapping and cheering. As I swam in a **lopsided** circle and came back to the riverbank some fifty yards below them, I saw Auntie Joyce fish into her huge black handbag for her purse. I crawled up out of the water, brushed through a patch of stinging nettles and ran up the bank. I may have been cold, muddy and stung by the nettles, but I could swim.

'Here you are, Ricky,' Auntie Joyce said. 'Well done.'

I looked at the ten-shilling note in my hand. It was large, brown and crisp. I had never held that amount of money before: it seemed a fortune.

'All right, everyone,' Dad said. 'On we go.'

It was then that I realised he too was dripping wet. He had lost his nerve and dived in after me. He gave me a massive hug.

TOP TIP

The story of somebody's life is called a *biography* (if somebody else writes it) or an *autobiography* (if they write it themselves). 'Autobiography' is a long word, but when you break it down it's actually easy, especially if you know any Greek! You might think that you don't, but most of us do, even though we don't realise it. It comes from three Greek words: *Auto* + *bio* + *graphy* = Self + life + writing.

EXPLORE

1. As you know, this extract is from an autobiography of one of the world's most successful businessmen. Did you find it easy or difficult to read? Explain your answer.

2. 'This snapshot of Branson's life shows us that he and his family are strong-minded and ambitious.' Do you agree with this statement? Explain your answer, using at least one example.

3. Did anything in this passage shock you?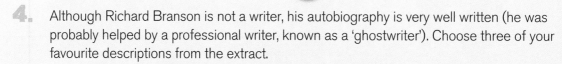

4. Although Richard Branson is not a writer, his autobiography is very well written (he was probably helped by a professional writer, known as a 'ghostwriter'). Choose three of your favourite descriptions from the extract.

5. Thinking about the **RAFT** structure (see the Top Tip on p. 40), can you identify the **role** of the writer here, the **audience**, the **format** and the **topic**?

6. After reading the passage (you might need to re-read it), imagine you are Richard Branson on the evening of the swimming incident described. Write a tweet to describe the experience. You may need to write a couple of drafts before you get it right.

SPELLING

Write down the fourteen words **bolded** in the text and then look up their meaning in your **dictionary**. Were there any other words in the extract that you didn't understand or words which you didn't know but worked out from the context? Write them down too.

Now learn to spell these words, and when you are confident that you know them, get another student to test you on them. Then choose five of these words and make up your own sentences with them.

TOP TIP

A tweet is a message which is currently 140 characters or less.
A 'character' includes a letter, space, comma, full stop or any kind of punctuation.

REMEMBER
The Safe Spelling Code: Look, Cover, Write, Check.

Imagine and then script (write) the dialogue (conversation) between Richard's parents as they watched him in the water trying to swim.

✱ Working with a partner, plan the conversation by jotting down key words that you think they might use; you can do this by using a plan or doing a brainstorm (see the next page for an example)

✱ Use your plan to draft the script

✱ Act it out quietly

✱ Redraft your work based on what you noticed when you acted out your first draft

Oral Group Assessment

Reflect on your classmate's contribution to the dialogue task and then write down two things you think they did well and one thing they could improve on. Now make some final changes based on the feedback you receive before acting it out for a larger group or the class.

REMEMBER Drafting and redrafting, p. 19.

Planning/Brainstorming

A plan or a brainstorm helps you to come up with and take note of key words or ideas to assist you in what you want to achieve, in this case writing a piece of dialogue.

To make a plan

- Write down words and phrases that will remind you of the ideas you want to include in your script.
- Put the ideas in order by numbering them according to when you want to use them. Cross out any ideas you decide not to use.
- You are now ready to write a first draft!

Planning/Brainstorming in Action

A dialogue between two teenage girls discussing going to a school disco

Key Words and Ideas

1 excitement

4 meeting beforehand

2 who's going?

5 how getting there?

6 takeaway afterwards?

3 getting ready? clothes and make-up

~~7 bring outfits into school~~

First Draft

Characters: Aoife and Katie

Aoife: Hey, Katie, are you going to the school disco on Friday?

Katie: Absolutely! I'm so excited! I can't wait. Is Emma going?

Aoife: Well, Emma's definitely going and I think Rachel's going too – if she's allowed!

Katie: Cool! Do you know what you're going to wear? We can get ready in my house if you like. You can come over after school.

Aoife: Yeah, sure. I think my dad can bring us, but I'll ask him again. Maybe we can get a takeaway too – do you want to stay over at my house afterwards? My sister's away on a school trip so you could have her bed.

Katie: Yes! I'll have to ask, but I'm pretty sure I'll be allowed. I'm so excited! I'm going home to find something to wear now. I'll text you later.

A Radio Documentary

What I will learn:

to listen actively to get the gist of a story and appreciate the features of a good opening

Do you know what a documentary is? Write down what you think it is. When you have done that, **compare and contrast** your answer with another student and combine your work. Now look up the definition in your **dictionary** and write it down in your copy. Finally, learn how to spell the word 'documentary'. When you are confident that you know the spelling, ask your classmate to test you.

'Clonehenge' (RTÉ Radio 1)

In the first collection you read the opening lines of some novels. Now you will listen to the opening of a radio documentary from RTÉ Radio 1. 'Clonehenge' is about a new structure that suddenly appeared on Achill Island, Co. Mayo, which became known as 'Achillhenge' to the locals and which certainly changed the landscape! You will hear the first three minutes of the documentary and you will listen to it three times.

FIRST LISTENING

Listen to the clip in its entirety to get the gist of it.

SECOND LISTENING

During the second listening the clip will be broken down into three parts.
Read the following questions before you listen to help you focus on the important information.

CLIP 1

1. What do we learn about where the narrator is going?

2. How do we know that the narrator is tired?

3. What is effective about this clip as an opening piece? What makes you want to keep listening?

CLIP 2

1. Listen carefully to the narrator's description and write down the things you learn about the structure.

2. Make a sketch of what you think the structure looks like.

CLIP 3

1. Make a list of anything you learn about the man who created this new structure (just write some key words as you won't have time to write down everything).

2. Did you want to keep listening to the documentary? Explain your answer.

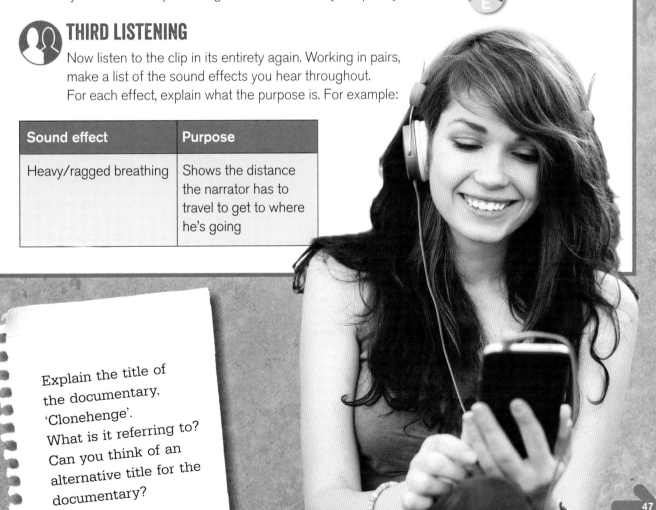

THIRD LISTENING

Now listen to the clip in its entirety again. Working in pairs, make a list of the sound effects you hear throughout.
For each effect, explain what the purpose is. For example:

Sound effect	Purpose
Heavy/ragged breathing	Shows the distance the narrator has to travel to get to where he's going

Explain the title of the documentary, 'Clonehenge'.
What is it referring to?
Can you think of an alternative title for the documentary?

SHOW WHAT YOU KNOW

You have learned many writing and speaking skills in this collection. Now it's time to *Show What You Know!*

My Portfolio Task

Your CSPE class has decided to organise an afternoon of activities for all first year students. The aim is to help everybody bond as a year group by challenging them to do something new as well as raise money for a charity/cause of your class's choice. On behalf of your class, you have been asked to **write a formal letter** to your principal requesting permission to hold this event.

SUCCESS CRITERIA

I should
- Politely ask my principal to reply with his/her decision
- Sign the letter off on behalf of the class

I must
- Use a formal structure and language
- Explain what will happen during the event
- Include the proposed date and time of the event
- Explain what the charity is and why this cause is important to the class
- Use the Proof-Reading Wheel to check my work
- Use a **dictionary** to check spellings I'm not sure of

Self-Assessment

Re-read what you have written and then write down two things you think you did well and one thing you could improve on.

I could
- Ask for a meeting with the principal to discuss the matter further
- Include a timetable for the afternoon's events or a diagram of where it will take place

Redrafting

Reviewing the success criteria again to make sure you have met all the requirements, and taking into account your own self-assessment notes, you can now revise your formal letter to create a second draft. When you are happy with it, you can put it in your **portfolio**.

Reflection Question
What might a reader enjoy most about the letter you wrote?

Oral Communication

Your event has been approved by the principal! Plan and then deliver an announcement (of 20–30 seconds) to be read to all first year students at their weekly assembly, the purpose of which is to:

- Inform the students all about the event which will take place the following week
- Explain the reasons for it
- Gain students' interest and enthusiasm
- Encourage them all to participate in the event

LISTEN

Before you begin

Listen to the sample announcement and then identify the elements which it addresses by ticking them off the success criteria list.

SUCCESS CRITERIA

I should

- Include a short description of the activities that will happen on the day
- Tell students what they will need to bring (e.g. money, equipment)
- Explain why this charity/cause is important to my class

I must

- Use formal register
- Include the time and date of the event
- Mention the name of the event
- Mention the charity, what the charge is and how the money will be spent
- Ensure the announcement lasts between 20 and 30 seconds

Peer Assessment

Reflect on your classmate's work and then write down two things you think he/she did well and one thing he/she could improve on.

I could

- Feature descriptions which refer to the senses (in order to gain students' interest and attention)
- Include a plea for students to come along and support the event

REMEMBER When you are speaking aloud and making presentations, speak slowly and clearly and maintain eye contact with your audience. See p. 2 for more tips on public speaking.

Mystery and Menace

Broadsheet and tabloid newspapers

Naming characters

The 5 Ws

TV news reports

Synonyms and antonyms

The Placemat Technique

Planning a story

Sound effects

As I explore this collection I will learn about:

Suspense and climax

Action verbs

Setting

Paragraphing

Dramatic dialogue

Stage directions

Using a dictionary and thesaurus

Learning Outcomes
OL4, OL5, OL7, R1, R6,
R8, R10, W5, W9

SHOW WHAT YOU KNOW

The skills you learn in this collection will enable you to **show what you know** in your final tasks at the end of this collection.

For my portfolio task I will:
Write the opening chapter of a mystery story that begins on a stormy night

For oral communication I will:
Record a scene for a radio play with sound effects and dialogue

Exploring the Theme – Mystery and Menace

Sharks are a **menace** to swimmers.

Menace *n.*

Definition: a worrying feeling of danger lurking in the background; a dangerous person or thing. A menace threatens harm, damage, danger or destruction. From the Latin word *minac*, meaning 'threatening'.
Synonyms: danger, risk, threat, peril

Mystery *n.*

Definition: something strange, mystifying, baffling, puzzling, out of the ordinary; a happening that you cannot understand or explain, an unsolved crime, a secret or hidden thing. From the Latin word *mysterium*, meaning a 'secret ceremony'.
Synonyms: puzzle, riddle, enigma

 Learn these two **dictionary** definitions of 'mystery' and 'menace'. Then, with a partner, recite them without looking at your book.

The baffling disappearance of the crew of the ship, the *Mary Celeste*, abandoned in the Atlantic Ocean in 1872, remains a **mystery** to this day.

 Using the **Placemat Technique**, in groups of four with a section each, brainstorm examples of:

* A mystery or a menace from history

* A mystery or a menace in the news

The Placemat Technique

A large sheet of paper is placed in the middle of the table and divided into four sections, with a box in the middle. Brainstorming the theme, 'Mystery and Menace', past and present, you write key ideas, words and phrases of that theme in your section.

When the alloted time is up, review what your classmates have written and then amongst yourselves decide which are the best ideas. One of you is then nominated to write these ideas in the centre box and report them back to the rest of the class.

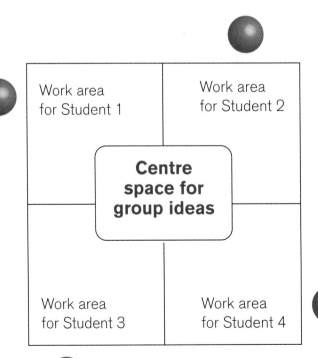

Work area for Student 1	Work area for Student 2
Centre space for group ideas	
Work area for Student 3	Work area for Student 4

A Nature Video

What I will learn:

dramatic words and phrases; how music and sound effects make a voiceover interesting and enjoyable

Great White Shark Attack (*Planet Earth*, BBC)

This spectacular three-minute hunt and chase video from BBC's *Planet Earth* programme shows an attack by a great white shark on a seal.

Sharks hunt by swimming just below the surface of the water, scanning for seals. When the shark strikes, the seals make desperate attempts to escape, using their speed and agility to try to avoid capture.

In this extraordinary clip, which took many weeks to find and film, the cameraman, Simon King, has slowed the footage right down to show viewers exactly how this massive, most powerful sea creature attacks and devours a tiny seal. The one-second leap then became a forty-second shot.

The ominous music especially composed and played by the BBC Orchestra reflects the danger and menace as the shark attacks. Notice how the sound of the ocean spray and the crashing of the shark and seal in the water can be clearly heard.

Now watch the clip.

Watch the clip again, but this time with the sound down. Write your own voiceover, describing what you see. Try to use dramatic verbs to describe the action. The words and phrases below will help you. Also, suggest the music that you would choose to accompany your voiceover.

A great white shark is on the prowl … soars from the ocean … massive head … razor-sharp, triangular teeth … long white underbelly … fin … leaps … dives … beats … tosses … takes its prey by surprise … twists … turns … chase … speed … seal attempts escape … dark blue ocean waves … menacing fin … white spray … burst in a great leap out of the water … final leap … seagulls overhead … helpless seal … above the water … last picture … falling back into the ocean … silence

A Newspaper Article

to plan and paragraph; to use descriptive language; to use the 5 Ws

How many newspapers, both Irish and international, can you name?

Pair and **share** your lists.

Divide the titles into two columns:

A. Serious newspapers that print detailed articles on politics and social issues

B. Popular newspapers that put celebrity gossip and shock headlines on their front pages

Those in column **A** are known as **broadsheet** newspapers. Those in column **B** are known as **tabloid** newspapers.

Broadsheet *n.*

Definition: a serious newspaper with long articles. So named because of its size, being printed on long 'broad' sheets of paper.

Tabloid *n.*

Definition: a newspaper with short articles. Smaller pages than a broadsheet, sensational headlines and large photographs – especially of celebrities. 'Tabloid' was an old word used in medicine for a small tablet or pill, therefore something easy to digest.

Learn these two **dictionary** definitions of 'tabloid' and 'broadsheet'. Then, with a partner, recite them without looking at your book.

The 5 Ws

It is important to know to look out for the **who, what, where, when** and **why** when reading an article or watching a news clip. These are known as the **5 Ws**. The 5 Ws are very useful to keep in mind when planning to write a news article or to present a radio feature of your own. The questions **Who, What, Where, When** and **Why** must all be answered. Who is my article for or who is it about? What happened? Where did it happen? When did it happen? Why did it happen or why are the public being made aware of the event?

The following broadsheet newspaper article warns of the threat of a shark attack in Massachusetts, USA, and uses the 5 Ws approach.

Shark Menace!

Following the sighting of an eight-foot great white shark off the coast of Massachusetts, a shark warning has been issued for this weekend. All visitors planning to visit coastal regions around the Maine and New Jersey areas are warned to be vigilant.

In her press statement, chief coastguard Natasha Kaminski advised the public: 'A great white shark that swims beneath the water would be happy to find a splashing paddler or a hand dangling from a boat.

Do not wear jewellery in the water; the reflected light looks like fish scales to a shark. Don't go into the water if you are bleeding from a wound. If you see a fin or an eight-foot shadow beneath the waves, get out of the water as fast as you can.'

Ms Kaminski also advised that swimmers should swim close to the shore, while boaters and kayakers should stay away from seal pods, which attract onlookers but also sharks. Unusually large populations of seals have drawn sharks to the area around Cape Cod. A close encounter between a small boat and a shark could end in tragedy.

Paragraph 1: States the facts – The 5 Ws

Paragraph 2: Press statement – Explains the danger to the public and gives advice to people who plan on going into the water; statement in inverted commas

Paragraph 3: Information – Dangers, more advice on how to stay safe

CREATE

W3.2

Write a three-paragraph newspaper article with the title: 'Jellyfish Menace!' In your article, the Head of the Irish Water Safety Association (name him or her) explains the danger to the public. Put the statement to the public in inverted commas, such as you saw in the article.

TOP TIP

Inverted commas are also known as speech marks. They go around a direct quote from a specific person.

Jellyfish Menace!

Paragraph 1: State the facts using the 5 Ws

Paragraph 2: Give the dos and don'ts about jellyfish

Paragraph 3: Give more information on how to stay safe or what to do if stung. You can include the following:

- Recent high temperatures
- Unusual number of jellyfish spotted
- Warning signs erected on beaches
- Jellyfish stranded on beach can sting
- Agonising pain from stings – blisters, cramps, vomiting, nausea, breathing problems, even heart failure
- Look down, be alert as you walk
- Don't panic – not all stings poisonous
- Wash wounds with vinegar, or put baking soda and water paste on sting
- Rinse with sea water, never fresh water
- Apply ice pack to sting
- Do not rub sting – spreads the poison
- Go to lifeguard hut for first aid; see doctor if you have allergic reaction

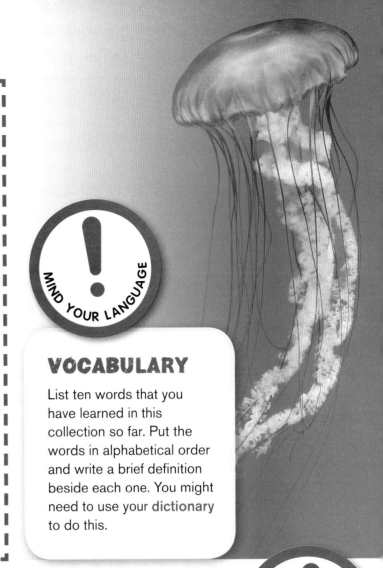

MIND YOUR LANGUAGE

VOCABULARY

List ten words that you have learned in this collection so far. Put the words in alphabetical order and write a brief definition beside each one. You might need to use your **dictionary** to do this.

A TV News Report

What I will learn:

to plan and write a television news item about a breaking news story; to use a dictionary and a thesaurus; to use strong verbs and a variety of nouns and adjectives

Big *adj.*

Synonyms: huge, large, massive, vast, enormous, immense, giant, gigantic, colossal

Antonyms: little, tiny, mini, puny, petite, small, miniature, minuscule

SYNONYMS AND ANTONYMS

MIND YOUR LANGUAGE

The Greek word *thesaurus* meant a **storehouse** or **treasure**. So a thesaurus (say: *th-saw-rus*) is a store of words of similar meaning. These words are called *synonyms* (say: *sin-in-im*). Each thesaurus entry will also give you words that are opposite in meaning. These words are called *antonyms* (say: *an-toe-nim*).

Now write the thesaurus synonyms and antonyms for the words **happy** and **horrible**.

PREPARE

Rewrite the sentences below, substituting a word of similar meaning – a synonym – for the underlined words.

(You'll do this very well if you use your **dictionary** and/or **thesaurus** to help you.)

- A <u>powerful</u> storm <u>battered</u> the Atlantic coast
- High tides <u>pummelled</u> cliffs and beaches
- The roadway was torn up by the <u>gale force</u> winds and <u>pounding</u> seas
- Corpses were <u>strewn</u> for miles
- <u>Boulders</u> <u>smashed</u> into <u>graveyards</u> and <u>demolished</u> headstones

READ

The following text is the script of a TV news report giving viewers information about a menacing storm that has caused damage on the west coast of Ireland. Read it and take note of any powerful words or images (pictures that form in your mind) that you find in the text.

Graveyard Ripped Apart In Storm

A powerful storm battered the Atlantic coast last night. As darkness fell, gusts of eighty miles an hour brought giant waves and high tides that pummelled cliffs and beaches. In Co. Galway, the roadway to Gurteen Cemetery in Ballyconneely was torn up by the gale force winds and pounding seas. Graves were opened, coffins ripped apart and corpses strewn for miles.

In Connemara the storm brought its own destruction to buildings and cemeteries. As hurricane force winds struck, a high wall protecting the cemetery was crushed to smithereens. Coffins and human bones were exposed when boulders thrown up by the sea smashed into the graveyard. A massive stone arch at the front of the graveyard was also reduced to rubble and then washed into the sea.

In the worst storm for decades, sea water crashed over flood barriers, uprooting trees and flooding coastal land.

Gale Force Winds Sweep Scotland (BBC News)

WATCH

You will now watch a video from the BBC News about a storm in Scotland. You will hear three different people:

1. The reporter as voice-over and on location

2. A politician speaking about the crisis

3. A weather forecaster

Watch and listen carefully. Take notes on what's being said so you can collect vocabulary for writing your own news item.

SPEAK

CREATE

Write an item for broadcast on the news about a storm under the heading: 'Gale Force Winds Batter the Country'. Think about adding different speakers, e.g. journalist on location, school principal commenting on the storm, weather forecaster giving further details on the progression of the storm, etc.

Now speak your news item aloud as if you were the TV newsreader. Give parts to different people to read. If you use flashcards, you can speak to the camera instead of looking down at your script. Fill in the grid on the next page as you listen to each other.

Peer Assessment

Peer Assessment Worksheet with Success Criteria for a News Broadcast

The quality of … was	Excellent	Very good	Good	Some room to improve (suggest briefly **how** to improve)
Information				
Eye contact with viewers				
Appropriate vocabulary				
Confident appearance				
Clear pronunciation				
Correct pacing, neither too slow nor too fast				
Any other point				

In this news broadcast	Comment
I liked	
I was surprised by	
I thought the best part was	
I think there could be some improvement in	

A Poem

to plan a mystery story in five parts, describing the setting, using sound effects, action verbs and dialogue, and giving the story an interesting title

READ

In the following poem, a man finds a ring on a skeleton after a storm has ripped apart a graveyard. For some mysterious reason, the ghostly skeleton will not let the ring be taken.

The Visitor

by Ian Serraillier

> **Title:** 'The Visitor' sounds innocent and pleasant, but you soon find out that this 'visitor' is sinister and threatening.

> **Setting:** Where? When? Sea; churchyard; crumbling graves; bedroom; midnight; darkness; house uphill from graveyard

A crumbling churchyard, the sea and the moon;

The waves had gouged out grave and bone;

A man was walking, late and alone...

He saw a skeleton on the ground;

A ring on a bony finger he found.

He ran home to his wife and gave her the ring.

'Oh, where did you get it?' He said not a thing.

'It's the loveliest ring in the world,' she said,

As it glowed on her finger. They slipped off to bed.

At midnight they woke. In the dark outside,

'Give me my ring!' a chill voice cried.

'What was that, William? What did it say?'

'Don't worry, my dear. It'll soon go away.'

'I'm coming!' A skeleton opened the door.

'Give me my ring!' It was crossing the floor.

'What was that, William? What did it say?'

> **Sounds:** crashing waves; voices; opening door, skeleton scuttling across floorboards; screams; bones clattering downhill

'Don't worry, my dear. It'll soon go away.'

'I'm reaching you now! I'm climbing the bed.'

The wife pulled the sheet right over her head.

It was torn from her grasp and tossed in the air:

'I'll drag you out of bed by the hair!'

'What was that, William? What did it say?'

'Throw the ring through the window! THROW IT AWAY!'

She threw it. The skeleton leapt from the sill,

Scooped up the ring and clattered downhill,

Fainter... and fainter... Then all was still.

Action verbs: ran; glowed; cried; crossing; reaching; climbing; pulled; torn; tossed; drag; throw; threw; leapt; scooped; clattered

Dramatic dialogue: 'THROW IT AWAY!'

EXPLORE

1. Quote between inverted commas the phrases in the poem that match these phrases:

- The sea had ripped skeletons from graves
- It shone and gleamed
- It was snatched from her
- Jumped from the window ledge
- Ran noisily downwards
- More and more quietly

2. Write the adjectives that are used to describe the following nouns in the poem:

- churchyard
- finger
- ring
- skeleton's voice

SPEAK

Now speak and record the poem aloud as a drama. You need four actors: the man, his wife, the skeleton, and a narrator. You will need a ring as a prop.

Prop *n.*

Definition: an object or item that is used by an actor or actress on stage. It aids the understanding of the story, e.g. if a scene was set in a kitchen, on stage there might be props like chairs, cutlery, pots and pans.

1. Solve the mystery behind the poem. Many years ago, someone was buried with a ring on his or her finger.

- How, where, when and why did he or she die?
- Why was the ring left on his or her finger?
- Why would the skeleton not be parted from this ring?

2. Following the **Five-Part Story Planner** (as detailed below) write the story of the poem to be read by a teacher to a group of fourth class pupils. Use a mixture of your own words and words and phrases from the poem.

THE FIVE-PART STORY PLANNER

1 Beginning
Describe the stormy night: darkness; moonlit graves; storm; bones; tombstones

2 Introduce the characters
Man walking alone; howling wind; skeleton; bony finger

3 Start the action
Runs home as fast as legs can carry him; terrified but excited; gives ring to wife; doesn't answer questions; sleep

4 Build-up to the dramatic climax
Voice from the darkness; 'Give me my ring!'; 'THROW IT AWAY!'

5 Ending
The Visitor's departure: the skeleton leaps; departs; clatters; eerie silence

Sound effect n.
Definition: a sound that is made artificially in a play, film or computer game to make the story more realistic

SPEAK

Now read aloud the story you wrote to a group of classmates as if they were the fourth class pupils. You could do this on your own or as an acting group. Use the following steps:

- Highlight in one colour the lines that you will speak loudly or quickly
- Highlight in a different colour the lines to be spoken softly or slowly
- Dramatise the story by using props, pictures or music
- Add sound effects like the man's footsteps, the howling of the wind, claps of thunder, rain falling, the clatter of dead bones on the floorboards …
- End with silence

Oral Peer Assessment

Reflect on your classmates' presentation and then write down two things you think they did well and one thing they could improve on.

RESEARCH ZONE

Do a poet profile on Ian Serraillier.

Extract from a Novel [1]

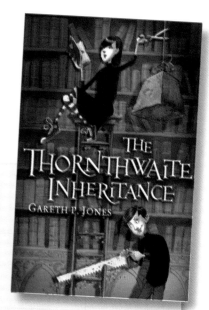

What I will learn:

to speak and write dialogue; to pay attention to facial expressions, gestures and tones of voice; to give characters unusual names

The Thornthwaite Inheritance, set in a creepy mansion, tells the tale of unusual thirteen-year-old twins who wear only black, live without electricity and are heirs to a vast fortune. The story is full of mystery and menace, skulduggery, unexplained deaths, threats, dangers, deceptions, trickery, twists, turns and chilling secrets. In this first chapter, the parents of twins Lorelli and Ovid are already dead. Today is the twins' thirteenth birthday. The opening sentence makes a surprising statement about their murderous aim in life.

Speak the story aloud as a drama. You need two actors, Lorelli and Ovid, as well as a narrator. 'Lorelli' and 'Ovid' have to decide on the accents they will use and also plan the way they will sit or stand while reading, e.g. straight, slumped, etc. The narrator needs to be ready to read at the right moments. As props, you need a table and two slices of cake.

Chapter 1, 'The Truce' from *The Thornthwaite Inheritance* by Gareth P. Jones

Lorelli and Ovid Thornthwaite had been trying to kill each other for so long that neither twin could remember which act of attempted murder came first. Was it Lorelli's cunning scheme to put on a play about the French Revolution, casting Ovid in the role of aristocrat to be executed using a working guillotine? Or could it have been that long hot summer when Ovid managed to produce an ice lolly containing a small but deadly explosive, triggered by the surrounding ice reaching melting point?

Whoever had struck first, trying to take each other's life was now simply something the Thornthwaite twins did, in the same way that other brothers and sisters might play together, enjoy watching cartoons or squabble over the remote control. Except that compared to playing, watching cartoons or squabbling, trying to kill your twin is much harder work, not to mention illegal, which was why on their thirteenth birthday, having clocked up over two hundred murder attempts between them, Ovid suggested they call a truce.

'I no longer want to kill you,' he announced, his bottle-green eyes meeting his sister's across the table. Two slices of cake sat in front of them. Neither had been touched.

'I have never wanted to kill you,' replied Lorelli, 'I have only ever acted out of self-defence.'

Ovid smiled, 'Whereas self-preservation has always been my motivation, and, as you were the last one to attack, I propose that we call it quits.'

'I wasn't the last one to attack,' stated Lorelli, pushing her straight black hair from her face.

'What about the flesh-eating piranha in my bath?'

'That was on Sunday. You booby-trapped my bed on Monday.'

'I'd been working on that for months. I couldn't let all that planning go to waste.' Ovid remembered with pride how he had set up a device in his sister's bedroom that was designed to fling the first thing that sat on the bed out the window. Lorelli's bedroom was at the top of the central spire of Thornthwaite Manor.

'Poor Cowell had the fright of her life,' said Lorelli.

Ovid had forgotten that the cat liked to jump on her bed for a snooze sometimes.

'Cats have nine lives,' he said. 'We only have one. It doesn't matter who started it if we both agree to stop it now.'

Lorelli eyed him suspiciously. She didn't trust her brother for one second. He had tried this tactic before, waiting for her to lower her guard before unleashing the next lethal scheme.

'I mean it this time,' he said, wearing an expression of deepest sympathy.

'OK,' she said finally, deciding she would go along with the ceasefire while remaining sensibly cautious. 'Truce.'

'Truce,' repeated her brother, grinning.

They leant forward and shook on it before sealing the deal with two slices of birthday cake, which they switched fourteen times before eating, ensuring that neither piece had been tampered with.

> Notice how the writer gives you details of his characters' tone of voice, gestures or facial expressions while they speak their lines, e.g., "'I no longer want to kill you,'" he announced, his bottle-green eyes meeting his sister's across the table.' In a play these would be called stage directions.

EXPLORE

1. Find and complete the words from this first chapter that match the following definitions.

Clever in a shrewd, evil or dishonest way	c _ nn _ ng
Part in a play, film or event	ro _ e
Machine to chop heads off	gui _ _ ot _ ne
Made to happen, the action that sets off a device	tr _ gg _ red
Argue over a small, unimportant, trivial thing	squa _ b _ e
Agreement to stop fighting	t _ _ ce
Hidden bomb designed to explode when touched	boo _ _ -tr _ p
Tall pointed tower, usually on a church	sp _ _ e
Large country house with land around it	m _ n _ r
Short sleep	sn _ _ ze
Clever move or strategy	t _ ct _ c
Something that can cause death or great damage	l _ thal
Military order to stop fighting for a short time	ce _ s _ fi _ e
Damaged deliberately by interference	t _ mp _ red with

2. Now working in pairs, test your memory of this first chapter. Assign **A** and **B** roles. **A** has the book and asks the questions. **B** answers the questions without the help of the book. Two points are given for each correct answer. Score out of 20.

i. In what had Ovid concealed a deadly explosive? (2)

ii. How many murder attempts had they clocked up between them? (2)

iii. What colour are Ovid's eyes? (2)

iv. Which of them claims to have always acted 'out of self-defence'? (2)

v. What does Ovid say has been his motivation? (2)

vi. What colour is Lorelli's hair? (2)

vii. What had Lorelli put in Ovid's bath? (2)

viii. What room is at the top of the central spire of Thornthwaite Manor? (2)

ix. What is the name of Lorelli's cat? (2)

x. How many times do they switch the slices of cake? (2)

Total: 20 points

Write a short, dramatic dialogue between Ovid and Lorelli. You can use some of the stage directions below, which give examples of expressions, gestures and tones of voice. Add some more of your own.

'_____,' announced Ovid, looking straight at Lorelli, his menacing eyes meeting hers across the table.

'_____,' replied Lorelli angrily, thumping her clenched fist.

'_____,' Ovid said, smiling.

'_____,' declared Lorelli, shrugging her shoulders.

'_____,' bellowed Ovid, laughing loudly.

'_____,' declared Lorelli.

'_____,' retorted Ovid, twisting his face in a sinister smirk.

'_____,' whispered Lorelli, looking menacingly at Ovid.

'_____,' declared Ovid coldly, without a trace of sympathy.

Gesture n.

Definition: a movement of the hand, the head, the shoulders, etc., that expresses what you are thinking or feeling

Synonyms: movement, body language

It is the morning after the near death of Lorelli in a mysterious accident.

Form pairs: **A** plays the detective; **B** plays Ovid.

Together, you will write and then perform a short drama, using these steps.

- Decide what kind of accident might have happened to Lorelli.
- Together, compose three questions that the detective would ask Ovid.
- Write the answers that you think Ovid might give.
- Add stage directions, telling the actors how to speak their lines.
- Learn the script you have written and perform your questions and answers aloud.

Extract from a Novel [2]

to create an atmosphere of suspense; to set a story in different seasons; to give imaginative names to minor characters

In the second chapter of *The Thornthwaite Inheritance*, we read about the deaths of Lorelli and Ovid's parents.

Six speakers need to be assigned for the following roles: the narrator; Mr Crutcher, the butler; District Inspector (DI) Lionel Skinner; Lady Thornthwaite; Lorelli and Ovid, who speak just one line, which they will say together. DI Skinner and Lady Thornthwaite have to decide on the accents they will use and what way they will each sit or stand, e.g. straight, slumped, etc. The narrator needs to be ready to read at the right moments. An old-fashioned telephone, a sherry glass and a torch would be excellent props.

Chapter 2, 'The Sudden Deaths of Lord and Lady Thornthwaite' from *The Thornthwaite Inheritance* by Gareth P. Jones

The twins' truce came thirteen years after the untimely demise of both their parents. When they were old enough to understand, it was the head servant, Mr Crutcher, who explained to Lorelli and Ovid the circumstances surrounding the deaths.

Lord Mycroft Thornthwaite had died first very suddenly one Tuesday night after a sumptuous four-course meal with his wife, Lady Martha Thornthwaite, the twins' mother.

The investigating officer was DI Lionel Skinner who, having spent his career failing to get a promotion in the big city had recently moved to Hexford County Police in order to become a detective inspector. Following the discovery of a slice of melon meringue wedged in the corpse's throat, Skinner concluded that Lord Thornthwaite had choked to death.

Lady Thornthwaite's story supported this conclusion. She claimed to have left the room during dessert to visit the lavatory only to find, upon her return, her husband dead. She said she had heard him coughing from the hallway but assumed he must have lit one of his stinky cigars. They always made him cough, she said. She had no idea he was choking to death.

'I loved my husband, Inspector Skinner,' she said. 'I can't believe he's gone.'

The story seemed perfectly plausible until the blood tests came back from the postmortem of the dead body, finding poison in his bloodstream. Further tests revealed traces of the same poison on the dirty dishes upon which the caviar had been served as a starter.

After questioning all the staff, Inspector Skinner learned that Lady Thornthwaite had given them all the night off, even Mrs Bagshaw, the cook, saying she wanted to prepare the meal herself. When asked by the detective, Mr Crutcher was forced to admit that she had access to all the ingredients that made up the poison that killed Lord Thornthwaite.

'Why did our mother kill our father?' Lorelli and Ovid had wanted to know.

'Greed can make people do terrible things,' Mr Crutcher had replied before continuing with his story.

It was a wild winter's evening when Mr Crutcher answered the door to DI Skinner and led him to the great hall, where Lady Thornthwaite was waiting, looking every bit the beautiful widow, draped entirely in black.

'Would you care for a sherry, Inspector?' she asked.

'No thank you, ma'am,' he replied.

'You don't mind if I do, do you?' she said, pouring herself a glass of sweet sherry from the decanter.

'Not at all, but I'm sorry to say this is not a social visit.'

Watching her take a sip from the glass, Skinner blurted out, 'I have evidence to suggest that you murdered your husband.'

Before Lady Thornthwaite could respond, the telephone began to ring.

'I'm sorry, Inspector, do you mind if I get that?' she said

Outside, the rain pounded on the long windows. Forks of lightning cut across the dark grey sky and thunder growled ominously, growing nearer each time.

Looking back on it, Mr Crutcher would reflect how Lady Thornthwaite had no idea she was about to utter her last words, or else she might have said something more profound. As it was, the last thing Lady Thornthwaite said was, 'I simply can't stand to leave a ringing phone unanswered.'

'I know exactly what you mean,' said Inspector Skinner, noting how calm she was for someone who has just been accused of murdering her husband.

She placed her glass of sherry on the mantelshelf above the fireplace and stooped to pick up the earpiece of the old-fashioned phone.

A clap of thunder sounded above, shaking the old manor to its foundations. The room went bright white as lightning struck, creating an image of Lady Thornthwaite that would haunt Inspector Skinner for the rest of his life, burnt into his mind like an overdeveloped photograph.

Immediately afterwards the power went dead and the room was thrown into darkness. 'Don't be alarmed, ma'am,' said the inspector. 'I carry a torch for just such occasions.'

He pulled a torch from his belt, switched it on and pointed it to where Lady Thornthwaite had been standing.

She wasn't there.

He lowered the beam of light and discovered her lying on the ground, dead, still clutching the telephone earpiece.

This time the forensic tests were conclusive. The twins' mother was killed by a bolt of lightning striking the telephone mast outside, sending one billion volts through the wire, frying the telephone and cooking Lady Thornthwaite's insides.

Inspector Skinner checked the phone records and found the person who made the call had been trying to get through to his wife to warn her about the storm. He hadn't even known the Thornthwaites.

In other words, Lady Thornthwaite was killed by a wrong number.

?
EXPLORE

1. Find and complete the words from this second chapter that match the following definitions.

Delicious	su_ _tuous
Dead body	co_pse
Police officer who investigates special crimes	d_ _ _ _ _ve
Test on a body to find cause of death	p_ _ _ ⁻ m_ _ _ _m
Expensive fish delicacy	c_ _i_r
Bright flash of light in a storm	li_ _ _ _ing
Holding tightly	cl_ _ ching
Glass container for wine	de_ _ nter
Part of a building below ground that supports its weight	fo_nd_ _ _ _ns

2. Now working in pairs, test your memory of this second chapter. Assign **A** and **B** roles. **A** has the book and asks the questions. **B** answers the questions without the help of the book. Two points are given for each correct answer. Score out of 20.

- **i.** How many years has it been since the deaths of Lorelli and Ovid's parents? (2)
- **ii.** What was Lord Thornthwaite's first name? (2)
- **iii.** On which night of the week did he die? (2)
- **iv.** What was Lady Thornthwaite's first name? (2)
- **v.** What was Mr Crutcher's job in the house? (2)
- **vi.** What was the detective inspector's name? (2)
- **vii.** What was found in the corpse's throat? (2)
- **viii.** What had been served as a starter? (2)
- **ix.** What was Mrs Bagshaw's job? (2)
- **x.** In which room of the house did Lady Thornthwaite receive the detective? (2)

Total: 20 points

CREATE

In the second chapter you read the following paragraph, which describes the winter setting for the arrival of DI Skinner.

> It was a wild winter's evening when Mr Crutcher answered the door to DI Skinner … Outside, the rain pounded on the long windows. Forks of lightning cut across the dark grey sky and thunder growled ominously, growing nearer each time. … A clap of thunder sounded above, shaking the old manor to its foundations. The room went bright white as lightning struck … Immediately afterwards the power went dead and the room was thrown into darkness. *(75 words)*

Now read this summer setting for the arrival of another official investigating a crime.

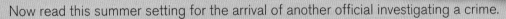

> It was a bright morning in July when Mrs DiCaprio answered the door to Garda Cillian McGrath. Outside, the cloudless sky and the early morning sunshine promised another hot day. The little side street was quiet but the distant roar of rush hour traffic could be heard from the main road. Who would have guessed that the scullery of Mrs DiCaprio's tiny terrace house had been the scene of a terrible crime? *(72 words)*

Now write your own descriptive opener to a murder mystery. Insert different names and a different season, month and time of day.

It was a _____ in _____ when _____ answered the door to _____. Outside, _____ ...

Self-Assessment

Re-read what you have written and then write down two things you think you did well and one thing you could improve on.

1. Fill in the gaps with the words used in the second chapter. Then, in each case, write a synonym for the word. Your dictionary or thesaurus can help you to complete this task.

Before Lady Thornthwaite could r _ _ _ _ _ d (..................) the telephone b _ _ _ n (.........) to ring.

Outside, the rain p _ _ _ _ _ d (...........................) on the long windows.

F _ _ _ s (..................) of lightning cut across the d _ _ k (.........) grey sky and thunder g_ _ _ _ _ d (...............) ominously, growing nearer each time.

A c _ _ p (.............) of thunder sounded above, s_ _ _ ing (............) the old m_ _ _ _ (............) to its foundations.

2. Complete the adverbs in the following sentences from the story you have just read.

Lord Mycroft Thornthwaite had died first v _ _ y s _ _ _ _ _ _ y one Tuesday night.

'OK,' she said f _ _ _ _ _ y.

DI Lionel Skinner had r _ _ _ _ _ y moved to Hexford County Police.

The story seemed p _ _ _ _ _ _ _ y plausible.

Thunder growled o _ _ _ _ _ _ ly.

I know e _ _ _ _ ly what you mean.

I _ _ _ _ _ _ _ _ ly afterwards the power went dead.

Extract from a Novel [3]

What I will learn:

the language of dramatic climax; to use powerful verbs and adjectives to describe fear; to use short followed by long sentences to create a dramatic effect

Here is an extract from a very famous short novel, *The Birds*, written by Daphne du Maurier in 1952. This story inspired an even more famous Alfred Hitchcock film of the same name. In this extract, we read of a terrifying attack by birds on a family home. The father, Nat, tries to defend his wife and children against the attack.

Extract from *The Birds* by Daphne du Maurier

The window was wide open. Through it came the birds, hitting first the ceiling and the walls, then swerving in mid-flight and turning to the children in their beds.

'It's all right, I'm here,' shouted Nat, and the children flung themselves, screaming, upon him, while in the darkness the birds rose and dived, and came for him again. 'What is it, Nat? What's happened?' his wife called. Swiftly he pushed the children through the door to the passage and shut it upon them, so that he was alone in their bedroom with the birds.

He seized a blanket from the nearest bed and, using it as a weapon, flung it to right and left about him in the air. He felt the thud of bodies, heard the fluttering of wings, but they were not yet defeated, for again and again they returned to the assault, jabbing his hands, his head, the little stabbing beaks sharp as pointed forks. The blanket became a weapon of defence; he wound it about his head, and then in greater darkness beat at the birds with his bare hands. He dared not stumble to the door and open it, lest in doing so the birds should follow him.

How long he fought with them in the darkness he could not tell, but at last the beating of the wings about him lessened and then withdrew, and through the density of the blanket he was aware of light. He waited, listened; there was no sound except the fretful crying of one of the children from the bedroom beyond. The fluttering, the whirring of the wings had ceased.

He took the blanket from his head and stared about him. The cold grey morning light exposed the room. Dawn and the open window had called the living birds; the dead lay on the floor. Nat gazed at the little corpses, shocked and horrified. They were all small birds, none of any size; there must have been fifty of them lying there upon the floor. There were robins, finches, sparrows, blue tits, larks, and bramblings, birds that by nature's law kept to their own flock and their own territory, and now, joining one with another in their urge for battle, had destroyed themselves against the bedroom walls or in the strife had been destroyed by him. Some had lost feathers in the fight; others had blood, his blood, upon their beaks.

Make a list of the ten best dramatic words and phrases that make this extract a powerful description of a frightening invasion.

Write an item for the evening news, informing viewers about an attack by flocks of birds on a coastal town.

FUN FACT

Alfred Hitchcock's film of this book had a huge publicity campaign. When the audience at its London premiere left the Odeon cinema, there were loudspeakers hidden in the trees in Leicester Square broadcasting the squawking and screeching of birds!

SHOW WHAT YOU KNOW

You have learned many writing and speaking skills throughout this collection. Now it's time to *Show What You Know!*

My Portfolio Task

Write the opening chapter of a mystery story in which a detective visits a large lonely house on a cliff near a graveyard overlooking the sea. It is a stormy winter's night. The house (give it a name) is seen by local people as a place of mystery and fear. There are local rumours of séances and black magic. A twelve-year-old boy who lived there and was heir to the house and family fortune has disappeared. The detective has come to interview a relative about the disappearance.

SUCCESS CRITERIA

I must

- Describe the setting, i.e. the cliff, the house, both inside and out, the time of night, the stormy weather
- Use some of the words and phrases from this collection to describe a storm (reviewing 'The Visitor' for examples)
- Include dialogue between my characters
- Arrange my chapter in paragraphs
- Read what I've written to check for missing punctuation marks (, . ! ?) or missing words
- Use a **dictionary** to check spellings I'm not sure of

I should

- Give my story an interesting and maybe mysterious title
- Use adjectives and action verbs
- Use a thesaurus to find synonyms so that I do not repeat words
- Include tone of voice, gestures and facial expressions when writing dialogue

I could

- Think of a good name for the house
- Think of interesting names for the detective and the relative
- Reveal what the detective is thinking as he or she walks/drives up the long avenue to the house
- Use a variety of sentence lengths, some short, some long, to give rhythm and flow to my story when it is read aloud
- Read my story aloud to check how it sounds, then make any changes necessary

Self-Assessment

Re-read what you have written and then write down two things you think you did well and one thing you could improve on.

Redrafting

Reviewing the success criteria again to make sure you have met all the requirements, and taking into account your own self-assessment notes, you can now revise your story opener to create a second draft. When you are happy with it, you can put it in your **portfolio**.

Reflection Question

Did I use stories or poems I have read to give me ideas for my storyline/dialogue/descriptions?

Oral Communication

In groups, pick your favourite opening chapter from your group. You will now perform it as a radio play and record it. Remember that your radio listeners are not reading the story; instead they are **hearing** it.

SUCCESS CRITERIA

We should

- Brainstorm the sounds needed to make this believable as a stormy night on a windswept cliff with a detective travelling up a long driveway and knocking on a door
- Appoint a sound engineer who, with the help of the group, will figure out how to create these sound effects using common items

We must

- Appoint a narrator to read the opening paragraph describing the setting
- Appoint actors to speak the character parts in the story, giving them directions regarding tone of voice so the actors know how they should speak their lines
- Create atmosphere by adding a piece of music in the background
- Add sound effects

We could

- Change the name of the story to something that will attract an audience hearing advance publicity for the programme

Peer Assessment

Reflect on your classmates' work and then write down two things you think they did well and one thing they could improve on.

TOP TIP

The job of the sound engineer is to find objects that can sound realistic; for example, howling wind, a fog horn out at sea, footsteps, the doorbell/knock on the front door, the creaking of the door as it opens, etc. You will have to use your imagination to come up with things you can easily find that will make realistic sound effects. For example, the sound of an umbrella rapidly opening and closing imitates bats flying; shaking a thin sheet of metal makes a stormy sound.

Celebrations

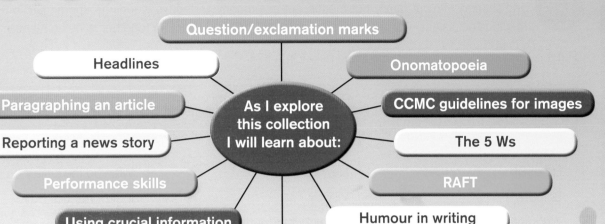

Question/exclamation marks

Headlines

Paragraphing an article

Reporting a news story

Performance skills

Using crucial information

As I explore this collection I will learn about:

Onomatopoeia

CCMC guidelines for images

The 5 Ws

RAFT

Humour in writing

Personal response

Learning Outcomes
OL2, OL5, OL10, OL11, R3, R6, R8, W1, W4, W11

SHOW WHAT YOU KNOW

The skills you learn in this collection will enable you to **show what you know** in your final tasks at the end of this collection.

For my portfolio task I will:
Write an article about a celebration

For oral communication I will:
Record or perform a news report

Exploring the Theme – Celebrations

There are so many different events that happen throughout our lives that we all enjoy celebrating and sharing with our family, our friends, our community. Birthdays, weddings, sporting victories, religious occasions – whatever the happy event, we enjoy coming together to celebrate it.

Put the various reasons to celebrate listed below into their relevant category.

Religion/Beliefs	Achievements	Festivals	Changes	Commemorations	Traditions	Emotions

Eid al-Fitr

Birthday

Wedding

St Patrick's Day

Exam results

Driving test

Joy

Birth of a baby

Christmas

New Year's Eve

VE Day

Winning the County Final

Hanukkah

Happiness

Pride

Honour

Homecoming

Finishing a show

Winning the lottery

Independence Day

Promotion

Relief

Anniversary

Excitement

New house

Easter

Fourth of July

A Newspaper Article

What I will learn:

to create a catchy headline; to use paragraphs in an article; to use the 5 Ws

Have you ever won a competition in school or with your local club? If you are lucky enough to have held a trophy or had a medal hung around your neck, you know the celebrations are immense and well-deserved. Often newspapers are filled with articles about people whose achievements most definitely should be celebrated.

Article n.
Definition: a piece of writing included in a magazine, newspaper, online or in other types of publication

PREPARE

Read these statements and spend one minute thinking about your response to them.

Now, when your teacher instructs you, turn to your partner and see if you have had any similar responses.

When you have finished, form groups of four to share your ideas. Then choose one speaker to share the group's responses with the rest of the class. Be able to explain each answer and give as much detail as possible.

STATEMENTS

- I know what an opinion is.
- I have heard other people give their opinions.
- I have read a piece of writing where someone shares their opinion.
- I would love if someone wrote about me.
- I would normally read opinions in/on:
  * Newspapers
  * Blogs
  * Magazines
  * Social media
- I normally hear opinions on/in:
  * Radio
  * Podcast
  * Television
  * School
  * Public meetings
- If I was giving my opinion, I would need to include:
  * Accurate information
  * Reasons for giving my opinion
  * Clear explanation
  * Appropriate tone and language
- I know what an article is: it is ...

These words are included in the article you will read next. In your copy, match up each word with the correct definition. You may need to use your **dictionary** to do so.

jabbed	previous place of education
basking	lasting
stellar	suddenly get excited
alma mater	all agreed
ballistic	exceptional
sparred	getting pleasure from
enduring	punched quickly and sharply
unanimous	trained/practised for a boxing match

It is important to learn new words so you can use them in your writing and speaking. Once you have completed the word match, you have sixty seconds to learn and remember as many of the definitions as possible. Afterwards, you and your partner will test each other.

READ

This article from the *Irish Independent* celebrates a magnificent achievement by Irish boxer, Katie Taylor.

In articles, it's important to have a catchy headline

'When Katie's Arm Went Up We All Went Ballistic'

by Brian Byrne

It's good to start with a catchy opening paragraph.

THE trophy shelf in Katie Taylor's home is beginning to strain under the weight of the Wicklow boxer's success as she claimed her fifth successive world title in South Korea.

The Bray woman **jabbed** her way to victory over Azerbaijan's Yana Alekseeva, and while her attention will now shift to Rio 2016 and retaining the gold medal she won at the London Olympics two years ago, relatives, friends and neighbours who yesterday followed her progress from the edge of their seats at home were **basking** in yet another **stellar** performance from their golden girl.

Next you can add in any other important information that you feel is necessary

Katie's nephew Jason King (14), who is in second year at her **alma mater**, St Kilian's Community School in Bray, said the whole family was delighted with the win. 'We'd be watching her matches in the house and every time she gets a good jab or to see her arm going up at the end of the match, everyone just goes **ballistic** in the house.'

Despite wearing her 17th gold medal in less than a decade around her neck, Katie hasn't forgotten where she comes from, a point made repeatedly by locals, and plainly visible at the school, where a number of students are already succeeding at the sport.

Among them is Shannon Reilly (14), who won bronze at the European Youth and Junior Championships in July and once even **sparred** against the 28-year-old.

Shannon said: 'Katie came down to the school after she won an earlier world championship title and she inspired me to get into the sport. It's a great sport, and women have taken it by storm.'

However, asked whether she knew the secret to the Bray woman's success, Shannon admitted: 'It's too complicated. She's just brilliant. She's very tough. She hits very hard. That's part of it, you have to learn how to take a shot.'

Fellow student Chloe Bishop (13), who won an individual bronze medal and team gold medal at the World Kick-Boxing Championships in October, said: 'She's inspired me a lot. When she won the Olympics she came down and she inspired me to go out to the world championships. Loads of girls have started doing boxing now. Kick-boxing is hopefully going to be in the Olympics in 2020 so there will be loads of girls getting into the sport.'

Katie's **enduring** career has left a mark that will last for generations in Bray, proof of which came in eight-year-old Finn Kelly, who described her as 'the best female boxer in the world', adding that he too had followed in his heroine's courageous footsteps.

But her successes have touched more than just the residents of the north Wicklow town. President Michael D. Higgins put into words the thoughts of the nation when he said: 'All of us are so proud of her.'

'I offer sincere congratulations to Katie and indeed her family on this outstanding win; where she again showed such remarkable skill, determination and courage at the very highest level.

'Katie Taylor is without doubt the outstanding Irish sportswoman of her generation and has set a standard for all Irish sportspeople to follow in decades ahead.'

The judges were **unanimous** in their decision to award Katie the title of AIBA World Elite Lightweight Champion after four intense rounds, despite the boxer characterising her competitor Alekseeva as 'very, very tricky'.

> When you have included the most essential facts, you can write about less important details

1. Based on your reading of the article, answer the 5 Ws:
   - **Who** is this article about?
   - **What** is it about?
   - **Where** is it referring to?
   - **When** it is referring to?
   - **Why** was it written?

2. What has Katie inspired others to do?

3. Do young people think of her as a role model?

4. How do you think the writer feels about Katie Taylor? What is his opinion of her and her success?

REMEMBER
The 5 Ws, p. 53.

A role model is someone you admire for a particular reason. Brainstorm five celebrities you consider to be role models and what you consider to be their greatest achievements or accomplishments. Now imagine you are writing an article about one of your chosen role models. Consider whether you are writing for a tabloid or a broadsheet newspaper. Design a catchy headline that would appear at the top of the page, e.g. 'The World Weeps for Mandela', 'Tom Cruises to Box Office Glory'.

RESEARCH ZONE

Do some research on one of your celebrity role models. Create a profile for him/her which includes the following details:

- Date of birth (and death, if applicable)
- Place of birth and background
- Family
- Major goals and achievements

You could use the following website to give you more ideas on how to create a profile:

http://www.readwritethink.org/files/resources/interactives/profile/

  Using the information you collected in your research zone task, write a headline, an introductory paragraph, and draw an image, for an article on your chosen role model.

REMEMBER   Use the 5 Ws.

TOP TIP

It is helpful to use Google as a search engine, but you must remember that not every website is trustworthy. Look at more than one site to make sure you are getting accurate information.

Social Media – Twitter

What I will learn:

to write a short message to get my point across

When things are going well for us or when something good or exciting happens to us, we are always very eager to share our joy with our family and friends, and sometimes with the world! Like article headlines, tweets have to get your attention using just a few words. Therefore words must be chosen carefully.

Ed Sheeran ✔
@edsheeran

1

11th week at #1 and 5 times platinum. UK, udabes

7:18 PM - 21 Dec 2014

↩ ⟲ 10,397 ★ 29,142

Katie Taylor ✔
@KatieTaylor

2

Thank you so much for all the support over the last few weeks. Can't wait to touch down in Dub with another Gold.

3:35 PM - 24 Nov 2014

↩ ⟲ 599 ★ 1,871

Adele ✔
@OfficialAdele

3

Wish I was there! Thank you for the grammy! (My 10th one! Whhaaa?) Have a wonderful night. I'm in bed, now feeling very restless x

11:17 PM - 26 Jan 2014

↩ ⟲ 7,529 ★ 9,775

The very popular social messaging service, Twitter, was launched in 2006. Twitter allows users to send and read short 140 character 'tweets'. These are some celebrity Twitter messages. They are tweeting about various moments of celebration. Can you guess what each one is about?

4

Barack Obama ✔
@BarackObama

Four more years.

4:16 AM - 7 Nov 2012

↩ ⟲ 749,935 ★ 287,316

Andy Lee ✔
@AndyLeeBoxing

5

I'm on top of the world!

5:43 PM - 14 Dec 2014

↩ ⟲ 969 ★ 2,255

Look at the following pictures of various celebrations. For each picture, write a Twitter message from a key personality who could be associated with each event.

Drama – A Play

What I will learn:

to write or speak about personal experiences; to practise my performance skills

In the last lesson, you will have noticed how Twitter messages can reveal what a person is feeling at a particular time. These celebrities were willing to share their thoughts with their followers. However, not all people are comfortable sharing their personal feelings. In this next drama, 'Happy Birthday Squirt!', a fourteen-year-old boy finds it very difficult to explain how disappointed he is when he thinks his family have forgotten his birthday.

What has been your favourite birthday so far? Why was it special? How did you spend it?

You will now get ready to perform 'Happy Birthday Squirt!'

In groups of five, practise a reading of the script. When you have finished, your group must assign roles, practise their drama skills and perform the script. Pay attention to movement and gestures. Remember – many of the characters have stage directions, so you should add these to your performance.

Characters: James, a boy of medium height with brown hair, wearing jeans, a t-shirt and Converse; his father; his mother; his twin sisters, Eve and Lucy.

Setting: A family kitchen on a Saturday morning. James enters the kitchen in an excited manner as today is his birthday and he is looking forward to receiving his present of an Xbox, which his father has promised him. In the kitchen, his father and mother sit reading: his father is reading the newspaper about Kerry's win in the previous Sunday's All-Ireland Football Final; his mother is flicking through a magazine. Both keep reading as James enters the room.

Props: Newspaper, magazine, teapot, permission slip, Xbox, birthday cake

Stage directions n.
Definition: part of the script of a play telling the actors how to move or to speak their lines

Happy Birthday Squirt!

James: (*excited*) Good morning!

Dad: (*grumbles quietly*) Eh? ... Yeah yeah ... Mornin'.

Mam: (*without looking up*) Mornin' love.

James waits for a moment, confused at their lack of attention.

James: (*coughs*) A-hem!

Neither his mam nor dad look up from their reading.

Dad: Jeez, you'd think that miserable blighter would accept defeat! No, he just keeps on wailin' about the referee and his Hawkeye. Sure if his own lads were able to hit a barn door, they might have had some chance!

James: Dad? ...

Dad: ... and Colm Cooper, what a credit to his county. I'd go so far as to say he's one of the greatest – yes, I've said it before and I'll say it again – one of the greatest footballers Kerry has ever seen. Mind you, he'd want to have a couple more Celtic crosses in the cabinet before he's considered a Kerry 'great'. James, make yourself useful there and put on the kettle before I die of thirst.

James: (*gets up to put the kettle on*) Dad, I was just wondering if you *remembered* ...

Mam: Ah sure of course he has – aren't you a darling to remind him about these things, James, but you know he will never forget to do the Lotto! Isn't that right, John, ten million euro tonight? Think of all the lovely cups of tea that would get you (*giggles to herself*).

Dad: (*chuckling*) Ah Mary, you're gas! Now James, don't be festerin' with the pot, pour that water in so it will stew. You should be able to trot a mouse across the top of it.

James: Yeah, but Dad, I was just wondering if you remembered what *day* it was ...

Dad: Sure course I do! That pair are off to town to spend all my hard-earned money. Mac make-up, Hollister hoodies – they'll clean me out. Actually, no sign of the double trouble act yet, they must be still snorin' away.

James: No Dad, not the twins. There's another promise you made …

Mam: Oh yes, how could we forget, James? Oh dear, we are *very* sorry, James, what diabolical parents we are – not remembering such a thing. But yes, yes, we remember the promise: of course you can go on that History trip. I'll sign the permission slip right away! (*Goes to the cabinet to get the slip and sign it*) All you young ones these days going on school trips here and there; the closest we ever came to a school trip was being sent to the local shop to get a message for the teacher.

Dad: Oh jeez, yeah, sorry son. Can you imagine us forgetting a thing like *that*? We are such dithering old fools. As the King once said, 'Education plus character – there is the true goal of education' … did I ever tell you about the time King …

Mam: John, not another Martin Luther King story, it's Saturday morning, we all need a break.

Dad: Ah now, Mary, you should savour the words of the King. I mean, remember what he said in Montgomery (*both Mam and James roll their eyes*): 'Darkness cannot drive out darkness: only light can do that. Hate cannot drive out hate: only love can do that.'

James: No Dad, not the History trip! By the way, this obsession with Martin Luther King is a little eccentric, don't you think?

Dad: What's eccentric about reciting inspirational words, James? Are they not teaching you anything in that school of yours? Maybe I'll have to give you extra History lessons meself (*laughs*).

James: You're okay Dad, but getting back to my original point. I was just hoping that you *remembered* …

At this point the teenage twins, Eve and Lucy, burst through the door.

Lucy: Morning, *a tuismitheoirí*!

Eve: (*to James, rubbing his head*) Morning, Squirt Face!

James: Ah would ya stop! Go away!

Lucy: Is someone a little irksome this morning? You're such a grump!

Mam: (*winking at the twins*) Now girls, tell me. Are you ready for your big shopping trip? Dad said he won't have a penny left with the two of you. Nothing left at all for any other extravagance for the foreseeable future.

James looks alarmed.

Lucy: We are going to paint the town red and enjoy ourselves silly. New outfits, new shoes, new makeup … a whole new us!

James: But what about me?

Eve: What about you, Squirt? Sure what would you need, you're so *young*?

Lucy: Yeah, you're just a baby!

James: No I'm not, it's my …

Eve: Stop blatherin' on, James. You won't get the girls that way – not that you really have much of a chance anyway.

Lucy: Yeah James, you really should look at doing something with that mop of hair. You look like you're hiding something under it. No girl will want to look at you, let alone kiss you!

James: Stop! I can't take my sisters talking to me about kissing. Please Mam, make them stop! (*Looking very disappointed, he says to himself*) I'm outta here.

Dad: James, where are you going? Haven't you forgotten something?

James: Oh, (*he sighs*) the tea (*going to pick up the teapot*).

Mam: Well, you might want to take down some cups too.

James opens the cupboard, only to find an Xbox wrapped up in a bow.

Dad, Mam, Eve & Lucy: Happy Birthday!

Mam and Dad run over to give him a hug.

James: Brilliant!

Dad: Well, you hardly think we forgot your birthday, James?

James: But I thought you said you wouldn't have any money left with the girls' shopping spree!

Eve: Ah, we were only winding you up, Squirt Face.

Lucy: Yeah – look! We were up super early this morning to get you this gigantic chocolate cake (*produces cake from the fridge*). Come on, let's have some!

Mam: Not only that, but we have loads of great things planned for today – we're off to town where you can get yourself some new clothes, and maybe pick out another game for that contraption.

James: I thought you had all forgotten. This is the best birthday ever!

1. In your own words, what did James' dad say about the Gaelic footballer, Colm Cooper?

2. Imagine you are acting one of the parts on stage. Describe the costume you would wear.

3. What kind of person do you think James is?

4. Lots of families play practical jokes on each other. Do you think this one was a good one?

Create a two-page drama script based on a celebration where something unexpected or out of the ordinary happens. You must decide on the celebration, the complication and an ending. You must have three characters and must include stage directions.

RESEARCH ZONE

Find out more about Martin Luther King Jr and why he is one of the most celebrated men in history. Create a character profile on him.

Peer Assessment

Read your classmate's work and then write down two things you think he/she did well and one thing he/she could improve on.

A Poem

What I will learn:

to use crucial information

New Year's Eve is one of the only festivals that is common to and celebrated in most countries. Saint Patrick's Day is an Irish religious occasion that has turned into a festival celebrated all around the world. Then there are some festivals which are specific to certain countries, for example Carniriv in Nigeria, Klaipeda Sea Festival in Lithuania and the Fourth of July in America.

W4.5

What is your favourite memory of a celebration? Describe what types of activities were involved. Did you have certain types of food and drink? If so, describe them. What emotions did you feel on the day? Who shared the memory with you?

READ

Poetry is an excellent way of writing about our personal experiences. Poems are ideal for exploring feelings because, like tweets, they use a limited amount of carefully chosen words to describe big ideas and feelings. In the following poem, the poet explores her feelings about an important celebration.

 ## Danitra's Family Reunion
by Nikki Grimes

On the Fourth of July,
my cousins and I
ran sack races,
played kickball
and tug-of-war
before
we heard
our stomachs
growl.

We stopped for
deviled eggs,
buttered corn,
coleslaw,
fried chicken,
potato salad, and
Strawberry Pie Jubilee.

We sipped lemonade
and listened to
Grandma Brown's stories
of when our folks were little.
Then Uncle Joe
handed out prizes
for this year's graduates
and for the best all-round student,
which I won.

By the time
the day was done,
I was full of fun
and food
and warm feelings,
knowing that I am more
than just me.
I am part
of a family.

CREATE

1. Imagine the poem is entitled 'Christmas Eve' or 'New Year's Eve'. Now change some of the lines to create your own poem based on your tradition of this celebration.

2. Imagine you are visiting your relatives in America during the Fourth of July. Write an email to your friend back home describing your experiences. It is important to gather factual information about the event to make it authentic (realistic). Read the following information to help you with the details:

REMEMBER

Writing an email, p. 10.

- The Fourth of July commemorates when America gained independence from Britain in 1776. (How many years ago was this?)
- It was on the fourth of July that the Declaration of Independence was signed by Thomas Jefferson.
- People celebrate the day with historical parades, re-enactments of battle scenes, picnics, trips to the beach, baseball games and American football games.
- Common foods eaten include hot dogs, hamburgers, corn on the cob, coleslaw and apple pie.
- Fireworks are often displayed in different states and are a huge attraction for both locals and tourists.

You could research this celebration some more to gather extra information for your email.

Self-Assessment

Re-read what you have written and then write down two things you think you did well and one thing you could improve on.

Images

to comment on photographs/images using CCMC

Images are at the heart of all aspects of society, whether they're on television, in newspapers, advertising cars, clothes, or whether they are used in books to illustrate stories or poems. With the introduction of new technology such as smartphones, taking pictures and capturing moments is a common occurrence in all our lives.

It is important to be able to look at an image and question why someone has chosen to set up a picture in a particular way, or why they have chosen a particular image to illustrate their work.

Photo Survey

Here are some questions to ask your partner:

1. Do you take photographs?
2. Why do you take photographs?
3. Do you put photographs up on social media?
4. Have you ever planned the shot to include specific things? Describe how you did this.
5. Do you think photographs should be studied? Explain your answer.
6. Do you like having your photograph taken?
7. If you were allowed to take only one photograph per year, on what occasion would you take it?

FUN FACT

The word 'selfie' was the word of the year in 2013, according to Oxford Dictionaries. Miley Cyrus had over 450 selfies on her Twitter account in that same year!

The CCMC Approach to Examining Photos

When you examine a photograph, this is what you need to look out for:

CONTENT
Who or what is in the photograph?

CONTEXT
When and where do you think the photo is set?

MESSAGE
Why did the photographer decide to take the shot at that exact moment? Did they want the message to be positive or negative?

COLOUR
Is the photo in black and white or in colour? Does the colour or lack of colour make you feel anything specifically about the picture?

CCMC in Action

The **content** of this photograph includes a long dragon puppet being carried by Chinese men. There is lots of confetti surrounding it. The **photo is taken** in a narrow street with buildings either side and Chinese signs and posters attached to the shop fronts. **I believe the photographer decided** to take the shot at that moment because they could capture the length of the dragon, showing how much work and preparation had gone in to creating this spectacle. The fact that there is lots of **colour** makes me feel that this celebration is fun and dazzling. It makes me want to visit the parade.

REMEMBER

The Five-Part Story Planner p. 61.

CREATE

1. Pick your favourite image from the selection given here and use the CCMC guidelines to help you to examine the photo and write about it.

2. Imagine you are at that parade or festival. Write a short story inspired by the image.

A Poem

What I will learn:

to use onomatopoeia

Celebrations and happy times are often associated with extravagance and big occasions. However, it is often the little things in life, the things we take for granted, that can make us happy: when your mother makes your bed for you, your brother gets you a drink, a friend sends you a nice message when you are feeling down …

  What are the things in your life that you can't live without? Why are they essential to your life?

 This writer's appreciation for the little things in life shines through in her very descriptive poem.

 ## Blessing
by Imtiaz Dharker

The skin cracks like a pod.
There never is enough water.

Imagine the drip of it,
the small splash, echo
in a tin mug,
the voice of a kindly god.

Sometimes, the sudden rush
of fortune. The municipal pipe bursts,
silver crashes to the ground
and the flow has found
a roar of tongues. From the huts,
a congregation: every man woman

child for streets around
butts in, with pots,
brass, copper, aluminium,
plastic buckets,
frantic hands,

and naked children
screaming in the liquid sun,
their highlights polished to perfection,
flashing light,
as the blessing sings
over their small bones.

1. If you were writing to the author of this poem, what questions would you ask her? Write three meaningful questions you have about this poem.

2. Write a note to the poet giving your personal response to the poem.

MIND YOUR LANGUAGE

ONOMATOPOEIA

W4.6

Onomatopoeia is another effective tool to add to your writing. Onomatopoeia (say: *on-o-mat-o-pay-a*) is a word that mimics the sound of the object or action it refers to, e.g. the *dripping* tap; the *tick-tock* of the clock; the ice *clinking* in the glass.

1. In the poem 'Blessing', the poet uses several examples of onomatopoeia to describe the precious rainwater. Can you find them?

2. Read the following sentences and insert an appropriate onomatopoeic word.

i. The lion _____ the cool water from the river.

ii. The teacher gave out to Adela because she _____ her pen non-stop.

iii. The egg _____ when it fell on the tiles.

iv. I am trying to focus on my novel but the _____ of the clock is distracting me.

v. Watching the latest horror film, Rachel _____ when she saw the monster.

vi. During Halloween, our cat gets upset when he hears the _____ of the fireworks.

vii. I hate walking past my neighbour's little dog, he always _____ at me.

viii. Cian's dad asked how his day was when he returned from school but he just _____.

ix. I awoke in the morning to find my dad making breakfast; the sausages were _____ on the frying pan.

x. The rain was pouring down as Daciana ran to the shop, she was _____ as the car drove through the puddle.

3. Having found the onomatopoeic words for the rain sounds in 'Blessing', try reading it, substituting the examples of onomatopoeia for the actual sounds. Then read aloud each sentence from question 2, also substituting the onomatopoeic words for the actual sounds.

A Speech

What I will learn:

to use RAFT to structure my writing; to explore and practise using question/exclamation marks; to appreciate the use of humour

When people achieve great personal glory or fame they also bring great pride to their local area. Communities come together to celebrate these achievements and to show the person or people involved how much they are appreciated. They might throw a big party or make a presentation to them.

  Think carefully and, with your partner, compile a list of any famous people from your county or local area. Now come up with the best way to honour them and celebrate their achievements.

  Some people like to discuss celebration in a serious manner, like in the poem 'Blessing'. Others, however, like to use humour, like Chris O'Dowd in this next piece. Chris O'Dowd, the well-known star of *Moone Boy*, *The IT Crowd* and the film *Bridesmaids*, is from Boyle, Co. Roscommon, and because of his great success internationally, he was awarded the freedom of the county in October 2014. The following edited text is the speech he gave when accepting the honour.

FUN FACT

The Freedom of the County is an honour given to a valued member of a particular county.

Acceptance Speech by Chris O'Dowd on being made a Freeman of Roscommon

Thank you so much first of all everybody for making this happen and for being so **resilient**. I know you asked me a while ago and I was playing hard to get but I am so glad to be here.

Today I am a freeman of Roscommon, a freeman of Roscommon I am today! The most alarming thing about that statement is that before today I hadn't been aware that Roscommon had enslaved me. Believe it or not I had gone about my daily business utterly **ignorant** as to my apparent on-going struggle for **liberation** beyond the county borders of Athlone and Lough Arrow. What a fool I was! In many ways I innocently, before today, saw Roscommon as my friend rather than my captor. All this time I'd been kidnapped.

And what can I tell you of my captor? How did it manage to **hoodwink** me into loving it all this time? Where do I start? And of course, I mainly consider myself a man of Boyle but I feel like I have a relationship with townlands up and down the county. Athleague, Roosky, Elphin and Drum are only some of the towns I have lost football matches in ... along with some of the people here today.

Frenchpark, Knockvicar, Tulsk and Ballyfarnon are among the very few towns that I've been caught underage drinking in ... along with some of the people here today.

Croghan, Castlerea, Cootehall and Keadue are only the tip of the iceberg when I think of places I've tried and failed to kiss girls in carparks ... I managed to do that on my own. Thankfully though there has been some progress in that area and I'm delighted to say that my lovely lady wife and I – mostly her – will deliver a fresh Roscommon child into the world next year. And we don't know whether it is to be a future Roscommon footballer or Camogie player, but I think it is safe to say that in the light of recent results, that even in its current state as a foetus, it could probably make either squad ... of course I'm joking!

And what would I tell my young one of my home? In research for today I discovered that Roscommon has the longest life expectancy in all of Ireland. I like to think that it is because Roscommon people have more to live for. But it is also possible that now that we're without an A&E department, we're simply too afraid to die ... they're jokes of course! What we lack in clean water, we make up for in dirty jokes ... at ease councillors, I know that it's nobody's fault.

But seriously, what will I tell my daughter or my son? I would tell her how that in an ever-changing Ireland, Roscommon stayed true to itself. For when I lose the run of myself, Roscommon stays put. I love it and not because it is perfect but because it's real. The truth is Roscommon is not a rich man's weekend **getaway**; it is breeding ground for artists and entertainers like John Reilly and Maureen O'Sullivan and John Carty. Roscommon is not a community built on the wings of a foreign computer company; it is a refuge for writers and scholars like John McGahern and Brian Leyden and Douglas Hyde.

Roscommon is not a destination for stag nights, it's the birthplace of Margaret Gillespie, one of the most extraordinary women of the global suffragette movement whose strength and will helped her become the first female magistrate in India.

Roscommon is not a satellite town for Dublin commuters. Roscommon is home. And if none of that works, I'll tell my child to blame its grandparents. Because my parents love Roscommon. When the time came for my mother to migrate from her homestead in Knockvicar in search of bright lights and adventure, she landed in Boyle … and refused to leave. She spent years listening to her children's problems and being a pillar of the community, and for **respite**, became a therapist. She helps local people heal themselves, so she's a local hero to me.

As a sign writer, my father spent his career literally telling people what's what. In semi-retirement he's doing much of the same. In his later years, my dad has **dedicated** his life to a website helping local people stay informed of events in their town. Realboyle.com. He serves his community near and far, so to me he is a local hero.

All you people here today, whether you ran my first drama class like Frank; or pulled my first pint … like a lot of you; or pushed me to adore King Lear, like Paddy and Tony; or made me look less useless on a football field, like Gay and everybody else; or laughed at jokes you knew weren't funny, or whistled with me at German boats at the wooden bridge; or gave me my first job or my first thump or been a brilliant sister, or a doctor or teacher or **remarkable** other; you're all local heroes to me.

And though I doubt that my new title grants me such power, today I give you freedom. I'd like to leave you now with a wonderfully short poem by a local poet called Percy French and it's called 'Remember Me':

'Remember me is all I ask, and yet if the remembrance proves a task, forget.'

EXPLORE

1. Why does Chris O'Dowd find the statement 'Today I am a freeman of Roscommon, a freeman of Roscommon I am today!' so 'alarming'?

2. Why does he call himself a 'fool'? **P I E**

3. What negative experiences did Chris claim he had when he was younger?

4. What does he discover about Roscommon while researching his speech?

5. Why does he regard Margaret Gillespie as an 'extraordinary' woman? **P I E**

6. Chris O'Dowd refers to a lot of 'ordinary' people as local heroes. Do you agree with his choice of local heroes? **P I E**

7. Pick out three examples of humour in the piece.

8. Look up the **bolded** words in your **dictionary** and write down the definition for each.

CREATE

Imagine you are a journalist. Write a short article for a newspaper outlining the details of an important local event.

Success Criteria

You must
- Use the 5 Ws
- Use paragraphs
- Give your opinion
- Give facts

You should
- Use **RAFT**
- Have a catchy headline

You could
- Use interesting vocabulary
- Use humour

RAFT GUIDELINES

When you write your article, use the **RAFT** structure to help you.

ROLE OF THE WRITER

Who am I as the writer? What is my personality? How will I react to the information or situation? My role depends on the situation; for example, am I a film critic writing a review, or a customer writing a letter of complaint?

AUDIENCE

To whom am I writing? Who needs to read this? Who am I trying to persuade? What is the goal or purpose of writing? What type of emotional reaction do I want from the reader?

FORMAT

In what format am I writing? There are numerous possibilities, for example an article, a diary entry, a speech, an opinion piece.

TOPIC

What am I writing about? What is the subject I am covering? What information do I have to share? What is the focus of my chosen format?

RESEARCH ZONE

Research some speeches made by famous people and find one that you enjoy reading or listening to. You might like to look up the actress Ellen Page accepting an award from the Human Rights Campaign for her commitment to Lesbian, Gay, Bisexual and Transgender (LGBT) equality: 'Ellen Page receives the HRC Vanguard Award' on YouTube.

Practise reading the speech you have researched, and then perform it for your class. You will be assessed by your peers based on the following criteria:

- Clear and confident delivery
- Appropriate tone, e.g. serious, passionate, emotional, humorous, light-hearted
- Correct pace and pausing, e.g. being aware that commas and full stops are there to make you take a pause at important moments
- Eye contact – even though you are reading, you should be able to look up from the speech several times to make eye contact and connect with your audience.

QUESTION MARKS AND EXCLAMATION MARKS

Chris O'Dowd's speech includes a lot of question marks (?) and exclamation marks (!).

Question mark n.

Definition: used to indicate where a question is being asked. Looks like this: ?

Oral Peer Assessment

Reflect on your classmate's oral communication task and, having reviewed the criteria above, write down two things that he/she did well and one thing he/she could improve on.

Exclamation mark n.

Definition: used to indicate a strong emotion. Looks like this: !

Asking questions during a speech is a good way to get people's attention or to introduce a piece of information.

1. How many questions does Chris O'Dowd ask during his speech?

2. Where in each paragraph does he usually ask the questions? Explain why he does this. **P I E**

3. How many exclamation marks are there in the text? What do they show?

4. Would the speech be very different without exclamation marks? Give reasons for your answer. **P I E**

Now rewrite this short dialogue between a mother and her daughter, putting in exclamation marks and question marks where appropriate.

Mother:	Did you win.
Daughter:	We won. We defeated them easily.
Mother:	Well I have a surprise for you.
Daughter:	Are we going shopping. Really. Awesome.
Mother:	I am giving you some spending money.
Daughter:	Excellent. What centre are we going to.
Mother:	I haven't decided yet. Which one would you prefer.

A TV News Report

What I will learn:

to report a news story

Festivals and traditions are often central to a community – like the Puck Fair in Co. Kerry or the Lisdoonvarna Festival in Co. Clare – or are more general traditions – like the annual St Patrick's Day parades that take place around the country, or the tradition of the Wren Boys, who go visiting on St Stephen's Day. Often over time traditions and festivals change, sometimes with positive effects, other times with negative effects. For example, the elderly in a community might still celebrate traditions which younger people have never heard of or have no interest in, or the symbolic and cultural importance of a festival might be overshadowed by a commercial aspect.

Study this picture of the Songkran Water Festival in Thailand. Write a paragraph explaining what you think the festival is about.

Tourists Dampen Traditional Thai Buddhist Celebrations (Al Jazeera News)

Now look up 'Tourists Dampen Traditional Thai Buddhist Celebrations' on YouTube – an Al Jazeera news report that looks at how the local festival has changed in recent years.

1. News reports use the 5 Ws. What are the 5 Ws in this news report?

2. Give one complaint that some people have with the development of the festival.

3. Write down two ways in which people are injured while attending the festival.

In groups, write and then record/perform a news report about a festival you are familiar with. Each person must have a speaking role in the task. The report should last for one and a half minutes.

REMEMBER
A TV news report, p. 55.

SUCCESS CRITERIA

You must
- Use the 5 Ws
- Research the topic, gathering important information

You should
- Use performance skills, for example actions, gestures, facial expressions and movement

You could
- Include two different reporters (people reporting news from different locations)
- Include an anchor man (the person who presents the news programme from a studio)
- Include an interview (where a reporter asks someone questions to gain more information)
- Include an expert speaker (a person who has a lot of knowledge about a particular subject)
- Include a witness (a person who saw the events taking place)

Oral Peer Assessment

Reflect on your classmates' oral communication task and, having reviewed the criteria above, write down two things you think they did well and one thing they could improve on.

If you want to look at some more models of news reporting, visit: http://www.rte.ie/news/player/news2day/

SHOW WHAT YOU KNOW

You have learned many writing and speaking skills throughout this collection. Now it's time to *Show What You Know!*

My Portfolio Task

You are a journalist reporting on one of the following celebrations:

- Commemorative, e.g. celebrating someone's life or celebrating an anniversary of an event, like the 1916 Easter Rising
- Milestones in a celebrity's life, e.g. an engagement or the birth of a baby
- Traditions, e.g. New Year traditions in a particular country

Write an article containing three paragraphs on the event.

SUCCESS CRITERIA

I could
- Use a humorous or serious tone

I must
- Use the 5 Ws
- Include a relevant accompanying photo
- Create an eye-catching headline
- Research my topic, gathering important information
- Use paragraphs to organise my ideas
  Paragraph 1: Introduction, saying what my article is about and why I am writing it
  Paragraph 2: Main body of the piece, where I mix facts with opinion
  Paragraph 3: Conclusion, where I attempt to convince the reader that my opinion is right
- Use RAFT
- Read what I've written to check for missing punctuation marks (, . ! ?) or missing words
- Use a **dictionary** to check any spellings I'm not sure of

I should
- Retell the events accurately and in the correct order

Peer Assessment

Read your partner's work and then write down two things you think he/she did well and one thing he/she could improve on.

Redrafting

When you have received your partner's assessment, and reviewing the success criteria again to make sure you have met all the requirements, you can now revise your article to create a second draft. When you are happy with it, you can put it in your **portfolio**.

Reflection Question

How did the article I read in this collection help me to write my own article for my portfolio task?

Oral Communication

Record/perform a ninety-second news report on one of the three options from your Portfolio Task (a commemoration, a milestone, a tradition).

SUCCESS CRITERIA

I must

- Use the 5 Ws
- Research the topic, gathering important information
- Retell the events of the story in the correct order

I should

- Use performance skills, for example actions, gestures, facial expressions and movement
- Present the news report in an appropriate tone of voice
- Include an interview (where a reporter asks someone questions to gain more information)

I could

- Include two different reporters (people reporting news from different locations)
- Include an anchor man (the person who presents the news programme from a studio)
- Include an expert speaker (a person who has a lot of knowledge about a particular subject)
- Include a witness (a person who saw events taking place)
- Use props and costume

Peer Assessment

Reflect on your classmate's oral communication task and then write down two things that he/she did well and one thing that could be improved on.

Magic Moments

Character, setting, props, dialogue

Listening skills

Acronyms

Mnemonics

Homophones

Memoir writing

Rhythm, volume, pace in speaking

Skills of the sports presenter

Structure of a sports article

As I explore this collection I will learn about:

Mind mapping a story

Short, simple opening sentences

Abstract nouns

Taking notes – main points/key words

Comparing and contrasting poems

More examples of onomatopoeia and alliteration

Learning Outcomes
OL2, OL4, OL5, OL6, OL8,
R8, R13, W5, W9

SHOW WHAT YOU KNOW

The skills you learn in this collection will enable you to **show what you know** in your final tasks at the end of this collection.

For my portfolio task I will:
Write about a magic moment in my life (or, pretending to be someone else, I will tell the story of a magic moment in his or her life)

For oral communication I will:
Speak as a NASA scientist, recording a radio broadcast or a short video

Exploring the Theme – Magic Moments

A magic moment happens when something wonderful, amazing and out of the ordinary occurs. It could be something very big and momentous, or something very small and seemingly insignificant, but special to you. Here are two examples.

The national anthem is playing. Lights are flashing as the cameras point at me. I stand alone on the highest point of the Olympic podium. Years of 5 a.m. alarms, early-to-bed when everyone else was going out, training until I was aching and beyond tiredness, have led me to this magic moment. I clutch the gold medal, hold my head high, as I proudly sing out the words.

I am three years old, looking out my bedroom window at my first snow. Big, fluffy white snowflakes fall silently in the darkness. Mam comes upstairs and says, 'Quick, quick, get dressed!' She puts my jumper over my pyjamas. We get my coat with the big hood, my scarf and gloves from the cubby and out we go. The air is ice cold; my dad is already there rolling the snow into a big ball. We make another and stick in pieces of coal for eyes and a nose. Back in bed I fall asleep, dreaming of giant snowmen.

RESEARCH ZONE

Find out the names and nationalities of the sportsman and sportswoman who have won the most Olympic medals of all time.

WRITE

Write a paragraph describing a magic moment in your life. Describe where you were, what you were doing, seeing or saying, and how you felt.

W5.1

Write another paragraph about a magic moment that you have heard about or seen in the news recently.

PREPARE

In your copy, complete the adjectives below that might be used to describe a magic moment.

F_ b_ _ _ _ s

Br_ l_ _ _ _ t

S_ _ c_ _ l

B_ _ _ t_ _ ul

E_ c_ _ _ ng

F_ sc_ _ _ _ _ ng

Un_ _ _ ie_ _ _ le

W_ n_ _ _ _ ul

En_ _ y_ _ le

Ch_ r_ _ ng

Unf_ _ _ _ _ _ _ ble

Ex_ _ _ _ r_ _ _ _ ry

Am_ _ _ ng

A Science Video

What I will learn:

to listen carefully, taking notes of main points; scientific words and information to help me to speak about stars and planets

PREPARE

NASA is an acronym. What do the initials NASA stand for? What does NASA do?

What three other acronyms do you know?

W5.2

REMEMBER

Acronyms, p. 8.

FUN FACT

SCUBA is an acronym for *self-contained underwater breathing apparatus*, but it's much easier and much quicker to say the word 'Scuba'!

READ

The following piece of text discusses the discovery of a new planet.

The Discovery of Kepler-186f

Using NASA's Kepler Space Telescope, which searches for distant planets, astronomers have discovered the first earth-size planet orbiting a star in the 'habitable zone', i.e. a zone not too hot and not too cold, capable of sustaining life. **'Kepler-186f'**, as the planet has been called, receives energy from the sun. The discovery of Kepler-186f is a significant step toward finding worlds like our planet earth,' said Paul Hertz, NASA's astrophysics division director. 'This planet, five hundred light years away from us, has many elements that resemble earth. That does not necessarily mean that it is inhabited.'

Astrophysics n.

Definition: the study of the structure of stars and planets

A New Planet (NASA)

W5.3

You will now watch a video about the newly discovered planet from NASA twice. The first time, just watch and listen carefully. The second time, write single key words that will help you to answer the questions below.

FUN FACT

NASA runs newsflashes on their website every day, and it invites schools to join the organisation as an 'explorer school'.

? EXPLORE

1. Name the two space experts who are interviewed in the clip (one of whom is pictured here).

2. In a series of bullet points (and referring back to your key words), write the facts that you learned from the first speaker.

3. In a series of bullet points (and referring back to your key words), write the facts that you learned from the second speaker.

4. Compare your points with the person beside you.

IS THERE LIFE OUT THERE?

MIND YOUR LANGUAGE

CREATE SPEAK 1 MIN

In your opinion, is there 'life out there'? Write down a few key words to support your opinion, and then speak for sixty seconds, attempting to convince your class with your evidence that there is/is not life out there.

MNEMONICS

A mnemonic (say: *nem-on-ic*; you don't pronounce the 'm' at the beginning) is any clever little sentence or rhyme that helps us to remember information. For example, **R**ichard **O**f **Y**ork **G**ave **B**attle **I**n **V**ain is a mnemonic to help you remember seven particular colours. Do you know what they are? **R**hythm **H**elps **Y**our **T**wo **H**ips **M**ove is a mnemonic to help you spell what word correctly?

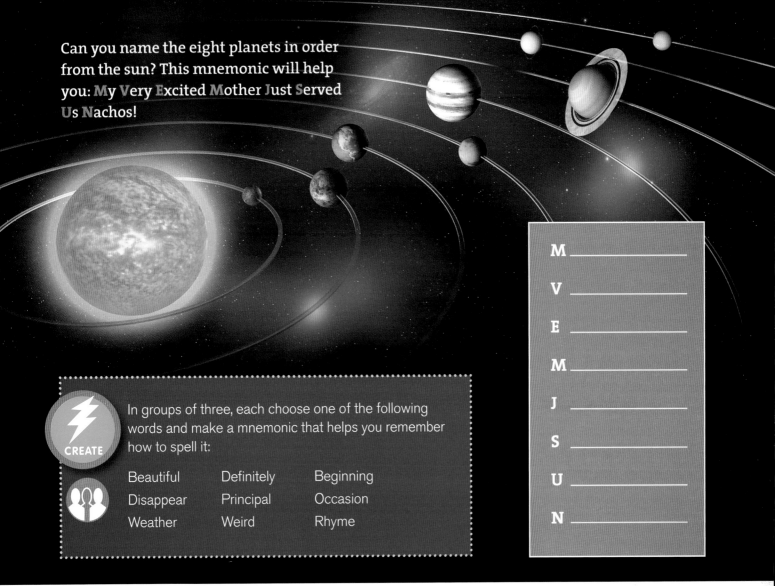

Can you name the eight planets in order from the sun? This mnemonic will help you: **My Very Excited Mother Just Served Us Nachos!**

CREATE

In groups of three, each choose one of the following words and make a mnemonic that helps you remember how to spell it:

Beautiful	Definitely	Beginning
Disappear	Principal	Occasion
Weather	Weird	Rhyme

M _____
V _____
E _____
M _____
J _____
S _____
U _____
N _____

An Image

What I will learn:

to comment on a photograph; an idea for a magic moment in life as remembered by an older person

This Irish soccer fan in the Polish city of Poznan is enjoying a magic moment before the Ireland–Italy match in the European Championships on 18 June 2012. It was eighteen years to the day since Ireland's victory over Italy in Giants Stadium, New York, in the 1994 World Cup finals. In Poznan that evening, Ireland lost 2-0.

REMEMBER CCMC p. 90.

Write a paragraph examining this photograph using the **CCMC** approach.

The **content** of this photograph includes …
The **photograph is taken** in a city with … in the background and … on the right. There are … in …. **The photographer decided** to take the shot at that moment because …. The **colour(s)** ….

In 2062 the man in this photograph has two grandchildren, Ella (aged 6) and Ivan (7). They ask their granddad to tell them about the photograph. Pretending to be him, write two paragraphs remembering what it was like to be in Poznan that afternoon.

An Audio Clip

What I will learn:

the communication skills of a radio broadcaster and a sports writer

Which sports broadcaster or commentator do you most enjoy on radio or television? Why do you like listening to this person? Can you speak a few sentences in which you imitate his or her voice and style?

LISTEN

W5.4

James Alexander Gordon Reads the Football Results

In 1974, James Alexander Gordon was a young newsreader. One day after reading the four o'clock news, he was asked to 'nip over' to the sports section and read the football results. He looked at the list of names and scores and said to himself, 'Well, I'm in the communications business, I should try and make it more interesting.' He made it so interesting, listeners got to enjoy his style for the next forty years.

In the clip you will hear, James explains how he matched his tone of voice to the feelings of the winning or losing team: 'I looked at Arsenal and I thought, "They've lost, I'm very sorry for them; Manchester United have won, I'm delighted for them". And being musical I thought, "I'll try and get a rhythm with this …"'

Listen out for his:

* Happy tone for winners
* Solemn tone for losers
* Rhythm and pace
* Volume rising and falling

SPEAK

Now try to imitate the voice, tone, rhythm, volume, pace and style of James Alexander Gordon by reading this poem aloud.

You Tell Me

by Michael Rosen

Here are the football results:

Manchester United won, Manchester City lost.

Crystal Palace 2, Buckingham Palace 1

Millwall Leeds nowhere

Wolves 8 a cheese roll and had a cup of tea 2

Aldershot 3 Buffalo Bill shot 2

Evertonill, Liverpool's not very well either

Newcastle's Heaven, Sunderland's a very nice place too

Ipswich one? You tell me.

HOMOPHONES

Homophones are words that sound the same but mean different things and have different spellings. For example:

W5.5

peace	**piece**	
steal	steel	
weigh	**way**	
pour	poor	
he'll	**heal**	**heel**
rain	reign	rein

1. In your copy, list at least three examples of homophones in the poem by Michael Rosen.

2. Rewrite the following sentences, filling in the correct spellings of the homophones.

i.   She th _ _ _ the ball t _ _ _ _ _ _ the hedge.

ii. When he was attacked, the forester killed the b _ _ _ with his b _ _ _ hands.

iii. T _ _ _ _ shoes were lost over t _ _ _ _ near the lockers.

iv. The white clouds b _ _ _ across the b _ _ _ sky.

v.   After his fall at the finish line, the runner was in a d _ _ _ for d _ _ _.

vi. The school p _ _ _ _ _ _ _ _ said she would not give in on p _ _ _ _ _ _ _ _ _.

vii. He told us a s _ _ _ _ about the collapse of a ten- s _ _ _ _ _ building.

viii. We m _ _ _ _ _ the bus because we didn't see it coming in the morning m _ _ _.

ix. The town was far t _ _ quiet for the t _ _ young girls t _ stay for a fortnight.

x.   There was a sticky chocolate s _ _ _ _ stuck to the carpet in the hotel s _ _ _ _.

READ

You will now read an article about the Polish footballer Robert Lewandowski and a moment of great accomplishment and triumph in his footballing career.

LEWANDOWSKI TRIUMPHS!

On Saturday afternoon, superstar Robert Lewandowski proved himself once again to be the man of the moment as he exploded into top form in the DFB Polka Final against Borussia Dortmund's old rivals, Bayern Munich.

Over the course of a blistering ninety minutes of play, the 26-year-old showed the talent and brilliance that have made him a superstar at Dortmund. His strength, accuracy and speed ensured that the outcome of the match was all but decided before the half-time whistle.

Kagawa opened up events for Dortmund in the third minute of play following what can generously be called a lapse in concentration on behalf of Bayern. Robben balanced things up for the Bavarian team with a well-taken penalty in the 26th minute, only for it to be cancelled out by a penalty awarded in the 41st minute and expertly taken by Hummels. In the extra minute of play before the half-time whistle, Lewandowski gave a glimpse of the brilliance that was to come in the second half, netting the ball to put Dortmund 3-1 ahead. Scoring two in the second half, Lewandowski was allowed to open up and show his class. It comes as no surprise that this remarkable centre forward was Polish footballer of the year in 2011, 2012 and 2013. The match finished 5-2.

The first paragraph gives general admiration for the player. As you read, take note of at least four admiring words and phrases.

SPORT 23

Choose a sports star you admire. Write a two-paragraph newspaper article about him or her under the heading:

'[*Name*] **TRIUMPHS!**'

CREATE

REMEMBER Paragraph 1 states general admiration. Paragraph 2 gives more specific details about a special triumphant victory. Refer back to the **RAFT** model, p. 97.

Extract from a Memoir [1]

What I will learn:

to describe characters, events and memories so vividly that the reader can imagine the scene exactly as it happened

A memoir is a book in which a person writes a collection of special, important or influential personal memories. *The Glass Castle* is a memoir about the childhood of Jeannette Walls (pictured). In the book, Jeannette tells lots of stories about her childhood experiences.

Aged three, she remembers making hot dogs on the stove on her own. As a teenager, she was so hungry that she rummaged in school bins to find thrown-out lunches. Yet, she says, her parents loved her, read to her and encouraged her to be independent and creative.

In this extract from her memoir, Jeannette remembers occasional Sunday evenings when her father had money and would bring them out to eat in the Owl Club, a local diner, which had a bar and a snooker table.

SPEAK

You will now get ready to perform – to dramatise – this story from Jeannette Walls' memoir. You will need eight actors and a narrator.

REMEMBER

Props, p. 60.

Characters: Dad; Mom (she says nothing, but she giggles and rolls her eyes while the narrator describes dad's stories); Lori, Jeannette and Brian (the kids, who speak their parts together); two men in the Owl Club bar, who throw their heads back, laughing and slapping one another between the shoulder blades; the Owl Club waitress; and the narrator (who in this case is the author, adult Jeannette).

Setting: You can seat the family at a table as if they are in the dining booth in the Owl Club. The two men at the bar will stand to the side.

Props: You can make this more realistic by having each actor wear something appropriate or hold a prop that helps him or her to be in character. For example, one of the men at the bar might hold a deck of cards or something to represent a snooker cue.

'Dinner at the Owl Club' from *The Glass Castle* by Jeannette Walls

Dad was a dramatic storyteller. He always started out slow, with lots of pauses. 'Go on! What happened next?' we'd ask, even if we'd already heard that story before. Mom giggled or rolled her eyes when Dad told his stories, and he glared at her. If someone interrupted his storytelling, he got mad, and we had to beg him to continue and promise that no one would interrupt again.

Dad always fought harder, flew faster and gambled smarter than everyone else in his stories. Along the way, he rescued women and children and even men who weren't as strong and clever. Dad taught us the secrets of his

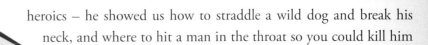

heroics – he showed us how to straddle a wild dog and break his neck, and where to hit a man in the throat so you could kill him with one powerful jab. But he assured us that as long as he was around, we wouldn't have to defend ourselves, because, by God, anyone who so much as laid a finger on any of Rex Walls's children was going to get their butts kicked so hard that you could read Dad's shoe size on their ass cheeks.

When Dad wasn't telling us about all the amazing things he had already done, he was telling us about the wondrous things he was going to do. Like build the Glass Castle. All of Dad's engineering skills and mathematical genius were coming together in one special project: a great big house he was going to build for us in the desert. It would have a glass ceiling and thick glass walls and even a glass staircase. The Glass Castle would have solar cells on the top that would catch the sun's rays and convert them into electricity for heating and cooling and running all the appliances. It would even have its own water purification system. Dad had worked out the architecture and the floor plans and most of the mathematical calculations. He carried around the blueprints for the Glass Castle wherever we went, and sometimes he'd pull them out and let us work on the design for our rooms.

All we had to do was find gold, Dad said, and we were on the verge of that. Once he finished the Prospector* and we struck it rich, he'd start work on our Glass Castle. […]

On Sunday night, if Dad had money, we'd all go to the Owl Club for dinner. The Owl Club was 'World Famous,' according to the sign, where a hoot owl wearing a chef's hat pointed the way to the entrance.

Off to one side was a room with rows of slot machines that were constantly clinking and ticking and flashing lights. Mom said the slot players were hypnotised. Dad said they were damn fools. 'Never play the slots,' Dad told us. 'They're for suckers who rely on luck.' Dad knew all about statistics, and he explained how the casinos stacked the odds against the slot players. When Dad gambled, he preferred poker and pool – games of skill, not chance. 'Whoever coined the phrase "a man's got to play the hand that was dealt him" was most certainly one pisspoor bluffer,' Dad said.

The Owl Club had a bar where groups of men with sunburned necks huddled together over beers and cigarettes. They all knew Dad, and whenever he walked in, they insulted him in a loud funny way that was meant to be friendly. 'This joint must be going to hell in a hand basket if they're letting in sorry-ass characters like you!' they'd shout.

'Hell, my presence here has a positively elevating effect compared to you mangy coyotes,' Dad would yell back. They'd all throw their heads back and laugh and slap one another between the shoulder blades.

We always sat at one of the red booths. 'Such good manners,' the waitress would exclaim, because Mom and Dad made us say 'sir' and 'ma'am' and 'yes, please' and 'thank you.'

'They're damned smart, too!' Dad would declare. 'Finest damn kids ever walked the planet.' And we'd smile and order hamburgers or chili dogs and milk shakes and big plates of onion rings that glistened with hot grease. The waitress brought the food to the table and poured the milk shakes from a sweating metal container into our glasses. There was always some left over, so she kept the container on the table for us to finish. 'Looks like you hit the jackpot and got something extra,' she'd say with a wink. We always left the Owl Club so stuffed we could hardly walk. 'Let's waddle home, kids,' Dad would say.

'The Prospector' was Jeannette's dad's invention. It was intended to sift through sand finding, separating and measuring gold nuggets from rocks and dirt.

TOP TIP

It's always good to start a memoir chapter with a short, simple opening sentence, because it immediately sets up a picture for the reader and gets them involved in your story. For example, in this piece, Jeannette says, 'Dad was a dramatic storyteller'. You get a really good idea of what sort of person her father is from this short, descriptive sentence.

True or False?

W5.6

Your teacher will call out the statements below one by one. Your job is to listen and decide if each statement is true or false. In pairs, very quietly agree on an answer before you hold up a **TRUE** or a **FALSE** sign between you. You must be ready to defend your opinions. Be able to quote a sentence from the story that gave you your answer, if you can. **P I E**

True

Statements

* The Walls children hero-worship their dad.

* He always has money.

* The 'Glass Castle' was built when they became teenagers.

* The children absolutely believed that the Glass Castle would be built for them.

* 'The Owl Club' is world-famous.

* Its customers enjoy the restaurant's French cooking and refined decoration.

* The waitress felt sorry for the Walls children.

EXPLORE W5.7

1. What was the Glass Castle? Describe it.

2. What are the two heroic skills that this dad teaches his children?

3. What does the mom think of her husband's stories? **PIE** How do you know what she thinks?

4. What do the Walls children think of their dad? **PIE**

5. What does the name of the club tell you about it? What does it look like inside? Who are its customers?

6. If you could interview Jeannette Walls, what three questions would you like to ask her?

7. Jeannette Walls uses many very descriptive phrases in her memoir, to really help the reader 'see', 'feel', 'smell' and 'taste' what it is she experienced. For example, we read of 'big plates of onion rings that glistened with hot grease'. Write three other phrases from the story that show that this writer is good at describing things, places or people.

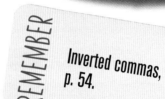

8. In inverted commas, write two other things said by two other characters in the story.

9. State in a sentence or two what these things tell you about the people who say them.

REMEMBER Inverted commas, p. 54.

MIND YOUR LANGUAGE

VERBS, ADJECTIVES AND DIALOGUE

Jeannette Walls uses a large and varied selection of verbs to tell her story.

1. Rewrite the following sentences, filling in the gaps to show the verb she uses to give you the best description.

W5.8

i. He (*stared hard and angrily*) at her   g _ _ _ ed

ii. He (*saved from death or great danger*) women and children   r _ _ _ _ ed

iii. Slot machines that were constantly (*making high-pitched, ringing sounds*)   c _ _ _ _ _ _ g

iv. The waitress would (*say loudly in surprise*)   e _ c _ _ _ m

v. Dad would (*say loudly and proudly*)   d _ c _ _ _ e

vi. Onion rings that (*shone and sparkled*) with hot grease   gl _ _ _ _ _ ed

vii. 'Let's (*walk heavily, full of food*) home, kids'   w _ _ _ e

2. Place the adjective used in the story in front of each of the nouns below.

d _ _ _ _ _ _ _ storyteller

w _ _ _ dog

p _ _ _ _ _ _ _ jab

w _ _ _ _ _ _ things

m _ _ _ _ _ _ _ _ _ _ genius

s _ _ _ _ _ _ project

g _ _ _ _ ceiling

s _ _ _ _ cells

s _ _ _ _ _ _ _ _ necks

m _ _ _ _ coyotes

g _ _ _ manners

h _ _ grease

3. Dialogue creates character. For example, when Jeannette's father speaks, he reveals his funny, confident, entertaining, loud, brash personality. He enjoys swearing, shocking, yelling, provoking people and making a big impression. He wants to be the man in charge and have everyone listen to him.

> 'Never play the slots,' Dad told us. 'They're for suckers who rely on luck.' Dad knew all about statistics …

> 'Let's waddle home, kids,' Dad would say.

> 'Hell, my presence here has a positively elevating effect compared to you mangy coyotes,' Dad would yell back.

> 'They're damned smart, too!' Dad would declare. 'Finest damn kids ever walked the planet.' And we'd smile …

Which of these adjectives do you think describes the dad's personality?

imaginative   boastful   **responsible**   quiet   protective   shy

optimistic   **happy**   timid   **cautious**   lovable   entertaining

Write three sentences about the dad in which you use at least three adjectives that describe his personality.

Extract from a Memoir [2]

FUN FACT

Jeannette Walls' memoir was on the New York Times bestseller list for 261 weeks. By 2007 it had sold over 2.7 million copies, been translated into twenty-two languages, and won numerous awards. Paramount has even bought the film rights to it.

What I will learn:

to set the scene, introduce characters, start the action; to create dramatic climax and bring a story to a quiet ending; how to use a mind-map either to plan or revise a story

Politicians, pop stars, sports stars, entertainers and 'ordinary' people often write memoirs. A chapter in a memoir might describe a memory of a special time, maybe a magic moment of pride or happiness, or maybe of a sadness still keenly felt; where they were, who else was there, their feelings and thoughts at the time.

PREPARE

See if you can match the words that you will find in this next extract from *The Glass Castle* with their meanings.

discarded	melted away, like a fizzy tablet in water
buzzard	optical illusion of water shimmering far off in the desert
toxic	can go up in flames easily
hazardous	rough, small wooden house or shed, with no foundations
flammable	thrown away, disused
shack	big, strong bird of prey, like a hawk or vulture
devour	poisonous
dissolved	dangerous, could do harm or damage
mirage	eat fast, hungrily and fiercely, demolishing the food

Now choose six of the above words and write one sentence for each of them. Each sentence should show that you understand what the word means.

READ

The Walls children enjoyed a freedom which allowed them to take risks; risks from which other children would have been protected by their parents' concern for safety. In this chapter from *The Glass Castle*, Jeannette remembers a day in the local dump. On this day, a magic moment of adventure turns in an instant to a nightmare moment. The magic returns when their father appears.

'The Scientific Experiment' from *The Glass Castle* by Jeannette Walls

Brian and I loved to go to the dump. We looked for treasures among the discarded stoves and refrigerators, the broken furniture and stacks of bald tyres. We chased after the desert rats that lived in the wrecked cars, or caught tadpoles and frogs in the scum-topped pond. Buzzards circled overhead, and the air was filled with dragonflies the size of small birds. There were no trees to speak of in Battle Mountain, but one corner of the dump had huge piles of railroad ties and rotting lumber that were great for climbing and carving your initials on. We called it the Woods.

REMEMBER It's good to start a memoir chapter with a short, simple opening sentence. For example, here the opening sentence is short and immediately descriptive: 'Brian and I loved to go to the dump.'

Toxic and hazardous wastes were stored in another corner of the dump, where you could find old batteries, oil drums, paint cans and bottles with skulls and crossbones. Brian and I decided some of this stuff would make for a neat scientific experiment, so we filled up a couple of boxes with different bottles and jars and took them to an abandoned shed we named our laboratory. At first we mixed things together, hoping they would explode, but nothing happened, so I decided we should conduct an experiment to see if any of the stuff was flammable.

The next day after school we came back to the laboratory with a box of Dad's matches. We unscrewed the lids of some of the jars, and I dropped in matches, but still nothing happened. So we mixed up a batch of what Brian called nuclear fuel, pouring different liquids into a can. When I tossed in the match, a cone of flame shot up with a whoosh like a jet afterburner.

Brian and I were knocked off our feet. When we stood up, one of the walls was on fire. I yelled to Brian that we had to get out of there, but he was throwing sand at the fire, saying that we had to put it out or we'd get in trouble. The flames were spreading toward the door, eating up that dry old wood in no time. I kicked out a board in the back wall and squeezed through. When Brian didn't follow, I ran up the street calling for help. I saw Dad walking home from work. We ran back to the shack. Dad kicked in more of the wall and pulled Brian out coughing.

I thought Dad would be furious, but he wasn't. He was sort of quiet. We stood on the street watching the flames devour the shack. Dad had an arm around each of us. He said it was an incredible coincidence that he happened to be walking by. Then he pointed to the top of the fire, where the snapping yellow flames dissolved into an invisible shimmery heat that made the desert beyond seem to waver, like a mirage. Dad told us that zone was known in physics as the boundary between turbulence and order. 'It's a place where no rules apply, or at least they haven't figured 'em out yet,' he said. 'You all got a little too close to it today.'

EXPLORE

W5.10

1. How many creatures appear in the first paragraph? Name them.

2. What dangers for children can you find in paragraphs 1 and 2?

3. What do you think the skulls and crossbones mean on the bottles?

4. Why do you think Brian called his mixture 'nuclear fuel'?

5. What do you think of their dad's reaction to the near disaster? What does his reaction tell you about him?

MIND YOUR LANGUAGE

ANTONYMS

Antonyms are words that have opposite meanings. For example, *turbulence* means unpredictable air currents that cause violent motion, as sometimes happens on a plane journey. In this story, *order* is used as an antonym for *turbulence*.

1. Write an antonym for each of these words that appear in the story:

small   loved   broken   huge   wrecked   yelled   quiet   nothing   furious

2. Write the line of the story that is closest in meaning to the following:

- The pool of water that had an impure coating of greyish froth on its surface
- To see if any of the things would go on fire
- A curved fiery shape rushed into the air with a short, sharp hissing sound
- Consuming that parched, ancient timber rapidly
- I charged up the road, yelling for assistance
- The line between chaos and calm

Mind Map

A mind map is a 'map' of key new vocabulary (words) from a story you have just heard, which help you to remember details of that story. Here is a sample mind map for this chapter from *The Glass Castle*.

MIND MAP for 'The Scientific Experiment' from *The Glass Castle*

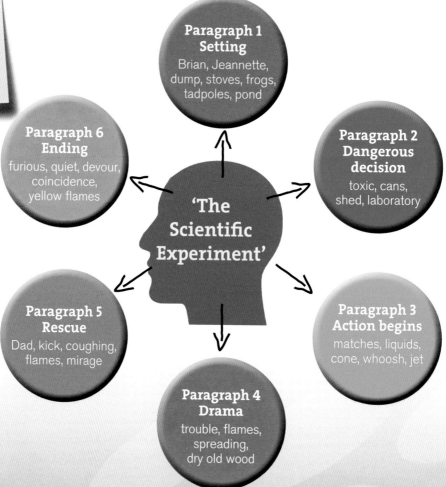

Paragraph 1
Setting
Brian, Jeannette, dump, stoves, frogs, tadpoles, pond

Paragraph 2
Dangerous decision
toxic, cans, shed, laboratory

Paragraph 3
Action begins
matches, liquids, cone, whoosh, jet

Paragraph 4
Drama
trouble, flames, spreading, dry old wood

Paragraph 5
Rescue
Dad, kick, coughing, flames, mirage

Paragraph 6
Ending
furious, quiet, devour, coincidence, yellow flames

'The Scientific Experiment'

Now make your own mind map about a special day (or a very dramatic day!) you remember from your own childhood. Plan five paragraphs, inserting key words for each paragraph just as you saw in the mind map for 'The Scientific Experiment'.

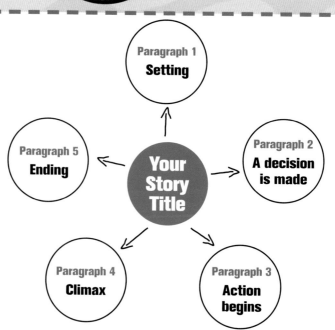

Paragraph 1 — **Setting**
Paragraph 2 — **A decision is made**
Paragraph 3 — **Action begins**
Paragraph 4 — **Climax**
Paragraph 5 — **Ending**
Your Story Title

Poetry

What I will learn:

abstract nouns, onomatopoeia and alliteration, dramatic storytelling in poetry;
to create my own poem

It is interesting to *compare* (spot similarities) and *contrast* (spot differences) between the next two poems, 'Jabberwocky' and 'f for fox'. Both poems tell a story. Both use onomatopoeia, alliteration and dramatic rhythm. Each poem has a hero and features animals.

'Jabberwocky' by Lewis Carroll has a human hero and is set in a forest, while 'f for fox' by Carol Ann Duffy has an animal hero and moves through town and country. Lewis Carroll makes up words and uses lots of punctuation marks. Carol Ann Duffy uses everyday words and lets the lines run on quickly without pauses.

After you have studied the two poems you will compare and contrast them, giving evidence for your comparisons and contrasts with quotations and examples you spot in the two poems.

The poem 'Jabberwocky' appeared in Lewis Carroll's book, *Through the Looking Glass*, the sequel to *Alice's Adventures in Wonderland*. When Alice reads the poem, she says:

TOP TIP

A sequel is a book or film that comes after the first book or film and continues the story; a prequel is a book or film that is also released after the first book or film, but tells the story before that told in the first release.

'It seems very pretty, but it's rather hard to understand! Somehow it seems to fill my head with ideas – only I don't exactly know what they are! Somebody killed something: that's clear, at any rate.'

Alice is right! The poem is hard to understand, being full of made-up, nonsense words. You have to speak it dramatically and think about the words to get the meaning. It starts in fear but then leads to a fabulous magic moment of triumph. Read it closely and see if you can figure out what's going on.

Jabberwocky

by Lewis Carroll

'Twas brillig, and the slithy toves
    Did gyre and gimble in the wabe:
All mimsy were the borogoves,
    And the mome raths outgrabe.

'Beware the Jabberwock, my son!
    The jaws that bite, the claws that catch!
Beware the Jubjub bird, and shun
    The frumious Bandersnatch!'

He took his vorpal sword in hand:
    Long time the manxome foe he sought —
So rested he by the Tumtum tree
    And stood awhile in thought.

And, as in uffish thought he stood,
    The Jabberwock, with eyes of flame,
Came whiffling through the tulgey wood,
    And burbled as it came!

PEACE: a time when there is no war, violence or conflict; a time of calm and quiet

COURAGE: being brave enough to meet danger, going into battle against the odds, coping with fear as you face a scary situation

EVIL: something that causes bad or harmful things to happen; wickedness, malevolence

One, two! One, two! And through and through
    The vorpal blade went snicker-snack!
He left it dead, and with its head
    He went galumphing back.

'And, hast thou slain the Jabberwock?
    Come to my arms, my beamish boy!
O frabjous day! Callooh! Callay!'
    He chortled in his joy.

'Twas brillig, and the slithy toves
    Did gyre and gimble in the wabe:
All mimsy were the borogoves,
    And the mome raths outgrabe.

TRIUMPH:
a great victory,
the feeling of success,
the defeat of a powerful
enemy or a very strong
opponent, especially in
a tough situation

PRIDE:
a feeling of happiness
or satisfaction in having
done something worthwhile;
delight in having worked
hard to achieve
something
difficult

LISTEN

Now listen to a recitation of the poem.
While you listen, follow the text again.
You could also look up the actor Benedict
Cumberbatch's brilliant recitation of the
poem on YouTube. You'll also find another
great performance of the poem on
YouTube by the Muppets!

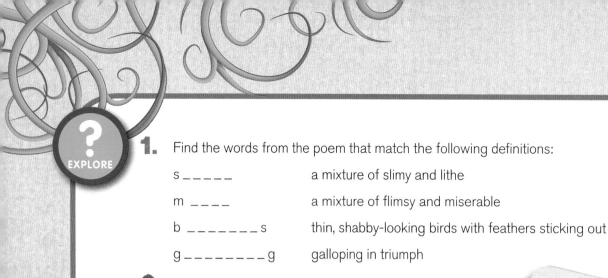

1. Find the words from the poem that match the following definitions:

s _ _ _ _ _   a mixture of slimy and lithe

m _ _ _ _   a mixture of flimsy and miserable

b _ _ _ _ _ _ _ s   thin, shabby-looking birds with feathers sticking out

g _ _ _ _ _ _ _ _ g   galloping in triumph

2. In Stanza 2, what dangerous creatures must the young hero be wary of?

3. Find words in Stanzas 4, 5 and 6 that are examples of onomatopoeia.

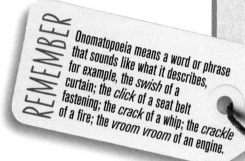

REMEMBER Onomatopoeia means a word or phrase that sounds like what it describes, for example, the *swish* of a curtain; the *click* of a seat belt fastening; the *crack* of a whip; the *crackle* of a fire; the *vroom vroom* of an engine.

4. Identify one or more verbs used in the poem to answer these questions:

- What did the toves do?
- What did the jaws do?
- What did the claws do?
- What did the hero do after he killed the monster?
- What did his father do to show his joy?

5. The five bubbles alongside the poem explain the abstract nouns *peace*, *courage*, *evil*, *triumph* and *pride*. Make the abstract noun from the following adjectives:

angry   beautiful   courageous   disappointed   good   happy
intelligent   miserable   proud   romantic   triumphant   victorious

6. The poem has been translated into many different languages. Read aloud and identify the languages of these two translations of the first verse. If you speak another language fluently, try to translate the original poem and read it aloud for the class!

1. Es brillig war. Die schlichten Toven
   Wirrten und wimmelten in Waben;
   Und aller-mümsige Burggoven
   Die mohmen Räth' ausgraben.

2. Briollaic a bhí ann; bhí na tóibhí sleo
   ag gírleáil's ag gimleáil ar an taof.
   B'an-chuama go deo na borragóibh
   is bhí na rádaí miseacha ag braíomh.

REMEMBER An abstract noun names an idea, a feeling, or a state of mind, rather than a thing that you can see, hear or touch.

ONCE·UPON·A·TIME

Write a short tale for young children beginning, 'Once upon a time …' Describe a character going into a forest, hunting out a dragon or monster that has been terrifying the villagers, battling with the creature, and coming back in triumph. You could use the Five-Part Story Planner below as a model. Keep your vocabulary simple for young listeners.

REMEMBER

The Five-Part Story Planner, p. 61.

1. Beginning: Describe the time and the place
Once upon a time, in a land far away, there was a dark and dangerous forest.

2. Introduce the characters
The hero/heroine, the people of the village, the monster

3. Start the action
'Into the forest, deeper and deeper …'

4. Build up to the dramatic climax
Sounds, distant rumble, the battle with the monster

5. Ending: The triumphant homecoming

Self-Assessment

Re-read what you have written and then write two things you think you did well and one thing you could improve on.

Peer Assessment

Read your partner's work and then fill in this grid.

In this story	Comment
I liked	
I was surprised by	
I thought the best part was	
I think there could be some improvement in	

READ

Like 'Jabberwocky', the following poem also begins in fear, describes a chase and ends with a magic moment of sheer relief. The chase is not through a forest but from a farm to a fairground, on through fields and back to the farm. This poem is also a supreme example of alliteration.

Alliteration n.

Definition: the use of the same letter or sound at the beginning of words in a sentence or piece of writing

 f for fox

by Carol Ann Duffy

The fox fled over the fields away from the farm
and the furious farmer.
His fur was freaked.
His foxy face was frantic as he flew. A few feathers
fluttered out of his mouth.

What feelings do you have for the fox in the first five lines?

The fox
had broken his fast with a feast of fowl!
The farmer had threatened to flay the fur
from his frame.

What had the fox done to make the farmer furious?

The frightened fox flung himself
at a fence.
The fox found himself in a fairground,
with a Ferris Wheel, flashing lights, fruit machines, fish
in plastic bags.
Furtively, he foraged for food—
fragments of candy floss, french fries—
but a fella folding fivers into his fist
flicked a fiery fag at the fox and the fox foxed off.

*What does 'furtively' mean? You might have to look up your **dictionary** to find out. What picture of the fox in the fairground forms in your mind? What is he doing? What happens to him?*

What adjectives in the final ten lines best describe the pitiful state of the fleeing fox?

Further and further fled the fox, through Forfar, Fife, Falkirk,
forests, fields, Fleetwood, Fazakerley, thunder and fog,
famished and fearful;
forcing his furry features
into family bins, filching thrown-away food.
Thief fox, friendless fox, thin fox. Finally
he came at first light to a faraway farm...
where the fox fed himself full
till his face was fat
and forlorn feathers floated away on the frosty air.

Describe your image of the fox in these final three lines.

?
EXPLORE

Compare and contrast the two poems, finding the lines that show how both poems tell a story, use language and display rhythm. As well as finding quotations and examples to show these similarities and differences, you must find new points in both poems to compare and contrast.

⚡
CREATE

W5.12

C is for cat ... D is for dog ... H is for hamster ... R is for robin ...

Choose a bird or animal and write an alliterative poem about them. Begin by doing some rough drafts, trying out lines and stanza lengths in your copy. Then, when you are happy with your work, write the complete poem in your worksheet.

SHOW WHAT YOU KNOW

You have learned many writing and speaking skills throughout this collection. Now it's time to *Show What You Know!*

SUCCESS CRITERIA

My Portfolio Task

Write a short chapter for a memoir that describes a magic moment in a life, either yours or someone else's.

I must

- Read back over some of the magic moments described in this chapter
- Arrange my writing in paragraphs
- Write a clear, short opening sentence
- Make a mind map of key words and special moments before I start
- Read what I've written to check for punctuation marks (, . ! ?) or missing words
- Use a **dictionary** to check any spellings I'm not sure of

I should

- Describe in detail the people and places mentioned so that readers can imagine the scene
- Use some of the new words I learned in vocabulary exercises in this chapter
- Include some dialogue, remembering to use inverted commas
- Include tone of voice, gestures and facial expressions when writing dialogue

I could

- Think of stories in the news at the moment to inspire me
- Be a NASA scientist remembering a great discovery
- End with a strong or a very gentle sentence that readers will not forget
- Use some images of taste, sight, smell or sound that I learned in poems or stories

> **REMEMBER**
> In a memoir, you recall some part of your life and tell the story of it.

Here are some suggestions for organising your chapter:

Paragraph 1

Start with a short simple sentence that tells your reader what is to come. You read some simple examples in this collection:

- *Dad was a dramatic storyteller*
- *Brian and I loved to go to the dump*

Now write your own starter sentence, telling your reader what you remember. Then write another three or four sentences to complete the paragraph, giving more information.

Follow-on paragraphs

Write good, detailed descriptions so that your reader can picture the people and places in your story. Remember some examples from what you read in this collection:

- *We'd smile and order hamburgers or chili dogs and milk shakes and big plates of onion rings that glistened with hot grease*

- *Slot machines were constantly clinking and ticking and flashing lights*

- *… a great big house he was going to build for us in the desert. It would have a glass ceiling and thick glass walls and even a glass staircase*

Verbs

Use good action verbs:

- *Brian and I were knocked off our feet. When we stood up, one of the walls was on fire. I yelled to Brian that we had to get out of there …*

Dialogue

Add dialogue:

- *'They're damned smart too!' Dad would declare. 'Finest damn kids ever walked the planet!'*

- *'Looks like you hit the jackpot and got something extra,' she'd say with a wink.*

Final paragraph

Your final paragraph should end with a strong or memorable sentence:

- *We always left the Owl Club so stuffed we could hardly walk. 'Let's waddle home, kids,' Dad would say.*

Self-assessment

Re-read what you have written and then write down two things you think you did well and one thing that could be improved on.

Redrafting

Reviewing the success criteria again to make sure you have met all the requirements, and taking into account your own self-assessment notes, you can now revise your memoir chapter to create a second draft. When you are happy with it, you can put it in your **portfolio**.

Reflection Question

Did I describe the people and places so well that someone reading my short chapter would be able to picture them as if seeing them on film?

Oral Communication

You are a NASA research scientist. Record a two-minute presentation for a radio broadcast or short video in which you explain to the public that NASA has discovered a new planet on which there may be life. Add music, pictures, sound effects or anything that helps to communicate your findings. Record the scene, with different voices speaking the dialogue and sound effects as necessary.

SUCCESS CRITERIA

I must

- Write a script that will be the voiceover
- Look back at the notes and key words I wrote while watching the NASA video clips for ideas and phrases
- Divide the presentation into paragraphs, each with a clear point
- Punctuate carefully to mark the pauses in speaking
- Explain clearly and speak slowly, like the two NASA research scientists

I should

- Rehearse speaking my script until I can say it naturally, using flash cards
- Practise making eye contact
- Illustrate my talk with photographs, pictures or diagrams
- Choose suitable music to make it more enjoyable for my listeners

I could

- Give my presentation a name that will excite curiosity and interest
- Include different speakers giving specialist information
- Vary my tone of voice like James Alexander Gordon did when he read the football results – sometimes light, sometimes solemn, as the piece requires
- End with an impressive closing sentence that excites the listeners

Peer Assessment

Reflect on your classmate's work and then write down two things you think he/she did well and one thing he/she could improve on. Use the feedback you receive from your partner along with the success criteria above to review and redraft your work if necessary before you present it to your teacher or your class.

Passions and Pastimes

- Similes
- Performing a poem
- Discussing poetry
- Mood
- Discussing memories
- Visuals, target audience and logos
- Presenting information creatively
- Multi-modal presentation
- Mime and gesture
- Speaking confidently
- Slogans

As I explore this collection I will learn about:

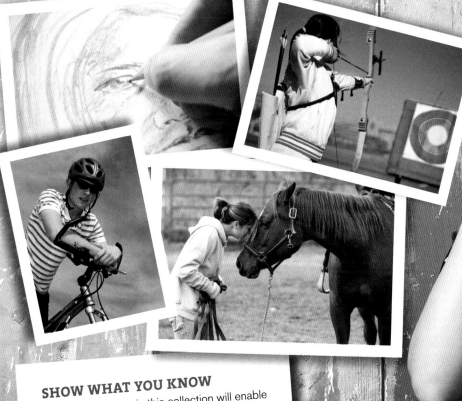

SHOW WHAT YOU KNOW

The skills you learn in this collection will enable you to **show what you know** in your final tasks at the end of this collection.

For my portfolio task I will:
Create a presentation on a poem

For oral communication I will:
Give a dramatic performance of a poem

Learning Outcomes
OL5, OL11, R1, R3, R6, R8, W3, W6, W11

Exploring the Theme – Passions and Pastimes

REMEMBER

Brainstorming, p. 45.

KWL

What I know	What I want to know	What I have learned

STEP 1 Using the heading 'What I know', brainstorm the title of this collection, 'Passions and Pastimes' and what it means to you, e.g. 'sport, enjoyment, clubs, friends'.

STEP 2 When you have finished, swap your brainstorm with your partner and read one another's. Write two questions under the heading 'What I want to know'. This can be anything – there are no wrong answers, e.g. 'Why is sport so popular?' or 'What is the most played instrument?'

STEP 3 Now read the following quotes and fun facts about the passions and pastimes of some famous people. Think about how these quotes and facts might have informed or changed your understanding of this collection's theme, 'Passions and Pastimes'. Write down any new thoughts or ideas that you have under the heading 'What I have learned', e.g. 'You need enthusiasm to participate in a pastime'.

'My mission in life is not merely to survive, but to thrive; and to do so with some passion, some compassion, some humour, and some style.'

Maya Angelou

'Red is such an interesting colour to correlate with emotion, because it's on both ends of the spectrum. On one end you have happiness, falling in love, infatuation with someone, passion, all that. On the other end you've got obsession, jealousy, danger, fear, anger and frustration.'

Taylor Swift

'Passion is energy. Feel the power that comes from focusing on what excites you.'
Oprah Winfrey

'There is no passion to be found playing small – in settling for a life that is less than the one you are capable of living.'
Nelson Mandela

'Winning isn't everything, it's the only thing.'
Vince Lombard
(American football coach)

Mila Kunis's hobby is playing World of Warcraft.

Albert Einstein played the violin and the piano all his life.

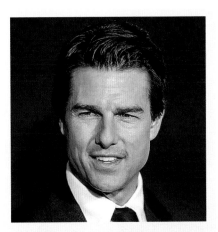

Tom Cruise loves to fence in his spare time.

Love Poems

What I will learn:

to read a poem aloud with meaning and give my opinion about a poem

People often speak of some of their pastimes being their 'passion'. But another interpretation of passion is the strong emotion of love. Valentine's Day is celebrated every February 14th, and it's a big event for many, with cards being exchanged and flowers delivered.

FUN FACT

Valentine's Day is named after St Valentine, a priest who, it is said, performed secret marriage ceremonies for soldiers and their sweethearts in Ancient Rome. They had to be in secret because soldiers were not allowed to be married, as the emperor of the time, Claudius II, believed single men made better soldiers. Valentine's Day was declared a holiday by King Henry VII in 1537.

PREPARE

Make a list of gifts you associate with Valentine's Day. When you have finished, choose one that you would like to receive from a secret admirer and explain your reasons for this choice.

Imagine you are sending a card to that lucky someone: come up with the short message you would write inside it.

READ

The first poem you will read is probably one of the world's most famous love poems. It still appears in greeting cards today.

Roses are Red

Roses are red
Violets are blue
Carnations are sweet
And so are you.

And so are they
That send you this
And when we meet
We'll have a kiss.

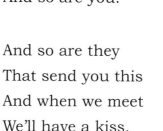

EXPLORE

1. These words first appeared in a book called *The Faerie Queene,* written by Edmund Spenser in 1590. How many years ago was this? What century was this in?

2. Many people have written different versions of the first stanza of this poem. Come up with your own version, starting 'Roses are red, violets are blue ...'

3. Do you think this is a convincing love poem? Why/why not?

This next poem by Elaine George is called a 'shape poem'. The poet has written it with its shape, or 'form', in mind, and intends for it to be printed as such in books or magazines or wherever it might appear.

She – is like a bubble by Elaine George

she
is like a bubble
a gentle floating kiss
blown from an angel's lips
made from melting rainbows
beads of heaven's morning mist
a floating ball of colour schemes
and constant changing themes
bursting into a twinkling down
scattering her joy all around
oh how I love the magic
of her sound

  Each person in the class must say one thing they notice about the poem. Begin with 'I noticed that …' Also mention one thing you liked and one thing you disliked about the poem.

 Create your own shape poem. It must be about a passion or pastime of yours.

EXPLORE

1. Based on your reading of the poem, what do you think the topic/object of the poem is? Remember to look at the shape of the poem to help you.

2. The poet cares a lot about the person she is writing about. What positive words does she use to show these feelings?

3. In the first two lines, the poet uses a simile to compare the person they are writing about to an object. Find the simile and explain why she uses it, making reference to the rest of the poem.

P I E

Simile n.

Definition: a figure of speech that compares two things or persons that are not similar. You'll recognise a simile by use of the words 'like', 'as' or 'than', e.g. 'My sister sings like an angel'; 'That film was as boring as watching paint dry'.

READ

This poem by Ian Serraillier (you might remember him from Collection 3) is very short but its message is simple. The speaker in a poem is not always the poet. Who do you think the speaker in this poem is?

Going Steady
by Ian Serraillier

Valentine, O, Valentine,
I'll be your love and you'll be mine.
We'll care for each other, rain or fine,
and in 90 years we'll be 99.

EXPLORE

1. The speaker makes two promises in this poem. What are they?

2. Make a list of the words that rhyme in the poem.

3. What age is the speaker in the poem?

4. Why do you think the poet decided to write from the perspective of this speaker?

READ

The next poem you will read is about an unlikely love story. It shows that love can overcome difficult challenges.

A Crow and a Scarecrow
by Carol Ann Duffy

A crow and a scarecrow fell in love
out in the fields.
The scarecrow's heart was a stuffed leather glove
but his love was real.
The crow perched on the stick of a wrist
and opened her beak:
Scarecrow, I love you madly, deeply.
Speak.

Crow, rasped the Scarecrow, hear these words
from my straw throat.
I love you too
from my boot to my hat
by way of my old tweed coat.
Croak.

The crow crowed back,
Scarecrow, let me take you away
to live in a tall tree.
I'll be a true crow wife to you
if you'll marry me.

The Scarecrow considered.
Crow, tell me how
a groom with a broomstick spine
can take a bride.
I know you believe in the love
in these button eyes
but I'm straw inside
and straw can't fly.

The crow pecked at his heart
with her beak
then flapped away,
and back and forth she flew to him
all day, all day,
until she pulled one last straw
from his tattered vest
and soared across the sun with it
to her new nest.

And there she slept, high in her tree,
winged, in a bed of love.
Night fell.
The slow moon rose
over a meadow,
a heap of clothes,
two boots,
an empty glove.

EXPLORE

1. Is it strange that a crow and a scarecrow should fall in love?

2. Describe how the crow and the scarecrow manage to stay together.

3. Draw your favourite image from the poem.

CREATE

Now choose your favourite poem from this collection so far. Remembering to use **PIE**, write a paragraph (10–11 lines) giving your opinion about the strengths of the poem. You will find some helpful phrases for stating your opinion on the next page. Some of the things you might like are:

REMEMBER

Alliteration, p. 126
Onomatopoeia, p. 93

- The name of the poem
- Its rhyme – when two words sound the same
- Its rhythm – the beat of the poem when you speak it
- Its musicality – how the poem sounds like a song when you speak it
- Its language – interesting choice of words (verbs, nouns, adjectives). Are the words simple or difficult? Did this affect your enjoyment of the poem? Is the language informal (causal) or formal (proper)?
- Its themes – what are the main ideas of the poem? Did you enjoy them or agree with them?
- Its images – what kind of pictures does the poet use? Did one or two stand out for you? Why did you enjoy them?
- Its alliteration – are there clever examples of alliteration? Why do you think the poet used it at that particular point?
- Its onomatopoeic words – are there any in the poem? Do they add humour or add to the sound imagery of the poem?

 in Action

The poem I like best is the shape poem, 'She – is like a bubble' by Elaine George. **This poem is very clever because the shape of the poem reflects the object – a bubble – from the first line. The poet also uses a simile to compare the girl to this delicate object: 'she is like a bubble'.** A bubble is a noun, a thing, and normally people are not compared to such unusual objects. Bubbles are light, clear and fragile; they are so light that when a person blows a bubble, they float up to the sky or they pop! I think the poet is trying to say that this person is special like the delicate bubble. Both the object and the person give the poet joy.

PASSIONS AND PASTIMES   **139**

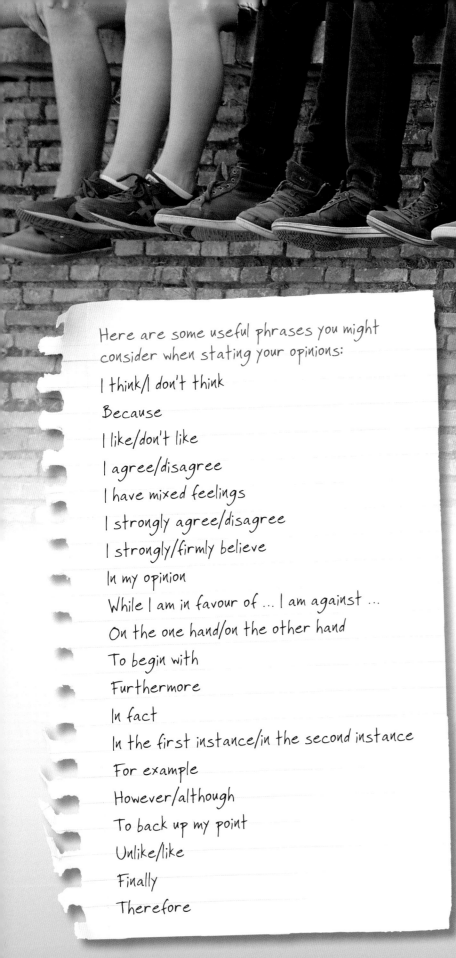

Here are some useful phrases you might consider when stating your opinions:

I think/I don't think

Because

I like/don't like

I agree/disagree

I have mixed feelings

I strongly agree/disagree

I strongly/firmly believe

In my opinion

While I am in favour of ... I am against ...

On the one hand/on the other hand

To begin with

Furthermore

In fact

In the first instance/in the second instance

For example

However/although

To back up my point

Unlike/like

Finally

Therefore

TOP TIP

Even if you are only writing a paragraph, you should briefly plan what you are going to include before you start writing it.

Peer Assessment

Read your partner's work and then write down two things you think he/she did well and one thing he/she could improve on.

* Pick a verse from the poem you enjoyed the most and draw a series of pictures illustrating it.

* Learn and practise a reading of the verse. Then perform your verse, showing the relevant images as you go. Your challenge is to present your verse as if it were a live animation film.

Advertising and Logos

to explain and give examples of mood, visuals and target audience; to explain and give examples of logos; to present information creatively

Most people have a particular hobby or pastime that they enjoy, and while we all might enjoy different types of pastimes, usually they have one outcome in common: they leave us in a particular mood. Can you think of a particular event or occasion when you were in a joyful, excited or disappointed mood? Was it at a match, a concert or just watching a film?

PREPARE

Discuss your favourite pastimes or hobbies with your partner. Then list companies associated with your hobbies; e.g. Hobby: soccer, Company: Nike

Mood n.

Definition: a particular feeling at a particular point in time
Synonyms: feeling, frame of mind, emotion

Advertising and Images

Advertising carefully chooses specific visuals to target our feelings. Companies spend vast amounts of money to create certain visuals for their target audience. The following visuals are unique images which aim to persuade specific groups of people to buy their products.

Visuals n.

Definition: pictures or images that are used in different genres such as advertising

Sponsored by Hyundai. Official Partner of the 2010 FIFA World Cup ™

Target audience n.

Definition: a group of people to which a product, service or advertisement is aimed

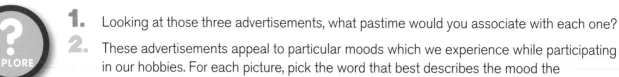

1. Looking at those three advertisements, what pastime would you associate with each one?

2. These advertisements appeal to particular moods which we experience while participating in our hobbies. For each picture, pick the word that best describes the mood the advertisements are trying to create. Explain your answer.

Advertisement ❶

a. bored   b. interested   c. fascinated   d. curious

Advertisement ❷

a. fun   b. embarrassed   c. moody   d. determined

Advertisement ❸

a. curious   b. bored   c. child-like   d. scared

1. Pick one of your favourite pastimes and think of a creative way to advertise it. You will need to make up the name of a company to appear in your advertisement. You can create a visual (picture/photograph/illustration) to help you. You should be able to explain the idea of your advertisement to your teacher.

2. Now examine the list of products below and say who the target audience is for each one:

* Washing powder   * Cheese strings   * Bicycle
* Lipstick   * Four-wheeled drive jeep   * Football jersey
* TV   * Tablet   * Dentures
* Milk   * Diamond earrings   * Aftershave

AIB/GAA All-Ireland Club Championships Advertisement

Team sports require both a personal and team passion, and they are a perfect example of a pastime pursued for enjoyment which quickly becomes a passionate quest for success. The next advertisement you will study is a TV advertisement for the GAA All-Ireland Club Championships. The GAA is a central part of Irish culture, and Gaelic football and hurling are the biggest spectator sports in the country.

This advertisement was produced by AIB Bank (sponsors of the championships) and it examines this quest for success.

Sponsor n.

Definition: a person or organisation that pays for or contributes to the costs involved in staging a sporting or artistic event in return for advertising space

Synonyms: backer, benefactor, promoter, patron

EXPLORE

W6.2

1. Only one person speaks during this advertisement. How would you describe the tone he speaks in?

2. List the sound effects you hear during the advertisement.

3. Write down two pieces of evidence to suggest that the supporters shown in the advertisement are passionate about their teams.

4. The slogan for this advertisement is #TheToughest. Do you know why it has the # sign in front of it?

5. Based on the advertisement, can you give two reasons why the producers felt this was a good slogan?

6. In your opinion, was this a convincing advertisement?

Slogan n.

Definition: a short, memorable phrase used in advertising

Synonyms: catchline, jingle

Logos

Logos are very important to company and product branding. For example, no matter where you are in the world, you instantly recognise the logo for McDonald's.

Logos n.

Definition: A company's emblem or symbol
Synonyms: brand, label

PREPARE

1. Can you think of five famous logos (apart from the examples on the left)?

2. Now looking at the logos on the left, can you figure out what companies they belong to and what pastimes they are associated with? (We've deleted the product name to see if you can recognise the company by the logo alone!)

CREATE

You are on work experience with an advertising company. They have four large corporations who want your company to create a name and logo for their products. You have been asked to think up a name and design a logo for one of these companies. The companies are selling:

- Dog food
- Milk
- Teenager's clothes
- Chocolate

Pick the product you wish to design for. Keep very clearly in mind what the company sells, and consider carefully the arrangement of text and use of colours and pictures, which are all very important in your design.

A Short Story

What I will learn:

to speak about personal feelings and memories

Advertising influences people to buy particular products, or to think a certain way about a product or organisation. However, family and friends are two of the most influential factors in our decision-making. If your mother was a tennis player, there is a high possibility you might become one too. If your best friend loves a certain celebrity, you might be persuaded to follow him or her also.

PREPARE

Do you think a teenager's peers are the most influential group in their life? Give reasons for your answer.

Peer n.
Definition: a member of one's age group or social group
Synonym: co-equal

READ

In this short story, the main character is influenced by his friends to take up a particular hobby. He soon develops a passion for it, but finds himself having to negotiate the trials and perils of being a champion.

Do you notice anything about the title of this story? Explain what the author of this short story has done and why.

Paul the Conkerer

Undefeated and indestructible, that autumn Paul was the one to beat. He was the yard kingpin. Every time the lunch bell tolled, Paul walked with an ever-increasing swagger to the ball alleys where his challengers jostled and elbowed each other, desperate to take him on. Yet he knew the order and knew the ones he wanted to beat. Paul had a 32-er. No one in his year had ever owned a 32-er. He smiled as he approached the crowd. 'So lads, which one of you losers am I going to beat today?'

Paul had been playing conkers since he was six but was never lucky with them. He had started because everyone on the road was playing, but as time passed a lot of the lads got bored with it. They'd rather belt the sliotar off the wall than play conkers. However, not long after starting in secondary school he noticed local bruiser, Johnny Kelly, playing conkers with some lads from a neighbouring village. He asked if he could have a go, but Kelly and his mates laughed at him. 'You're rubbish at football and you'll be rubbish at this. Don't be wasting our time, four-eyes.'

Paul's champion conker was a beauty. Every year he combed the orchard behind his house in an effort to find a champion but the best he had ever mustered was a 5-er. A pretty miserable level of performance, considering there were at least twenty die-hard conker players in his year. There was no special formula for finding a great conker, just blind luck, and it was blind luck that had led Paul to stumble across the 32-er. Mid-search his father had bellowed from the top of the hill, 'Stop acting the eejit down there and give me a hand with the feeding.' Paul was afraid of his father, a man with purpose and authority. In his haste to get to him as quickly as possible, Paul had stumbled over a root. He sprawled forward with his hands outstretched in a desperate attempt to avoid nettles and stones, grimacing as he crashed into the dirt.

In the competition, a victorious conker adds all the victories of its defeated opponent to its own score. If your conker has three victories (3-er) and defeats a conker with five victories (5-er) it becomes a 9-er (3-er + 5-er + the latest match = 9-er).

There he had seen it, unearthed like some miracle before his eyes, nestled beneath the moss-covered roots of the largest horse chestnut tree in the orchard. The outer skin was just breaking and revealing the tough, brown interior. He knew that for some reason this was special. Slipping it into his pocket, he jogged down the hill to join his father and proceeded to carry out the farm jobs with unusual energy. He was excited by his find but he wasn't sure why. It would surely be just another failure in a long line of failures.

'Playing conkers is more technical than people give it credit for. It is 40 per cent preparation, 50 per cent skill and 10 per cent luck,' remarked his father while they were both forking in silage to the cattle. It was one of his rare comments on the subject, or any subject for that matter. Paul was bolstered by his father's interest, so once the farm work was complete, he set about ensuring that the 40 per cent was in place before next year. The shed where he practised was bitterly cold, but nothing could break his concentration. Carefully he removed the prickly green exterior to reveal the velvety sheen inside. Using his grandfather's old manual drill and a tiny bit, he secured the conker in the vice and drilled a hole through the centre of it. He had split dozens of conkers in the past doing this, and was petrified that this one would suffer that fate. But he managed it, and threading the blackened string though the hole he then secured it with a solid knot. Once it was wrapped up in an oily cloth and stowed away at the back of an old wardrobe to harden, he drilled one more conker for the next day's game.

That second conker lasted three cracks of Ciaran Donoghue's 12-er, but he knew that he was playing the long game, biding his time until the following year when he would unleash his secret weapon.

One year on, the ball alleys loomed over Paul and the intensity of the gathering crowd was bearing down on him. Johnny Kelly eyeballed him, but this was not about physical strength. Kelly would realise that he might be able to push him around at football training, but that in this game Paul had the upper hand. It was obvious from the dull complexion of Kelly's conker that he had cooked it overnight. This was frowned upon as bad sportsmanship, but no one was going to challenge Kelly on this. Finally the time came for Paul to challenge Kelly in the contest. Kelly's shoddy conker lasted two cracks of Paul's champion, and he stormed away, furious that he had been beaten by the weakling four-eyes he so despised. Kelly scowled as Paul shouted after him, 'Better luck next time, Kelly'. Later that day, Ciaran Donoghue invited Paul to play football, but he told him he had better things to do. After all, he was now the King of the Conkers.

* STOP AND THINK *

What do you think is going to happen next? *Now read on …*

That evening as usual, Tom Byrne's bus dropped Paul at the local GAA club. It was about a half-mile walk to his house from there. Paul was baffled as to how Johnny Kelly managed it, but as he rounded the corner half-way up his road, there was Kelly, waiting for him. From the moment Paul laid eyes on him, he knew the deal. Outrunning him was unrealistic, so Paul walked towards him.

'You seem to think winning a few conker matches makes you important. You made a fool outta me today, Brennan, and no one makes a fool outta me,' he snarled. 'I beat you fair and square. Why can't you take your beating,' Paul retorted, shocked at his bravery. 'What did ya say, ya little maggot?' Kelly spat back. Paul was bolder now, foolishly showing courage because he was the conker champion. 'Why can't you take your beating?' he repeated forcefully. *Bang!* Paul's head took the powerful blow from Kelly and he could immediately taste the blood. Kelly then pushed him hard in the chest, knocking him off balance. Paul had no defence as Johnny jumped on him. But he wasn't punching him. He was scrambling around Paul's pockets. 'What are you doing?' Paul croaked. Then he realised that Kelly was after the conker. 'A 32-er is it? A 32-er?' Then he had it! 'What does it feel like, Brennan? Does it hurt? Who is the King of the Conkers now?' Kelly bellowed, as he lashed out at Paul with the conker. Then he turned to the wall, and started hammering it off it, cursing and swearing all the while. Paul picked himself up and started shuffling away. Kelly had forgotten about him but Paul waited just long enough to know it

took a lot of cracks – at least twenty – to finally break the champion conker.

Paul couldn't hide his swollen and bloody lip from his parents. He was refusing to say a word and his mother was in a terrible frenzy in the kitchen. 'Who did it? Why did they do it? I'm ringing the school!' His father sat motionless in the corner. 'Anne, can you boil the kettle, please?' he said calmly. Now Paul wasn't sure what had him in more discomfort: the pain from the punch or his father's calmness about it. His mother was still fussing over him while his father continued to muse in the corner, tapping his fingers on the arm of the chair. When his mother went rooting in the back kitchen for cotton wool and Dettol, Paul's father finally spoke again. 'What happened?'

'Johnny Kelly attacked me because I'm the King of the Conkers. He stole my champion conker and broke it off the wall.' The pain from his mouth and the intensity of his father's stare were starting to get too much for Paul, and tears began to sting his eyes. 'He's just jealous because I beat him today even though he tried to cheat. Sore loser, that's all he is. I'm the best'.

Paul's father was silent for a moment. Then he spoke. 'I had a 212-er, son. I was the envy of the parish. I defeated all challengers for six Octobers running until I retired it, undefeated. My biggest rival was Seanie Kelly, Johnny's father. Our match was usually to decide the champion and he never once beat me in six years. We never came to blows over it though. He was often frustrated, but we respected the game. If he knew what his son did to you today, he'd be very disappointed. Conkers is a great game. But if I'm not mistaken, you started to believe you were some kind of a big man, prancing around like the mayor of the town. I was chatting with your teacher, Mr Byrne, in town on Saturday. He was worried that something like this might happen if you continued to rub your success in the lads' faces. If Johnny is anything like his father, I don't think he would tolerate anyone that thought they were better than everyone else. Now there's no excuse for him attacking you over it, but you need to clear the air with Johnny. I'll talk to Seanie about it.'

With that, he stood up and left the room, but returned shortly with a small black box in his hands. Unlocking it, he handed it to Paul. 'Play with this tomorrow but play like a man. Forget these airs and graces. You won't lose, but when October is over you are going to hand me this back and start again. Johnny Kelly won't be able to say anything because he'd have to admit he took your conker and broke it.'

Paul didn't know what to say. They spoke for a few more minutes, and Paul realised his father must have given his mother some sort of signal to leave because she hadn't reappeared. He now spoke openly about the process of preparation and the skill involved, and Paul wondered why his father had never told him all his secrets before. So he asked him. 'Paul, the fun of something like this is in the discovery of it. If I gave away all the secrets, you would have missed out on all the fun. Now I never thought you'd catch a beating over it, but I've seen the time you have spent searching, discovering, preparing and playing. Would you have enjoyed me telling you how to do that as well?' With that he went

to the hall and picked up the phone. Paul wasn't quite sure what had just happened, but he knew that it was important.

The next day Johnny Kelly even managed a mumbled apology, and he couldn't help but grin when Paul mumbled an apology back. 'So, do you think you might want a game tomorrow?' asked Kelly. 'Yeah okay, I think I might have found another champion but I'd have to test it against the best first'. 'Damn right,' smiled Kelly as he pulled out a fresh conker. 'Maybe he's learning,' thought Paul. Maybe they both were.

FUN FACT

The World Conker Championship takes place each year in Northamptonshire, England.

1. Find the words in the story that match these definitions.

Contestant, competitor	ch _ l _ _ _ _ _ r
Nickname for someone who wears glasses	f _ _ r-e _ _ s
Area where you would find fruit trees	or _ _ _ _ d
Blueprint, instructions you follow	fo _ _ _ l _
Fall, trip, stagger	st _ _ _ _ e
A vision, wonder	m _ r _ _ _ e
Strong, hard	t _ u _ _
Supported, strengthened	bo _ _ _ _ _ _ d
Angrily, resentfully, severely	b _ t _ er _ _
Destiny, future	f _ _ e
Boring, darkened	d _ _ l
Young insect	m _ g _ _ _

2. For a trickier challenge, find the words in the story that match these definitions.

Everlasting, durable	in _ _ _ _ _ _ _ _ _ _ e
Knocked against others deliberately	j _ _ _ _ _ _
Gathered up, managed	m _ _ _ _ _ _ d
Shouted loudly	b _ l _ _ _ _ _
Fell with outstretched arms	sp _ _ _ _ _ _
Sheltered, put in a comfortable position	ne _ _ _ _ d
Clamp, an object which holds something in place	v _ _ e
Stood above in a threatening way	l _ _ _ _ d
Colour or quality of the skin	co _ _ _ _ _ _ _ n
Confused, puzzled	b _ _ _ _ _ d
A state of uncontrolled emotion	fr _ _ _ _
To think something over	m _ _ _

Create a storyboard for 'Paul the Conkerer'. You could use the storyboarding apps Penultimate, Paper or Storyboarder to help you to create it.

W6.4

Storyboard n.
Definition: a sequence of drawings/pictures that show the layout of a story

Have you been influenced by a family member or friend in following a passion or pastime? Take one minute to think about a time when you began to take an interest in a particular sport, hobby, singer, instrument, and who or what might have influenced your decision, and then discuss it with your classmate.

Listen to Katy's story and Cian's story about how they got involved in their passions. After you have listened, speak about a time when you became involved in a pastime.

In the short story, 'Paul the Conkerer', Paul is influenced by his friends and later his father. Following on from your discussion with your classmate, write a mini-memoir about how a particular person influenced you to become involved in your pastime. It should be about two paragraphs long.

What is a memoir, p. 111.

REMEMBER

Photo collage n.

Definition: a piece of art made from various clippings of newspapers, magazines, comics and other printed material generally relating to a specific theme, all assembled together

If you like, you can make a photo collage, with your memoir in the middle surrounded by pictures, words, newspaper clippings, ticket stubs, music sheets – it all depends on your particular pastime.

In your memoir, remember to include the following:

- Your **perspective**, using some personal pronouns; e.g. 'Seeing *my* favourite band's powerful performance live in Galway inspired *me* to take up the electric guitar'

- **Description**, to help recreate the scene for your reader, e.g. 'The *chalky texture* of the pastels almost discouraged me from finishing the picture, but I soon became used to them and now they are my favourite art material'

- **New vocabulary**, for example some new words you might have picked up from 'Paul the Conkerer'

A Short Video

What I will learn:

to speak confidently in front of an audience

So far you have examined popular pastimes that lots of people get great enjoyment from. But not everybody's pastime is a popular one.

Can you think of any unusual pastimes? Does anyone in your class have an unusual pastime? Do a survey and find out.

What do you think are the most popular pastimes in the world? In groups of three, create two lists. One list is of what your group believes are the most popular pastimes in the world. The second list is what you and your group believe to be the most unusual pastimes in the world. To help you make your list, remember that hobbies/pastimes can be divided into the following categories:

- Doing
- Making
- Collecting
- Learning

Black: My Journey to Yo-Yo Mastery (TED Talk)

The video you will watch is about a young man from Japan, Tomonari 'Black' Ishiguro, and his favourite hobby, the yo-yo. It might not be on everyone's list of top ten pastimes, but the yo-yo is his passion and he has reached an incredible level of skill with it. In this talk, Ishiguro also speaks about a personal memory. Watch the video and then answer the questions.

EXPLORE

1. What did Black expect to happen after winning his first world yo-yo championship?

2. What major changes did he make to his performance after winning his first world yo-yo contest?

3. Why did Black decide to pursue this passion?

4. Do you think that the audience were impressed with Black's performance?

CREATE

Write a letter to Black inviting him to perform at your school.

How to write a formal letter, p. 35.

REMEMBER

SPEAK

Yo-yo champion Black has accepted your invitation to visit your school and perform at assembly. You have been given the responsibility of introducing him to the students of the school. Write your introductory words. Then speak them to a partner.

Oral Peer Assessment

Reflect on your partner's oral communication task and write down two things you think he/she did well and one thing he/she could improve on.

Check out these links for access to more personal stories:

www.rte.ie/radio1/doconone/

www.ted.com/talks

When we talk casually with our friends and family, we often include personal stories, feelings and memories in our conversations. If you look out for it, you'll notice that people often tell stories from their own lives: 'Oh, that reminds me of when …'; 'That happened to me once too. I was …' Sometimes we might get to speak about these personal matters in a more formal way, like many of the speakers in the TED talks, or like people who appear in radio documentaries.

You will now write some notes and then prepare a short talk on a personal memory that would be suitable to present to a group of primary school students.

REMEMBER

You may want to create a mind map to help you prepare your talk. Mind mapping, p. 120.

Here are some suggestions on what you might like to share with them:

- Your first day in primary school
- A funny episode during class in secondary school
- When you met your best friend
- The first time you ever went to the cinema

STORY TIPS

Use **anecdotes** (an event or episode from your life) to demonstrate your opinion on a topic. For example:

I remember a Friday night back in October when my piano exams were looming. I really wanted the top grade so I practised the same pieces every day, twice a day for two months. It was the day before the exam and I just felt like giving up. The enjoyment was crushed under the weight of my ambition. I did my exam, received the top grade, but then gave myself a break. In the week after, I made sure to play songs I loved just to remind myself of how much I actually enjoyed playing the piano.

Use **humour**, as this will make your audience enjoy your experiences too. For example:

Golf is my passion. It makes sense, as golfers are amazing and extremely good looking – it's a proven scientific fact. In fact, the year I started playing was the year this fact was formally established.

Use **description**, another useful tool in helping your audience understand your memories and feelings. For example:

I remember vividly bringing my new horse, Holly, home for the first time. When I led her out of the horse box, she stamped the ground, flaring her nostrils and taking in the new environment. Her bright chestnut coat shone in the sun, and her big brown eyes took in everything in the yard.

Can you add any more criteria?

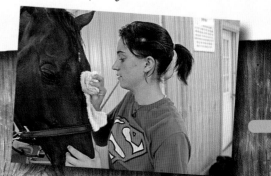

A Short Film

What I will learn:

to create a multi-modal presentation

Multi-modal *n.*

Definition: the use of many different methods to present information, e.g. a webpage containing text, images and audio/visual recordings

Question:

What do the following people have in common?

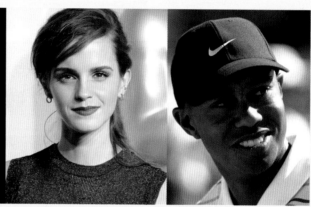

(You will find the answer at the bottom of this page)

Beyoncé (singer)   Emma Watson (actress)   Tiger Woods (golfer)

WATCH

Rockmount (Dave Tynan, dir.)

Like Ishiguro, our next character is strong-minded in his dreams to succeed as a footballer. Based on a real-life story, this short film, *Rockmount*, shows how ambition and enthusiasm begins at an early stage in life.

Answer: Apart from being famous for what they do, they were all driven to succeed at a young age. **Beyoncé** set up her first singing group with her friend, Kelly Rowland, when she was just nine. They entered a talent competition but didn't win. Her dad gave up his job to become their manager. **Emma Watson** wanted to be an actress since the age of six. She joined Stagecoach Theatre Arts and landed her first big acting job in *Harry Potter and the Philosopher's Stone*. **Tiger Woods** began playing golf at the age of two. He putted against the famous comedian Bob Hope on an American TV programme. At the age of eight he won the Junior World Gold Championships in his age category.

While you watch this film, jot down some notes about the following parts of the story:

- Opening
- Problem
- Climax
- Ending

 Roy always wanted to be a footballer. What is your dream job? Create a multi-modal social media page (background, status updates, etc.) where you imagine your future self.

- What year is it?
- What age will you be in that year?
- Who will you be friends with?
- What type of events will you be attending?
- What type of issues will you be commenting on?

Drama – Romeo and Juliet

What I will learn:

to practise my acting and performance skills; to use mime and gesture

Determination, ambition and passion can definitely be positive elements in a person's life, as we saw with Roy from *Rockmount*. However, sometimes these characteristics spill over into negative feelings and behaviours. When passion erupts, it can often lead to conflict. Drama is a very powerful way to see these passions and frustrations play out.

Turn the word *hate* into *love* in three attempts, by changing one letter at a time and making a new word each time.

Hate ? ? ? **Love**

(Hint: the second word is something you'd find on a calendar, the third word is a man's name, and the fourth word is a type of bird.)

What does the word **conflict** mean? Write a **dictionary** definition for this word.

Can you think of any news items you have heard recently that feature conflict? Who is involved? What are the problems that have occurred?

TOP TIP

It is useful to do warm-up exercises before you play a part in a drama!

 In this drama extract from *Romeo and Juliet* by William Shakespeare, conflict is translated not only by the words that Shakespeare has written but also by the way the actor performs them. This scene is set in Verona, Italy, in the fourteenth or fifteenth century. Two powerful families run the city but they hate and distrust each other. Even their servants fight with each other. In this opening scene, the servants of the house of Capulet meet servants from the house of Montague, and passions erupt.

In groups of six, practise a performance of the drama. You might need to read this extract a few times to become comfortable with it. Remember, you must emphasise your words when the character's emotions are heightened or more measured and calm. (To make things a bit easier, included is a modern English translation of the piece.)

Characters: *House of Montague:* Abram, Balthasar, Benvolio

House of Capulet: Sampson, Gregory, Tybalt

Setting: The streets of Verona

Props: Swords

Romeo and Juliet

by William Shakespeare

ACT 1 SCENE 1

Verona. A public place.

GREGORY

Tis well thou art not fish; if thou hadst, thou hadst been poor-John. Draw thy tool! Here comes two of the house of Montagues.

[Enter two other Servingmen, ABRAM and BALTHASAR]

SAMPSON

My naked weapon is out. Quarrel! I will back thee.

GREGORY

How! turn thy back and run?

MODERN ENGLISH TRANSLATION

GREGORY

It is good that you aren't a fish. If you had been a fish, you would have been a shrivelled salted hake. Draw your sword! Here comes two servants of the Montague family.

[Entering are two servants, ABRAM and BALTHASAR]

SAMPSON

My sword is out of its sheath. Start the fight. I will back you up.

GREGORY

How? By turning and running?

SAMPSON

Fear me not.

GREGORY

No, marry. I fear thee!

SAMPSON

Let us take the law of our sides; let them begin.

GREGORY

I will frown as I pass by, and let them take it as they list.

SAMPSON

Nay, as they dare. I will bite my thumb at them, which is a disgrace to them, if they bear it.

ABRAM

Do you bite your thumb at us, sir?

SAMPSON

I do bite my thumb, sir.

ABRAM

Do you bite your thumb at us, sir?

SAMPSON

[Aside to GREGORY] Is the law of our side if I say ay?

GREGORY

[Aside to SAMPSON] No.

SAMPSON

No, sir, I do not bite my thumb at you, sir, but I bite my thumb, sir.

GREGORY

Do you quarrel, sir?

ABRAM

Quarrel sir! No, sir.

SAMPSON

But if you do, sir, I am for you. I serve as good a man as you.

SAMPSON

Don't worry about me.

GREGORY

No, indeed. I fear you!

SAMPSON

Let's defend our side. Let them start the fight.

GREGORY

I will scowl at them as I go by and let them respond however they want.

SAMPSON

No, let them take it as they dare. I will bite my thumb as an insult to them.

ABRAM

Are you biting your thumb at us, sir?

SAMPSON

Yes, I am biting my thumb, sir.

ABRAM

Do you bite your thumb at us, sir?

SAMPSON

[In private to GREGORY] Is it legal if I say yes?

GREGORY

[In private to SAMPSON] No.

SAMPSON

No, sir, I am not biting my thumb at you, sir, but I am biting my thumb, sir.

GREGORY

Do you want a fight, sir?

ABRAM

A fight, sir? No, sir.

SAMPSON

But if you do want a fight, sir, I will attack you. I serve as worthy a master as you do.

ABRAM

No better.

SAMPSON

Well, sir.

[Enter BENVOLIO]

GREGORY

[Aside to SAMPSON] Say 'better'. Here comes one of my master's kinsmen.

SAMPSON

Yes, better, sir.

ABRAM

You lie.

SAMPSON

Draw, if you be men. Gregory, remember thy swashing blow.

[They fight]

BENVOLIO

Part, fools! Put up your swords. You know not what you do.

[Enter TYBALT]

TYBALT

What, art thou drawn among these heartless hinds?

Turn thee, Benvolio, look upon thy death.

BENVOLIO

I do but keep the peace. Put up thy sword,

Or manage it to part these men with me.

TYBALT

What, drawn, and talk of peace! I hate the word,

As I hate hell, all Montagues, and thee. Have at thee, coward!

[They fight]

ABRAM

Your master is no better than mine.

SAMPSON

I see, sir.

[Enter BENVOLIO]

GREGORY

[Privately, to SAMPSON] Say our master is better. Here comes a relative of the Capulets.

SAMPSON

Yes, my master is better, sir.

ABRAM

You are lying.

SAMPSON

Draw you swords, if you are real men. Gregory, remember your killer slice.

[They fight]

BENVOLIO

Stop, fools! Put up your swords. You don't know how dangerous this is.

[Enter TYBALT]

TYBALT

What is this? Are you attacking these weakling cowards?

Turn, Benvolio! Face your death.

BENVOLIO

I am trying to make peace. Put up your sword, or use it to help me stop this fight.

TYBALT

You aim your sword and talk about peace? I hate peace as I hate hell, the Montague family, and you. I challenge you, coward!

[They fight]

True or False

Your teacher will call out the statements below one by one. Decide if the statement is true or false. Show the teacher your answer by holding up a **TRUE** or **FALSE** sign.

Statements

- The author of this play is William Shakespeare
- *Romeo and Juliet* was written in 1999
- The play is set in the fourteenth century
- Sampson and Gregory are servants of the Capulet House
- Benvolio is a member of the Montague family
- Tybalt is a peacemaker

REMEMBER Props, p. 60.

Now answer these questions in your copy.

1. What impression do you get of Tybalt?

2. This play is about two groups that hate each other. If this play was set in today's world, can you think of two other groups that might find themselves in a similar situation?

3. What are the props used in the extract?

Using Mime

Mime is extremely important for actors, particularly Shakespearean actors. In Shakespearean times, actors did not have access to good props or special effects. They had to be able to demonstrate emotions and actions clearly for the audience and use their whole body to tell the story. Mime also helps an actor to react and play for time if they forget their lines!

Mime *n.*

Definition: suggesting action, character or emotion without using any words or sound, but by gesture, expression and movement alone
Synonyms: impersonate

1. Use mime to act out the following situations:

- Eating breakfast
- Packing a bag
- Sweeping the floor
- Baking a cake
- Making a sandwich
- Starting a car
- Using a laptop
- Playing basketball
- Cleaning a window
- Food shopping

2. Imagine you need to communicate an urgent message to a complete stranger. Your only way of communicating is through gesture and facial expression. With a partner, come up with an urgent message and try to communicate it to another pair in the class. Here are some suggestions:

- You need help with directions
- You need to see a train timetable and someone is standing in your way
- You have lost your backpack and your passport was inside
- You have been involved in an accident and you need medical assistance
- Your car has broken down and you need a mechanic
- You need help lifting something heavy
- Your home is on fire and someone is still inside

W6.8

CREATE

Design the front page for the next day's newspaper in Verona. You must write the main article/report which is about the brawl. You can write for a broadsheet or tabloid newspaper. You must include the following on your front page:

- A name for your newspaper
- A catchy headline
- Your main article comprising the 5 Ws
- Quotes from eye-witnesses
- A secondary article (another news article on the front page, smaller than the main article, either related in some way to the main story or about something else entirely)

REMEMBER
The difference between a tabloid and a broadsheet, p. 53.

SHOW WHAT YOU KNOW

You have learned many writing and speaking skills throughout this collection. Now it's time to *Show What You Know!*

My Portfolio Task

Choose a poem (any poem) that you would like to perform. Create a presentation on your chosen poem, making sure to fulfil the success criteria as listed here.

SUCCESS CRITERIA

You may wish to use presentation software like Prezi or slides.com to help you create your presentation.

I must

- Include the full text of the poem
- Write or type my presentation
- Include a profile of the poet
- Present the information creatively
- Read what I've written to check for punctuation marks (, . ! ?) or missing words
- Use a **dictionary** to check any spellings I'm not sure of

I should

- Give my opinion on different aspects of the poem
- Use quotes from the poem to support my opinion

I could

- Explain the poet's use of mood and tone in the poem

Self-Assessment

Re-read what you have written and then write down two things you think you did well and one thing you could improve on.

Redrafting

Reviewing the success criteria again to make sure you have met all the requirements, and taking into account your own self-assessment notes, you can now revise your presentation to create a second draft. When you are happy with it, you can put it in your **portfolio**.

Reflection Question

What particular part of my presentation do I think an audience would enjoy and why?

Perform a dramatic reading of your chosen poem.

SUCCESS CRITERIA

I should

- Use an appropriate tone, making my voice lower or higher, softer or stronger as necessary
- Recite the poem at a suitable pace
- Acknowledge where pauses occur

I must

- Learn the poem off by heart
- State the title of the poem and the poet at the beginning of my reading
- Project my voice when reciting the poem
- Make eye contact

I could

- Emphasise certain words that the poet intended to be emphasised
- Use gesture to aid the audience's understanding of the poem

Peer Assessment

Reflect on your classmate's oral communication task and then write down two things that he/she did well and one thing he/she could improve on.

Fables, Fairy Tales and Folklore

As I explore this collection I will learn about:

- Writing creatively
- Characterisation
- First and third person narrative
- Plot twists
- Italics
- Endings
- Elements in a story
- Formal and informal dialogue
- Well-known tales and characters
- Register

SHOW WHAT YOU KNOW

The skills you learn in this collection will enable you to **show what you know** in your final tasks at the end of this collection.

For my portfolio task I will:
Plan and write a short story featuring two characters from very different backgrounds

For oral communication I will:
Prepare and deliver a fairy tale suitable for an oral storytelling event

Learning Outcomes
OL5, OL7, R9, R13, W3, W5

Exploring the Theme – Fables, Fairy Tales and Folklore

Do a brainstorm around all the words you associate with fables, fairy tales and folklore.

Folklore *n.*

Definition: the traditional beliefs, customs and stories of a community, passed on through generations by word of mouth

Synonyms: tradition, folk story, ballad

Fable *n.*

Definition: a short story, often with animals as characters, designed to teach a lesson/moral

Synonyms: legend, myth, yarn

Fairy tale *n.*

Definition: a simple children's story about magical creatures including elves, goblins, dragons and fairies

Synonyms: mythical story

Creative Writing

What I will learn:

to write creatively, using images to generate ideas; to practise using the main elements in a story (setting, main character, complication, climax and resolution)

What is a writer? What do they do exactly? Make a list of the different things writers do other than write, e.g. researching. Now share your ideas with your partner and combine your answers. Working with your partner, complete the sentence:

'A writer is …'

Discuss your ideas as a class and agree on a class definition of a writer.

WRITE

5 MIN

Now that you've talked about writers, who they are and what they do, it is time for you to do some writing. For the next five minutes you will write about a good memory from your childhood by continuing the sentence below. You won't have to read this out, so don't worry if it isn't perfect!

'One of the best days of my life was …'

Creative Writing Tips

- Don't lift your pen up or pause to think about what you are going to write once you start – just keep writing. Even if it's hard, or it doesn't make sense at the time or isn't interesting at first, something good will come out if you keep writing.

- Don't edit your work at this stage.

- If you are using a tablet or computer, keep typing and don't delete or edit anything at all.

CREATE

W7.2

Working in groups, plan a story using three of the images below as inspiration.

- One image should help you to write the beginning of the story, i.e. to set the scene, introduce the main character(s) and start the action (this will lead up to the complication)

- The second image will assist you with the middle of the story (resulting in the climax)

- The last image should give you ideas about how to end the story (the resolution)

REMEMBER

The *beginning* of your story should introduce your setting, main character(s) and start the action. The *end* of your story should resolve the story. The *middle* contains the action and the conflict – this is why the story exists. Without conflict, there would be no story.

165

A Radio Documentary

*to create a character for a story by
listening to an interesting documentary*

Storytelling is an art as ancient as man. Before there were books, folklore and history were transferred orally (passed on by telling them out loud) from generation to generation. While you may not realise it, many stories you heard in childhood, like fairy tales and legends, are hundreds of years old.

'Lumps of Coal' (RTÉ Radio 1)

Listen carefully to this short extract from the radio documentary 'Lumps of Coal' from RTÉ Radio 1. It describes a character who is the antithesis (opposite) of Santa. As you listen, make a list of everything you learn about Santa. When you have finished you will work in groups and do a quiz which requires you to remember as much information as possible.

Mythological *adj.*

Definition: relating to myths or legends, ancient stories told about a place or tradition, usually involving supernatural elements

1. Work in groups to create a new character who is the antithesis of a known mythological character (e.g. the tooth fairy, the Easter bunny, Santa Claus).

Try to imagine:

- What it looks like
- The countries where it is known
- What exactly it does to undo the good work of another character
- Its darkest secret
- Its strength/power

2. Working in pairs or small groups, you have five minutes to make up a scene where this character meets a young child/some children, and what might happen next. The scene should have a definite beginning, middle and end.

Group Assessment

Reflect on your classmate's work and then write down two things you think they did well and one thing they could improve on. You might like to make changes to your scene now based on the feedback your group receives.

Act out your scene for another group or for the class. Everyone in the group should have a role (director or actor).

Storytelling – An Irish Folktale

What I will learn:

to read stories with interesting endings and suggest alternative endings

Ireland, like many countries, has a tradition of fables and folklore. Think about some of the tales you heard or learned about in primary school.

Working in pairs, write up a list of traditional stories/legends you know (either from Ireland or from other countries). Tell your partner if you know any folklore from other countries.

Now join up with another pair of students and take turns to tell one of those stories to your group of four. Select the best story from the group and write it together (three or four paragraphs is enough). When it is complete, read it out to the rest of the class. You might like to include dialogue in your story. Everybody in your group should take a turn to read – one person can be the narrator and the others can speak the dialogue.

REMEMBER

Dialogue, p. 61.

Design a poster to advertise a reading of a traditional Irish story at a book festival in your local area. The poster is targeted at parents, teachers and children aged 8–12. Your poster must answer the 5 Ws.

Success Criteria

Your poster must

- Include the name of the festival (What)
- Include the date, time and venue for the reading (When/Where)
- Include the reasons why children would enjoy this event (Why/Who)

Your poster should

- Include an image from the traditional Irish story or something linked to the event

Your poster could

- Include a catchy slogan or memorable line

The following tale is not very well known so you may not be familiar with it. You will read it, and near the end you will stop and try to guess the ending. You will later compare your ending with the actual ending.

'The White Wolfhound' retold by Eithne Massey

Fionn had a sister called Tuiren, who was so kind that everyone loved her. Everyone, that is, except a witch called Ukdelv, who was jealous of Tuiren's kindness and loveliness and long fair hair. So, one day, Ukdelv went to Tuiren's palace, and, waving her magic hazel wand, she turned the princess into an Irish wolfhound. But because Tuiren had been fair-haired and beautiful, the hound was beautiful too, and its coat was as white as snow. Ukedelv took Tuiren by the scruff of her neck and dragged her to the house of a very grumpy man called Fergus.

Fergus really hated dogs. When he saw Ukdelv and the big white wolfhound coming towards his house, he ran outside and barred the door.

'That dog can't come in here,' he said to Ukdelv.

'She's smelly and dirty and she'll drop hairs everywhere.'

Tuiren looked at him sadly and tried to lick his hand. He pushed her away.

'Get off me, you big hairy dribbler,' he said.

'But Fionn wants you to take this dog in,' said Ukdelv. She was sure that Tuiren would have a terrible life in Fergus's care.

Now, everyone did as Fionn asked, so, with a sigh, Fergus took the dog into his house. Ukdelv smiled as she watched Tuiren follow him inside with her tail tucked between her legs and her ears down.

But, although the witch had been able to change Tuiren's shape, she could not change her nature. Every time Tuiren saw Fergus, she would try to lick him. She tripped him up with balls, begging to play. She pined when he wasn't there. She was also the best hunting dog in the country, and the two of them spent many happy days together out in the woods and the mountains and the marshes.

So, as time went on, Fergus grew very fond of Tuiren. 'That dog is nearly human!' he would tell his friends, not realising that that was exactly what she was! He called her Princess, not realising that that was what she really was, too.

He was delighted when she had two little puppies, which he called Bran and Sceolan. They would roll around on the floor in front of the fire, and Fergus would find himself laughing at them. He sometimes thought Tuiren looked as if she were laughing too.

Fergus's life was much happier because of Tuiren. He was no longer grumpy.

But Fionn missed his sister and was afraid that something bad had happened to her. He used his magic thumb to discover that she was in Fergus's house. He travelled there, and as soon as he saw the big white dog, he knew that it was Tuiren. She ran to Fionn and put her paws on his shoulders, licking him all over the face.

Fergus explained how he had got the dog. They quickly realised that Ukdelv had put a spell on Tuiren. Together they went to the witch's house and forced her to turn Tuiren back into a woman. Fergus was very sad to lose his faithful friend, but Fionn got him a new puppy for company. Bran and Sceolan became Fionn's faithful hunting dogs and stayed with him always.

* STOP AND THINK *

The story is almost over – the last couple of paragraphs explain the difficulties that Tuiren experienced readjusting to life in the palace again after being a dog. Before you read on, working in small groups:

- Make a list of the difficulties you think that Tuiren may have experienced after returning home.

- Discuss how you think the story ends. Working together, come up with an appropriate ending.

- Share your ending with the rest of the class before you continue reading.

Now read on …

As for Tuiren, she was very happy to be back with her family and friends in the palace. But because of her time as a dog she had changed. She sometimes got over-excited when someone mentioned going for a walk. At dinner, there were times when she really, really wanted to pick up the bones from her plate and chew them by the fire. She missed running after rabbits. She missed rolling on her back in the long grass. She missed being able to scratch behind her ear with her foot. She missed being able to lick people she liked and bite people she didn't.

And there were summer evenings when Fionn would come upon her sitting on the grass outside the palace, gazing into the sinking sun and sniffing the wind, as if waiting for someone to call her home.

1. Why did Ukdelv turn Tuiren into a dog?

2. How does Fergus change as a result of having a dog?

3. What does the writer mean by the sentence, 'although the witch had been able to change Tuiren's shape, she could not change her nature'?

Working with a partner, discuss these questions:

1. Were you surprised by the ending?

2. Which ending did you prefer – your ending or the original ending?

Imagine the moment when Fionn and Fergus go to the witch's house to force her to turn Tuiren back into a woman. Write a script for this scene, as you imagine it. You can include stage directions if you wish (describing movements, tones of voices, props, setting, etc.). Clearly indicate who is speaking, e.g. **Fionn:** (*knocking*) Let me in … **Fergus:** Yes, open the door and come in …

Peer Assessment

Read your partner's work and then write down two things you think he/she did well and one thing he/she could improve on. Based on the feedback you receive, make any necessary changes. When you are happy with the script, act it out or swap it with a classmate's and act out each other's.

Persuasive Writing – An Article

What I will learn:

to think about the purpose of fairy stories; to appreciate the characters, setting, story and action

When you listened to stories as a child, you probably didn't realise that other young boys and girls in many other countries around the world were also listening to the same or similar stories. Think about the stories you were told when you were young, like *Snow White and the Seven Dwarfs* or *Hansel and Gretel*. These classic 'universal' tales (tales known all around the world) draw the young reader into the world of heroes and villains, scary moments and 'happily-ever-after' endings.

FUN FACT

It is believed that one of the most popular versions of *Cinderella* was written in French by Charles Perrault in 1697 – it was called *Cendrillon*.

SYNONYMS AND ANTONYMS

The following words are **bolded** in the article you will read:

successful	essence
palatable	slain
chilling	extinguished
gruesome	vindictive
hapless	familiar

For each of the words, use a **thesaurus** to:

- Find its synonym
- Find its antonym (where possible)

Then

- Learn its spelling

PREPARE

1. On your own, choose your favourite fairy tale story. Write three sentences to sum up the story for someone who mightn't be familiar with it and explain why you like it (you must give at least one reason). **PIE**

2. Now read your answer to a partner to see if it makes sense to them. For example, have you made your point clearly, illustrated it with an example and then explained it? Make sure you do all three steps of **PIE** in this process. Based on your discussion, you may need to rewrite what you have written.

3. Finally, take it in turns to read your work and discuss it with a group of other students. When you have discussed different fairy tales, consider the things they have in common, e.g. the same type of hero/villain appears in several stories; the main character often has to complete a task.

REMEMBER

The Safe Spelling Code – Look, Cover, Write, Check.

We're now going to dig a little deeper into fairy tales and consider what other role they might play other than entertaining young children. This piece of writing is what is called **persuasive writing** – it hopes to convince the reader of a certain point of view, to persuade them. This particular article explains a little about the history of fairy tales and some of the psychology behind them.

Psychology n.

Definition: the scientific study of the human mind and its functions

The Importance of Fairy Tales

Fairy tales have been with us for a long time. Some of the earliest date back to seventeenth-century Italy. The most popular ones are **successful** because they're universal, being understood by millions of children regardless of where they are in the world. There are slight cultural variations; for example, the glass slipper may become a grass one in some countries, but the **essence** of the tales and morals remain unchanged.

The current versions of much-loved stories like 'Little Red Riding Hood' and 'Cinderella' are thought to be a little scary, but in fact the originals were far more violent, involving cannibalism, mutilation and even infanticide (the killing of babies). The versions most children are familiar with were made more **palatable** by writers like the Brothers Grimm in Germany, Hans Christian Andersen in Denmark and Charles Perrault in France.

So why read such frightening tales to children? Why subject innocent minds to stories like 'Little Red Riding Hood', the little girl who wanders through the lonely woods only to meet a wolf who has devoured her grandmother and will do the same to the girl herself, before being violently **slain** by an axe-wielding hunter? It's all a little **chilling** really!

Some academics and psychologists would argue that there are great benefits to these stories. First – they say – the characters are either benevolent or malevolent (goodies or baddies), so children can easily identify the nasty characters and direct their own angry feelings toward them. Characters like the wicked witch, the big bad wolf and the evil stepmother are safe targets for children's anger or frustration, which they are not normally allowed to express.

This is often a child's first experience with siding with the good character, as they join them on a journey to rescue poor grandma from the wolf or save Cinderella from the tyranny of her stepmother and whisk her into the arms of the prince. In this way fables allow the child to step into a world in which violence and evil will be **extinguished** and hope can live on. That lesson of hope is a very important one for a child.

Another benefit is teaching children about morals. In fairy tales, deception and dishonesty are punished severely, while good, honest people are rewarded. Similarly promises must be honoured and silliness punished. However, many would argue that most children who read these stories are not drawn to the morals; rather, they enjoy the **gruesome** images of **vindictive** wolves chasing **hapless** pigs before plummeting down chimneys into vats of hot water!

The most satisfying and indeed the safest part of these tales is that, despite the gory descriptions, fairy tales are all told in the secure context of 'Once upon a time' – a place removed from a child's own world. This is a place where, it is assured, the evil will suffer and the good will not only be saved, they will actually live happily ever after.

Children love being told fairy tales – through these **familiar** stories, they learn morals, are soothed by repetition and relax in the knowledge that good will triumph over evil. And who could possibly argue with something that entertains, educates and comforts a child?

EXPLORE

1. Some parents are reluctant to tell their children fairy tales, as they worry about scaring them with violent images. This article aims to convince people about the benefits of fairy tales. Were you convinced by this writer? List and explain your reasons (at least three). **P I E**

2. The author uses 'rhetorical questions' to make their case. Find an example of a rhetorical question in the article and explain why it is rhetorical.

Rhetorical Question *n.*

Definition: a question that does not expect an answer, either because it doesn't have an answer or because it is asked to introduce or emphasise a point; e.g. 'And who could argue with that?', 'Do you think money grows on trees?', 'How should I know?'

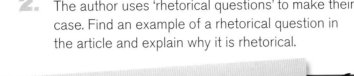

CREATE W7.5

Based on everything you have read about fairy tales, make a list of the success criteria for a good fairy tale, e.g. there should be a hero/heroine and a villain. When you have completed your list, share it with another student and combine your ideas to form one list. Now share those ideas within a group of two other students and combine the best ideas before you share them with the class.

RESEARCH ZONE

Now that you have learned about the history of fairy tales, research any of the following fairy tale writers and write an author profile on them. It might help to find some examples of their work.

The Brothers Grimm (authors of *Hansel and Gretel*, *Snow White and the Seven Dwarfs* and many other fairytales)

Hans Christian Andersen (author of *The Little Mermaid*, *The Snow Queen* and others)

Charles Perrault (author of *Cinderella*, *Little Red Riding Hood*, *Sleeping Beauty* and others)

Lewis Carroll (author of *Alice's Adventures in Wonderland* and others)

Carlo Collodi (author of *Pinocchio*)

Wilhelm Hauff (author of *The Dwarf Nose*, *The Cold Heart* and other fairy tales popular in German-speaking countries)

Any other fairy tale writer you know of from any culture

Your research should:

- Be presented neatly – use your best handwriting, or type and print the information

- Include details about when and where they grew up

- Mention anything that might have influenced their work

- List some of their most famous fairy tales

- Feature a photo of the chosen writer

You might like to present your author profile orally to a group of students or to the class.

A Short Story

What I will learn:

to anticipate a twist in a tale; to know how to tell the difference between first and third person narratives in a story; to appreciate a variety of registers and understand their use in the written word; to understand and practise using italics to create emphasis

First impressions count, there's no question about it. So, too, do final impressions. There's nothing worse than watching a good film or reading a good book, only to be disappointed by the ending. That's why it's important to consider the end of your stories very carefully. So what makes a good ending? How can we recognise one and how can we write one?

THE END

Think about some books you have read or films you have seen. Is there one in particular that you like because of the ending? In four lines, describe the ending.

Now explain **why** you like it – does it have a twist, a happy/funny ending, or does the hero/heroine beat the villain?

Popular Endings to Books and Films

- A union or reunion of two characters
- A surprise (a twist)
- A separation
- A triumph where the hero/heroine beats the villain
- An epiphany (a realisation)
- A change in a character's way of thinking

Can you add to this list? Think about the endings of books and films you have seen/read recently to get some ideas.

TOP TIP

Every story (poem, short story, book or film script) is told from a certain perspective. Some writers prefer to write using the first person narrative, which is when a story is told from one (or more) character's point of view. In first person narratives, the main character speaks directly to the reader using the personal pronouns, 'I' or 'we'. Other writers prefer to write in the third person. They tell the story of someone else using personal pronouns such as 'he', 'she', 'it' or 'they'. Usually the person writing isn't directly involved in the action.

READ

The following story by Roald Dahl has a number of strong elements, including a twist. Read it carefully and see if you can anticipate the twist. You should also try to identify why this is still such a popular short story many years after it was written.

The Hitch-hiker
by Roald Dahl

I had a new car. It was an exciting toy, a big BMW 3.3 Li, which means 3.3 litre, long wheelbase, fuel injection. It had a top speed of 129 mph and terrific acccleration. The body was pale blue. The seats inside were darker blue and they were made of leather, genuine soft leather of the finest quality. The windows were electrically operated and so was the sun-roof. The radio aerial popped up when I switched on the radio, and disappeared when I switched it off. The

powerful engine growled and grunted impatiently at slow speeds, but at sixty miles an hour the growling stopped and the motor began to purr with pleasure.

I was driving up to London by myself. It was a lovely June day. They were haymaking in the fields and there were buttercups along both sides of the road. I was whispering along at 70 miles an hour, leaning back comfortably in my seat, with no more than a couple of fingers resting lightly on the wheel to keep her steady. Ahead of me I saw a man thumbing a lift. I touched the brake and brought the car to a stop beside him. I always stopped for hitch-hikers. I knew just how it used to feel to be standing on the side of a country road watching the cars go by. I hated the drivers for pretending they didn't see me, especially the ones in big cars with three empty seats. The large expensive cars seldom stopped. It was always the smaller ones that offered you a lift, or the old rusty ones or the ones that were already crammed full of children and the driver would say, 'I think we can squeeze in one more.'

The hitch-hiker poked his head through the open window and said, 'Going to London, guv'nor?'

Guv'nor: British, particularly London, slang for 'boss'; short for 'governor'

'Yes,' I said. 'Jump in.'

He got in and I drove on.

He was a small ratty-faced man with grey teeth. His eyes were dark and quick and clever, like a rat's eyes, and his ears were slightly pointed at the top. He had a cloth cap on his head and he was wearing a greyish-coloured jacket with enormous pockets. The grey jacket, together with the quick eyes and the pointed ears, made him look more than anything like some sort of a huge human rat.

'What part of London are you headed for?' I asked him.

'I'm goin' right through London and out the other side' he said. 'I'm goin' to Epsom, for the races. It's Derby Day today.'

'So it is,' I said. 'I wish I were going with you. I love betting on horses.'

'I never bet on horses,' he said. 'I don't even watch 'em run. That's a stupid silly business.'

'Then why do you go?' I asked.

He didn't seem to like that question. His little ratty face went absolutely blank and he sat there staring straight ahead at the road, saying nothing.

'I expect you help to work the betting machines or something like that,' I said.

'That's even sillier,' he answered. 'There's no fun working them lousy machines and selling tickets to mugs. Any fool could do that.'

There was a long silence. I decided not to question him any more. I remembered how irritated I used to get in my hitch-hiking days when drivers kept asking *me* questions. Where are you going? Why are you going there? What's your job? Are you married? Do you have a girlfriend? What's her name? How old are you? And so on and so forth. I used to hate it.

'I'm sorry,' I said. 'It's none of my business what you do. The trouble is I'm a writer, and most writers are terribly nosey parkers.'

'You write books?' he asked.

'Yes.'

'Writing books is okay,' he said. 'It's what I call a skilled trade. I'm in a skilled trade too. The folks I despise is them that spend all their lives doin' crummy old routine jobs with no skill in 'em at all. You see what I mean?'

'Yes.'

'The secret of life,' he said, 'is to become very very good at somethin' that's very very 'ard to do.'

'Like you,' I said.

'Exactly. You and me both.'

'What makes you think that *I'm* any good at my job?' I asked. 'There's an awful lot of bad writers around.'

'You wouldn't be drivin' about in a car like this if you weren't no good at it,' he answered. 'It must've cost a tidy packet, this little job.'

'It wasn't cheap.'

'What can she do flat out?' he asked.

'One hundred and twenty-nine miles an hour,' I told him.

'I'll bet she won't do it.'

'I'll bet she will.'

'All car-makers is liars,' he said. 'You can buy any car you like and it'll never do what the makers say it will in the ads.'

'This one will.'

'Open 'er up': slang for 'make the car go as fast as possible'

'Open 'er up then and prove it,' he said. 'Go on, guv'nor, open 'er right up and let's see what she'll do.'

There is a traffic circle at Chalfont St. Peter and immediately beyond it there's a long straight section of divided highway. We came out of the roundabout onto the dual carriageway and I pressed my foot hard down on the accelerator. The big car leaped forward as though she'd been stung. In ten seconds or so, we were doing ninety.

'Lovely!' he cried. 'Beautiful! Keep goin'!'

I had the accelerator jammed right down against the floor and I held it there.

'One hundred!' he shouted ... 'A hundred and five! ... A hundred and ten! ... A hundred and fifteen! Go on! Don't slack off!'

I was in the outside lane and we flashed past several cars as though they were standing still – a green Mini, a big cream-coloured Citroën, a white Land-Rover, a huge truck with a container on the back, an orange-coloured Volkswagen Minibus ...

'A hundred and twenty!' my passenger shouted, jumping up and down. 'Go on! Go on! Get 'er up to one-two-nine!'

At that moment, I heard the scream of a police siren. It was so loud it seemed to be right inside the car, and then a policeman on a motorcycle loomed up alongside us on the inside lane and went past us and raised a hand for us to stop.

'Oh, my sainted aunt!' I said. 'That's torn it!'

The policeman must have been doing about a hundred and thirty when he passed us, and he took plenty of time slowing down. Finally, he pulled in to the side of the road and I pulled in behind him. 'I didn't know police motorcycles could go as fast as that,' I said rather lamely.

'That one can,' my passenger said. 'It's the same make as yours. It's a BMW R90S. Fastest bike on the road. That's what they're usin' nowadays.'

The cop got off his motorcycle and leaned the machine sideways onto its prop stand. Then he took off his gloves and placed them carefully on the seat. He was in no hurry now. He had us where he wanted us and he knew it.

'This is real trouble,' I said. 'I don't like it one little bit.'

'Keep mum': slang for 'keep quiet'

'Don't talk to 'im more than is necessary, you understand,' my companion said. 'Just sit tight and keep mum.'

Like an executioner approaching his victim, the policeman came strolling slowly toward us. He was a big meaty man with a belly, and his blue breeches were skin-tight around his enormous thighs. His goggles were pulled up onto the helmet showing a smouldering red face with wide cheeks.

We sat there like guilty schoolboys, waiting for him to arrive.

'Watch out for this man,' my passenger whispered, ''e looks mean as the devil.'

The policeman came around to my open window and placed one meaty hand on the sill.

'What's the hurry?' he said.

'No hurry, officer,' I answered.

'Perhaps there's a woman in the back having a baby and you're rushing her to hospital? Is that it?'

'No, officer.'

'Or perhaps your house is on fire and you're dashing home to rescue the family from upstairs?'

His voice was dangerously soft and mocking.

'My house isn't on fire, officer.'

'In that case,' he said, 'you've got yourself into a nasty mess, haven't you? Do you know what the speed limit is in this country?'

'Seventy,' I said.

'And do you mind telling me exactly what speed you were doing just now?'

I shrugged and didn't say anything. When he spoke next, he raised his voice so loud that I jumped.

'*One hundred and twenty miles per hour*!' he barked. 'That's *fifty* miles an hour over the limit!'

He turned his head and spat out a big gob of spit. It landed on the wing of my car and started sliding down over my beautiful blue paint. Then he turned back again and stared hard at my passenger.

'And who are you?' he asked sharply.

'He's a hitch-hiker,' I said. 'I'm giving him a lift.'

'I didn't ask you,' he said. 'I asked him.'

''Ave I done somethin' wrong?' my passenger asked.

His voice was soft and oily as haircream.

'That's more than likely,' the policeman answered. 'Anyway, you're a witness. I'll deal with you in a minute. Driver's licence,' he snapped, holding out his hand.

I gave him my driver's licence.

He unbuttoned the left-hand breast pocket of his tunic and brought out the dreaded book of tickets. Carefully, he copied the name and address from my licence. Then he gave it back to me. He strolled around to the front of the car and read the number from the number-plate and wrote that down as well. He filled in the date, the time and the details of my offence. Then he tore out the top copy of the ticket. But before handing it to me, he checked that all the information had come through clearly on his own carbon copy. Finally, he replaced the book in his breast pocket and fastened the button.

'Now you,' he said to my passenger, and he walked around to the other side of the car. From the other breast pocket he produced a small black notebook. 'Name?' he snapped.

'Michael Fish,' my passenger said.

'Address?'

'Fourteen, Windsor Lane, Luton.'

'Show me something to prove this is your real name and address,' the policeman said.

My passenger fished in his pockets and came out with a driver's licence of his own. The policeman checked the name and address and handed it back to him. 'What's your job?' he asked sharply.

'I'm an 'od carrier.'

'A *what?*'

'An 'od carrier.'

'Spell it.'

'H-o-d c-a-'

'That'll do. And what's a hod carrier, may I ask?' 'An 'od carrier, officer, is a person who carries the cement up the ladder to the bricklayer. And the 'od is what 'ee carries it in. It's got a long 'andle, and on the top you've got bits of wood set at an angle …'

'All right, all right. Who's your employer?'

'Don't 'ave one. I'm unemployed.'

The cop wrote all this down in the black notebook. Then he returned the book to its pocket and did up the button.

'When I get back to the station I'm going to do a little checking up on you,' he said to my passenger.

'Me? What've I done wrong?' the rat-faced man asked.

'I don't like your face, that's all,' the cop said. 'And we just might have a picture of it somewhere in our files.' He strolled round the car and returned to my window.

'I suppose you know you're in serious trouble,' he said to me.

'Yes, officer.'

'You won't be driving this fancy car of yours again for a very long time, not after we've finished with you. You won't be driving any car again, come to that, for several years. And a good thing, too. I hope they lock you up for a spell into the bargain.'

'You mean prison?' I asked alarmed.

'Absolutely,' he said, smacking his lips. 'In the clink. Behind the bars. Along with all the other criminals who break the law. *And* a hefty fine into the bargain. Nobody will be more pleased about that than me. I'll see you in court, both of you. You'll be getting a summons to appear.'

He turned away and walked over to his motorcycle. He flipped the prop stand back into position with his boot and swung his leg over the saddle. Then he kicked the starter and roared off up the road out of sight.

'Phew!' I gasped. 'That's done it …'

'We was caught,' my passenger said. 'We was caught good and proper …'

'I was caught you mean …'

'That's right,' he said. 'What you goin' to do now, guv'nor?'

'I'm going straight up to London to talk to my solicitor,' I said. I started the car and drove on.

'You mustn't believe what 'ee said to you about goin' to prison,' my passenger said. 'They don't put nobody in the clink just for speedin'.'

'Are you sure of that?' I asked.

'I'm positive,' he answered. 'They can take your licence away and they can give you a whoppin' big fine, but that'll be the end of it.'

I felt tremendously relieved.

'By the way,' I said, 'why did you lie to him?'

'Who, me?' he said. 'What makes you think I lied?'

'You told him you were an unemployed hod carrier. But you told me you were in a highly skilled trade.'

'So I am,' he said. 'But it don't pay to tell everythin' to a copper.'

'So what *do* you do?' I asked him.

'Ah,' he said slyly. 'That'll be tellin', wouldn't it?'

'Is it something you're ashamed of?'

'Ashamed?' he cried. 'Me, ashamed of my job? I'm about as proud of it as anybody could be in the entire world!'

'Then why won't you tell me?'

'You writers really is nosey parkers, aren't you?' he said. 'And you ain't goin' to be 'appy, I don't think, until you've found out exactly what the answer is?'

'I don't really care one way or the other,' I told him, lying.

He gave me a crafty little ratty look out of the sides of his eyes. 'I think you do care,' he said. 'I can see it on your face that you think I'm in some kind of a very peculiar trade and you're just achin' to know what it is.'

I didn't like the way he read my thoughts. I kept quiet and stared at the road ahead.

'You'd be right, too,' he went on. 'I *am* in a very peculiar trade. I'm in the queerest peculiar trade of 'em all.'

✳ STOP AND THINK ✳

Before continuing, think about what you have just read. What do you think is the hitch-hiker's trade? What do you think will happen now? Discuss this with a partner. *Now read on …*

I waited for him to go on.

'That's why I 'as to be extra careful oo' I'm talkin' to, you see. 'Ow am I to know, for instance, you're not another copper in plain clothes?'

'Do I look like a copper?'

'No,' he said, 'you don't. And you ain't. Any fool could tell that.'

He took from his pocket a tin of tobacco and a packet of cigarette papers and started to roll a cigarette. I was watching him out of the corner of one eye, and the speed with which he performed this rather difficult operation was incredible. The cigarette was rolled and ready in about five seconds. He ran his tongue along the edge of the paper, stuck it down and popped the cigarette between his lips. Then, as if from nowhere, a lighter appeared in his hand. The lighter flamed. The cigarette was lit. The lighter disappeared. It was altogether a remarkable performance.

'I've never seen anyone roll a cigarette as fast as that,' I said.

'Ah,' he said, taking a deep suck of smoke. 'So you noticed.'

'Of course I noticed. It was quite fantastic.'

He sat back and smiled. It pleased him very much that I had noticed how quickly he could roll a cigarette.

'You want to know what makes me able to do it?' he asked,

'Go on then.'

'It's because I've got fantastic fingers. These fingers of mine,' he said, holding up both hands high in front of him, 'are quicker and cleverer than the fingers of the best piano player in the world!'

'Are you a piano player?'

'Don't be daft,' he said. 'Do I look like a piano player?'

I glanced at his fingers. They were so beautifully shaped, so slim and long and elegant, they didn't seem to belong to the rest of him at all. They looked more like the fingers of a brain surgeon or a watchmaker.

'My job,' he went on, 'is a hundred times more difficult than playin' the piano. Any twerp can learn to do that. There's titchy little kids learnin' to play the piano in almost any 'ouse you go into these days. That's right, ain't it?'

'More or less,' I said.

'Of course it's right. But there's not one person in ten million can learn to do what I do. Not one in ten million! 'Ow about that?'

'Amazing,' I said.

'You're darn right it's amazin',' he said.

'I think I know what you do,' I said. 'You do conjuring tricks. You're a conjurer.'

'Me?' he snorted. 'A conjurer? Can you picture me goin' round crummy kids' parties makin' rabbits come out of top 'ats?'

'Then you're a card player. You get people into card games and you deal yourself marvellous hands.'

'Me! A rotten cardsharper!' he cried. 'That's a miserable racket if ever there was one.'

'All right. I give up.'

I was taking the car along slowly now, at no more than forty miles an hour, to make quite sure I wasn't stopped again. We had come onto the main London–Oxford road and were running down the hill toward Denham.

Suddenly, my passenger was holding up a black leather belt in his hand. 'Ever seen this before?' he asked. The belt had a brass buckle of unusual design.

'Hey!' I said. 'That's mine, isn't it? It *is* mine! Where did you get it?'

He grinned and waved the belt gently from side to side.

'Where d'you think I got it?' he said. 'Off the top of your trousers, of course.'

I reached down and felt for my belt. It was gone.

'You mean you took it off me while we've been driving along?' I asked flabbergasted.

He nodded, watching me all the time with those little black ratty eyes.

'That's impossible,' I said. 'You'd have had to undo the buckle and slide the whole thing out through the loops all the way round. I'd have seen you doing it. And even if I hadn't seen you, I'd have felt it.'

'Ah, but you didn't, did you?' he said, triumphant. He dropped the belt on his lap, and now all at once there was a brown shoelace dangling from his fingers. 'And what about this, then?' he exclaimed, waving the shoelace.

'What about it?' I said.

'Anyone round 'ere missin' a shoelace?' he asked, grinning.

I glanced down at my shoes. The lace of one of them was missing.

'Good grief!' I said. 'How did you do that? I never saw you bending down.'

'You never saw nothin',' he said proudly. 'You never even saw me move an inch. And you know why?'

'Yes,' I said. 'Because you've got fantastic fingers.'

'Exactly right!' he cried. 'You catch on pretty quick, don't you?'

He sat back and sucked away at his home-made cigarette, blowing the smoke out in a thin stream against the windshield. He knew he had impressed me greatly with those two tricks, and this made him very happy.

'I don't want to be late,' he said. 'What time is it?'

'There's a clock in front of you,' I told him.

'I don't trust car clocks,' he said. 'What does your watch say?'

I hitched up my sleeve to look at the watch on my wrist. It wasn't there. I looked at the man. He looked back at me, grinning.

'You've taken that, too,' I said.

He held out his hand and there was my watch lying in his palm. 'Nice bit of stuff, this,' he said. 'Superior quality. Eighteen-carat gold. Easy to sell, too. It's never any trouble gettin' rid of quality goods.'

'I'd like it back, if you don't mind,' I said rather huffily.

He placed the watch carefully on the leather tray in front of him.

'I wouldn't nick anything from you, guv'nor,' he said. 'You're my pal. You're givin' me a lift.'

'I'm glad to hear it,' I said.

'All I'm doin' is answerin' your question,' he went on. 'You asked me what I did for a livin' and I'm showin' you.'

'What else have you got of mine?'

He smiled again, and now he started to take from the pocket of his jacket one thing after another that belonged to me, my driver's licence, a key ring with four keys on it, some pound notes, a few coins, a letter from my publishers, my diary, a stubby old pencil, a cigarette-lighter, and last of all, a beautiful old sapphire ring with pearls around it belonging to my wife. I was taking the ring up to a jeweller in London because one of the pearls was missing.

'Now there's another lovely piece of goods,' he said, turning the ring over in his fingers. 'That's eighteenth century, if I'm not mistaken, from the reign of King George the Third.'

'You're right,' I said, impressed. 'You're absolutely right.'

He put the ring on the leather tray with the other items.

'So you're a pickpocket,' I said.

'I don't like that word,' he answered. 'It's a coarse and vulgar word. Pickpockets is coarse and vulgar people who only do easy little amateur jobs. They lift money from blind old ladies.'

'What do you call yourself, then?'

'Me? I'm a fingersmith. I'm a professional fingersmith.' He spoke the words solemnly and proudly, as though he were telling me he was the President of the Royal College of Surgeons or the Archbishop of Canterbury.

'I've never heard that word before,' I said. 'Did you invent it?'

'Of course I didn't invent it,' he replied. 'It's the name given to them who's risen to the very top of the profession. You've 'eard of a goldsmith and a silversmith, for instance. They're experts with gold and silver. I'm an expert with my fingers, so I'm a fingersmith.'

'It must be an interesting job.'

'It's a marvellous job,' he answered. 'It's lovely.'

'And that's why you go to the races?'

'Race meetings is easy meat,' he said. 'You just stand around after the race, watchin' for the lucky ones to queue up and draw their money. And when you see someone collectin' a big bundle of notes, you simply follows after 'im and 'elps yourself. But don't get me wrong, guv'nor. I never takes nothin' from a loser. Nor from poor people neither. I only go after them as can afford it, the winners and the rich.'

'That's very thoughtful of you,' I said. 'How often do you get caught?'

'Caught?' he cried, disgusted. '*Me* get caught! It's only pickpockets get caught. Fingersmiths never. Listen, I could take the false teeth out of your mouth if I wanted to and you wouldn't even catch me!'

'I don't have false teeth,' I said.

'I know you don't,' he answered. 'Otherwise I'd 'ave 'ad 'em out long ago!'

I believed him. Those long slim fingers of his seemed able to do anything.

We drove on for a while without talking.

'That policeman's going to check up on you pretty thoroughly,' I said. 'Doesn't that worry you a bit?'

'Nobody's checkin' up on me,' he said.

'Of course they are. He's got your name and address written down most carefully in his black book.' The man gave me another of his sly ratty little smiles.

'Ah,' he said. 'So 'ee 'as. But I'll bet 'ee ain't got it all written down in 'is memory as well. I've never known a copper yet with a decent memory. Some of 'em can't even remember their own names.'

'What's memory got to do with it?' I asked. 'It's written down in his book, isn't it?'

'Yes, guv'nor, it is. But the trouble is, 'ee's lost the book. 'Ee's lost both books, the one with my name in it and the one with yours.'

In the long delicate fingers of his right hand, the man was holding up in triumph the two books he had taken from the policeman's pockets. 'Easiest job I ever done,' he announced proudly.

I nearly swerved the car into a milk-truck, I was so excited.

'That copper's got nothin' on either of us now,' he said.

'You're a genius!' I cried.

''Ee's got no names, no addresses, no car number, no nothin',' he said.

'You're brilliant!'

'I think you'd better pull off this main road as soon as possible,' he said. 'Then we'd better build a little bonfire and burn these books.'

'You're a fantastic fellow!' I exclaimed.

'Thank you, guv'nor,' he said. 'It's always nice to be appreciated.'

EXPLORE

1. Whose perspective is this story written from? What kind of narrative is this called?

2. The ending of this story has a twist. Did you like it? Explain.

3. What is your impression of the two main characters? Write one paragraph about each character. Each paragraph should include at least two adjectives about the character.

4. Roald Dahl uses vivid images which allow the reader to clearly imagine the scenes. Choose your favourite image from this short story and explain what you like about it.

SPEAK

5. Roald Dahl often uses italics to emphasise words or phrases. Find one example of this and write the entire sentence in your copy. Then read the sentence aloud to another student, emphasising the italicised word/phrase. Now try reading the sentence without the emphasis and, with your partner, discuss how it changes the meaning of the sentence.

FUN FACT

Italics is a typeface that looks like this. Italics is usually used to draw the reader's attention to a particular word or phrase.

MIND YOUR LANGUAGE

DIALOGUE

The use of dialogue is very effective in this story. Mostly it tells us about the three very different characters in the story.

W7.6

1. Identify at least two features of the hitch-hiker's speech (register) and explain what it tells us about him.

2. For each of the three characters in the story, pick out something that they say, decide whether it is formal or informal, and then find more examples to back up your opinion.

CREATE

Now imagine an alternative ending for the story. Take it from the point where the policeman roars off on his motorbike. You should write it in the same style as the author. Two or three paragraphs is enough.

REMEMBER Register, p. 32. Formal and informal language, pp. 33–34.

SPEAK
2 MIN

Working with another student, do a two-minute role play of a telephone conversation. Take it in turns to pretend to be one of the characters from the list below and ring the other person (they can just be themselves). For example, if you are pretending to be someone's best friend, you might start the conversation by saying, 'Hi Mark, what's the story?' They must then respond in the appropriate manner.

Characters

* A good friend ringing another friend with some important news
* A manager of a company calling a customer who wrote a letter of complaint
* The principal of a school ringing to tell a student some important news
* A telemarketer (phone salesperson) trying to persuade someone to donate money to a charity
* A person calling a restaurant to book a table for a big event
* A radio talk show host calling to tell a listener they have won a big prize

After you have finished, write up one of these conversations in the appropriate language (formal or informal). To show that particular words should be stressed, underline them (these would usually be in italics in a typed text).

Adapting a Short Story into a Film

What I will learn:

to consider how a story can be adapted into a film;
to understand film terminology and apply it to an adaptation

PREPARE

Imagine you were asked to direct an adaptation of 'The Hitch-hiker' as a film. Plan how you would do this, taking the following questions into consideration.

1. Which actors would you choose to play the three characters in the story?

2. Where would you set this film?

3. What kind of music would you use?

4. What props and costumes would you need?

5. Would you need any stunts to be done? If so, what would they be?

TOP TIP

If you are making a novel or story into a film, you can use 'artistic licence', which means changing small details to suit the filming, e.g. cutting a scene, character etc.

Match the terms below with the correct definitions.

Film terminology	What is it and how is it used?
Setting	Presenting one form as another (e.g. turning a play into a musical or a book/short story into a film)
Score	A part of a film in which the action stays in one place for a continuous period of time. Scenes are usually divided by location or period of time, e.g. a wedding scene
Props	Music in a film (often in the background) to create a certain mood or enhance emotion
An adaptation	The location where a film is made. In some films the setting is more important than others, e.g. in a war film the setting is very important
Scene	What the characters wear. Costumes need to be appropriate for the period the film is set in. Characters should be dressed in a way that is appropriate to their social status, occupation, personality, etc.
Costumes	Other items needed for the filming, e.g. a car, a notebook

W7.7

Now draw a storyboard to accompany your film. On your storyboard, make a list of music or sound effects that you would use to accompany each scene.

FUN FACT

Many of Roald Dahl's short stories and books have been adapted into films: Willy Wonka and the Chocolate Factory, Matilda, Beware of the Dog, The Witches, Esio Trot.

REMEMBER Storyboarding, p. 150.

Storytelling

What I will learn:

to listen to an interesting story from a different era; to appreciate a variety of registers and understand their use

PREPARE

Look up these words (elements of oral language) in your **dictionary** and write out their definitions. Discuss them as a class to ensure you know what they mean. ➔

* Pronunciation

* Phonetic writing

* Colloquialism

* Vernacular

* Slang

The following is the transcript (the typed text of something said aloud and recorded) of a story from the Bible, in the speaker's own words. It has been typed exactly as it was spoken and some words are written phonetically to reflect how they were pronounced. The transcript also contains repetition and other elements consistent with oral language. You will read it first and later you will listen to the original recording. As you are reading, try to imagine who is telling the story and who their audience is.

Mary's Retelling of the Story of John the Baptist from *Give Up Yer Aul Sins* (Cathal Gaffney, dir.)

He grew up and they called him John the Baptist cos he used to go round, em, telling everybody, baptising all the big people and kids and all and telling people to do penance and give up their aul sins. And so didn't he come to the terrible *wicked* woman and he said to her, 'Do penance and give up yer aul sins.'

And so, she knew penance was hard and so she said, 'No, I won't give up me, I won't do penance and I won't give up me aul sins.' And so he said, 'Well then, you'll end up in hell in the big fire.' And then she got raging and she said to herself, 'I'll get me own back.'

And so he got thrown into jail, and this day didn't a man come to visit him and St John the Baptist said to him, 'Will you do me a favour?' And he said, 'Yeh.' And so he said, 'Will ya go to Jesus and ask him is he really God or is he a *shockin'* holy saint?'

And so the man went to Jesus and said, 'Poor John the Baptist is in prison and he wants to know are you *really* God or a *shockin'* holy saint?' And so he said, 'Tell him what you're after seein': the leopards are cured; the people that are blind can see and the people that are on crutches can walk.' And 'leopards' means that we're all full with sores all over them.

And so he came back and the man told him all – John the Baptist – all about it. And so John the Baptist said, 'Oh they're all miracles. That's God.'

And so, then, the same wicked woman, em, knew this wicked king. And so the wicked king had a party and so … so … they asked the woman to it, and the wicked young one. And so he said to her: 'Do you want to come to the party?' And she said, 'Yeh.' And he asked the wicked young one, she said, 'Yeh.'

And so they went to the party and so, em, he said to her, 'Will you do a dance for me?' And so she was only learning and she said, 'Yeh.'

And so she went up and did a dance and he went up to see a ... she was real common. And so it was finished and the king said: 'Oh that was *gorgeous*. I'll give you anything you want'.

And instead of taking earrings or a necklace or a watch or a bracelet or something, or a ring or a gold brooch – cos rich are, kings are always rich, they have *loads* of gold – and so instead of doing that she went over to her mother and said, 'What'll I take?' And she said, 'John the Baptist's head on a plate'.

And wasn't he in jail when he sent out all his soldiers. And so, and they came and they cut off his head.

1. Make a list of any words which are spelt phonetically in the transcript (e.g. yeh). Beside each word, write the correct spelling in standard English – as it would normally be written.

2. Based on the transcript, do you think this story was told by a child, a teenager, or an adult? Give reasons for your answer.

3. Mary talks about 'leopards' in her story – what does she actually mean?

4. The transcript above reflects the way the story was told orally. Identify any elements which are unique to oral language (e.g. repetition).

Write a summarised version (no more than 100 words) of this story in standard English using appropriate spelling, vocabulary and grammar.

Now watch a cartoon made using this original recording. Paying attention particularly to what is said, answer these questions.

1. Having read the transcript first, did anything surprise you about the recording?

2. When and where do you think this recording was made? What gives you this impression?

3. These recordings have become extremely popular with audiences of all ages since they were discovered. In groups, discuss why this might be so.

SHOW WHAT YOU KNOW

You have learned many writing and speaking skills throughout this collection.
Now it's time to *Show What You Know!*

My Portfolio Task

Write a short story about two people from different backgrounds whose paths cross for a short period of time, during which one unexpectedly helps the other. Illustrate your story with images (you can draw them yourself or find graphics online).

SUCCESS CRITERIA

I must

- Set the scene
- Introduce two main characters from very different backgrounds
- Start the action as soon as possible and introduce a complication
- Build up to a climax
- Bring the story to a close (the resolution)
- Show a change in at least one character
- Include illustrations (hand-drawn or digital)
- Use my proof-reading wheel (p. 19)
- Read what I've written to check for punctuation marks (, . ! ?) or missing words
- Use a **dictionary** to check any spellings I'm not sure of

I should

- Use the RAFT structure (p. 97)
- Use dialogue
- Include powerful verbs and adjectives (see p. 7)
- Consider referring to some of the five senses in my descriptions (see p. 4)

I could

- Use the first person narrative or phonetic dialogue, like in 'The Hitch-hiker' and 'Give Up Yer Aul Sins'
- Use italics or underline words to create emphasis
- Have a twist in my story

Peer Assessment

Read your partner's work and then write down two things you think he/she did well and one thing he/she could improve on.

Redrafting

When you have received your partner's assessment, and reviewing the success criteria again to make sure you have met all the requirements, you can revise your story to create a second draft. When you are happy with it, you can put it in your **portfolio**.

Reflection Question

What do you need to do to write a successful short story and how have you addressed this in your work?

Joey Blogg
@ JosephBlogg

If you wish to put your story on your class/school website, you can tweet a link and include the hashtag #Fantasticfairytales.

Reply   Retweet   Favorite

Oral Communication

You have decided to enter an oral storytelling competition called 'The Young Storyteller'. This year the theme is 'Fantastic Fairy Tales'. Draft and tell/record an original fairy tale which is suitable for one of the following groups:

* 3–5 year old boys/girls or both
* 6–8 year old boys/girls or both
* 9–12 year old boys/girls or both

Your story can be read aloud or recorded.

SUCCESS CRITERIA

I must

- Read some fairy tales before I start planning
- Have a beginning which introduces the main character(s) and setting
- Feature a setting beginning with the letter B (it can be a real or imaginary place)
- Include at least two characters
- Include an element of magic
- Have a complication and resolution
- Show evidence of a change in at least one of the characters

I should

- Include dialogue
- Feature a villain who is punished
- Include a moral at the end

I could

- Introduce a twist
- Have accompanying illustrations
- Have a happy or sad ending
- Use rhyme
- Write in the first or third person narrative

Peer Assessment

Reflect on your classmate's work and then write down two things you think he/she did well and one thing he/she could improve on.

Parents and Children

The language of storytelling through the centuries

Children past and present

Responding to a child's letter

Speaking my opinion

Proof-reading

As I explore this collection I will learn about:

Terms for writing about drama

The narrator in a stage play

Script-writing and stage design

Voice and facial expressions in film

Family relationships in stories

Dialogue and storyline

Describing eyes, faces, hair, skin, clothes

Settings for stories on screen and stage

Main Learning Outcomes
OL1, OL2, OL5, OL11, R1, R3, R5, R6, W6

SHOW WHAT YOU KNOW

The skills you learn in this collection will enable you to **show what you know** in your final tasks at the end of this collection.

For my portfolio task I will:
Write the script for a scene in a film or a play

For oral communication I will:
Speak for or against the following statement: '*A child born in the 21st century has a greater chance of happiness than a child of the past.*'

Exploring the Theme – Parents and Children

Life for parents and children has changed over the years, decades and centuries. We live longer now than in past centuries, and in most countries (unfortunately not all) the law says that children must go to school rather than work. Parents care for their children and in time children care for their parents. In rare cases, a child can be given to the wrong parents. And it can sometimes happen that a parent's right to name their child can lead to some strange choices!

READ

Hundreds of thousands of children are used as soldiers in armed conflicts around the world. Many are abducted, others join military groups to escape poverty. They take part in armed combat or serve as porters, carrying ammunition or injured soldiers. Some act as lookouts or messengers. Others have been used as suicide bombers.

Deaths of Babies and Children

In 1615, five out of every hundred children born in England died in the first month of life. By the age of six, a further thirty-six would have died, and by age sixteen only forty would still be alive.

A French court has prevented parents from naming their child Nutella. The judge renamed her Ella, saying that a child cannot be given a name that might cause mockery.

In 1833 an English law was passed saying that children aged nine to thirteen could work a maximum of twelve hours a day. A law of 1842 banned those under ten from working in mines. By 1850, one in three children aged ten to fifteen were working in factories or in mines where they climbed through tunnels too low and narrow for adults. Until the law forbade it in 1875, small boys would climb up chimneys to clean them. Finally, in 1880, the law said that from ages five to ten, children must attend school.

In 2013, the Chinese government passed a law stating that children who did not visit their elderly parents would be fined or jailed. Increasing numbers of old people had died unnoticed in their apartments. Following many decades of population control, there are now not enough careworkers to look after older people.

Heading n.
Definition: a short title at the top of a piece of writing that tells you what to expect, as in a newspaper headline

In 2011, two Russian families, one Christian, the other Muslim, found out that their daughters, Anya and Irina, born minutes apart, had been wrongly tagged at the hospital in December 1998. DNA tests had uncovered the mistake.

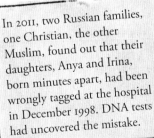

CREATE

1. Only one paragraph above has a heading. Write a heading for each of the other paragraphs.

2. Write another short paragraph about parents and/or children. It could be something you read about or heard in the news. Give your paragraph a heading.

Novel Extracts

storytelling language over the centuries

The following extracts from books from the last three centuries describe parent and child relationships. You will notice different styles of writing and different descriptions of appearance and personality.

The oldest book was published in 1847 (the nineteenth century), the most recent in 2006 (the twenty-first century).

The writers of Extracts 3 and 5 would be astonished to read the English used in Extract 2.

The writer of Extract 6 would never refer to a mother as 'mama' as in Extract 5, and this mother would not have been 'doing things on computers' as the parents in Extract 1.

SPEAK

Six students will read one extract each for the class. Prepare by taking a few minutes to read silently, getting the sense of the piece.

Speaking Tips

- Speak in a strong, clear voice.
- Try not to read your extract straight off the page – try glancing up at your audience every now and again.
- Read slowly to give your listeners time to imagine the scene and the characters.
- Vary the volume. Speak some lines softly, others loudly, as necessary.
- Dramatise the voices, as if you were an actor on stage, e.g. put lightness in your voice when a character is cheerful, put a whinge in your voice if a character's words should be spoken with great emotion.
- Pause as appropriate, at commas and full stops.
- Slow down as you read the last line to add to its impact.

LISTEN

TOP TIP

You can listen to these extracts being read aloud. This will help you to practise and perfect your own reading.

Extract 1

It was time to talk to her father.

Coraline's father was home. Both her parents worked, doing things on computers, which meant that they were home a lot of the time. Each of them had their own study.

'Hello Coraline,' he said when she came in, without turning round.

'Mmph,' said Coraline. 'It's raining.'

'Yup,' said her father. 'It's bucketing down.'

'No,' said Coraline, 'it's just raining. Can I go outside?'

'What does your mother say?'

'She says, "You're not going out in weather like that, Coraline Jones".'

'Then, no.'

'But I want to carry on exploring.'

'Then explore the flat,' suggested her father. 'Look – here's a piece of paper and a pen. Count all the doors and windows. List everything blue. Mount an expedition to discover the hot-water tank. And leave me alone to work.'

Extract 2

It's a funny thing about mothers and fathers. Even when their own child is the most disgusting little blister you could ever imagine, they still think that he or she is wonderful.

Some parents go further. They become so blinded by adoration they manage to convince themselves their child has qualities of genius.

Well, there is nothing very wrong with all this. It's the way of the world. It is only when the parents begin telling us about the brilliance of their own revolting offspring, that we start shouting, 'Bring us a basin! We're going to be sick!'

School teachers suffer a good deal from having to listen to this sort of twaddle from proud parents, but they usually get their own back when the time comes to write the end-of-term reports. If I were a teacher I would cook up some real scorchers for the children of doting parents. 'Your son Maximilian', I would write, 'is a total wash-out. I hope you have a family business you can push him into when he leaves school because he sure as heck won't get a job anywhere else.'

Extract 3

Only three people got out of the 11.54. The first was a countryman with two baskety boxes full of live chickens who stuck their russet heads out anxiously through the wicker bars; the second was Miss Peckitt, the grocer's wife's cousin, with a tin box and three brown paper parcels; and the third —

'Oh! my Daddy, my Daddy!' That scream went like a knife into the heart of everyone in the train, and people put their heads out of the windows to see a tall pale man with lips set in a thin close line, and a little girl clinging to him with arms and legs, while his arms went tightly round her.

'I knew something wonderful was going to happen,' said Bobby, as they went up the road, 'but I didn't think it was going to be this.'

Extract 4

The boy was smaller than Bruno and was sitting on the ground with a forlorn expression. He wore the same striped pyjamas that all the other people on that side of the fence wore, and a striped cloth cap on his head. He wasn't wearing any shoes or socks and his feet were rather dirty. On his arm he wore an armband with a star on it.

✡

When Bruno first approached the boy, he was sitting cross-legged on the ground, staring at the dust beneath him. However, after a moment he looked up and Bruno saw his face. It was quite a strange face too. His skin was almost the colour of grey, but not quite like any grey that Bruno had ever seen before. He had very large eyes and they were the colour of caramel sweets; the whites were very white, and when the boy looked at him all Bruno could see was an enormous pair of sad eyes staring back.

D

Extract 5

John Reed was a schoolboy of fourteen years old; four years older than I, for I was but ten: large and stout for his age, with a dingy and unwholesome skin … He gorged himself habitually at table, which made him bilious, and gave him a dim and bleared eye and flabby cheeks. He ought now to have been at school; but his mama had taken him home for a month or two, 'on account of his delicate health.' Mr Miles, the master, affirmed that he would do very well if he had fewer cakes and sweetmeats sent him from home; but the mother's heart turned from an opinion so harsh, and inclined rather to the idea that John's sallowness was owing to over-application and, perhaps, to pining after home.

E

Extract 6

Johnny Cade was last and least. If you can picture a little dark puppy that has been kicked too many times and is lost in a crowd of strangers, you'll have Johnny. He was the youngest, next to me, smaller than the rest, with a slight build. He had big black eyes in a dark tanned face; his hair was jet-black and heavily greased and combed to the side, but it was so long that it fell in shaggy bangs across his forehead. He had a nervous, suspicious look in his eyes, and that beating he got from the Socs didn't help matters. He was the gang's pet, everyone's kid brother. His father was always beating him up, and his mother ignored him, except when she was hacked off at something, and then you could hear her yelling at him clear down at our house. I think he hated that worse than getting whipped. He would have run away a million times if we hadn't been there. If it hadn't been for the gang, Johnny would never have known what love and affection are.

F

EXPLORE

1. Match the photographs with the extracts.

2. Match the extracts with the book titles:
   - *The Boy in the Striped Pyjamas* by John Boyne
   - *The Railway Children* by E. Nesbit
   - *Matilda* by Roald Dahl
   - *The Outsiders* by S. E. Hinton
   - *Jane Eyre* by Charlotte Brontë
   - *Coraline* by Neil Gaiman

3. What do extracts 4, 5 and 6 tell you about the child's eyes in each case?

4. In the case of each statement below, identify the book, **P I E** giving evidence for your answer.
   i. One of the books was written in England in 1847
   ii. One book was written by an American teenager in 1967
   iii. One book was made into a graphic novel and a film
   iv. One book is set during World War II
   v. One book describes the arrival of a train and an unexpected passenger
   vi. One book was written by a famous children's author with a wicked sense of humour

5. Which extract describes:
   i. A child who has been spoiled by a doting parent who refuses to see the truth
   ii. A child who has been neglected, mistreated and lacks confidence
   iii. A child who is silently sad
   iv. A child who is astonished to be reunited with her father
   v. An author who is sick of listening to parents bragging about their children
   vi. A child whose parents have very little time for being parents

6. In your opinion, which child or parent is most interesting? Why?

7. Highlight one phrase or sentence in each extract that you think is the best or that you most enjoyed reading.

8. Which book would you most like to read, having read the extracts above? Why?

FUN FACT

Charlotte Brontë published *Jane Eyre* under the pseudonym (say: *soo-de-nem*; it means 'fake name') 'Currer Bell', so that readers would think she was a male author and therefore be taken more seriously. Joanne Rowling used the initials 'J. K.' because she thought 'Joanne' would put male readers off reading her books.

TOP TIP

A good writer will describe not only a character's outer appearance (face, eyes, clothes, height etc.), but also his or her inner self (personality, confidence, shyness, good humour, crankiness etc.)

RESEARCH ZONE

The authors of these books are Irish, British and American.

1. Identify their nationality in each case.

2. Which of the stories was published in 1906?

3. Which was published in 1988?

4. How many of these books have been made into a film or a television series?

5. Which of these books has been adapted many times into film?

Thinking of a child or parent whom you know personally, or one that you have seen in a film, write a description of him or her. Your words should describe both appearance and personality, like the authors of the extracts did.

A Child's Letter

What I will learn:

to respond sensitively to a child's letter; to proof-read

Can you remember any letter that you wrote when you were a child? You might be astonished at the influence a child's letter (and a reply received) can have on later life.

In 1973, nine-year-old Anthony Hollander, having found a dying bird in his garden, wrote this letter to a British TV children's programme called *Blue Peter*. He asked them to help him to become a person who could 'make people or animals alive'.

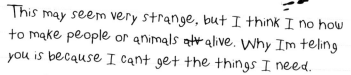

Dear Val, Jhon, ~~pe~~ Peter and Lesslie,

This may seem very strange, but I think I no how to make people or animals ~~alv~~ alive. Why I'm teling you is because I cant get the things I need.

A list of what I need.

1. Diagram of how evreything works. [inside youre body.]

2. Model of a heart split in half. [both halvs.]

3. ~~Ts~~ The sort of sering they yous for cleaning ears. [Tsering must be very very clean.]

4. Tools for cutting people open.

5. Tools for stiches.

6. Fiberglass box, 8 foot tall, 3 ~~fot~~ foot width.

7. ~~Pic~~ Picture of a man showing all the arteries.

Sorry but in number 6 in the list ~~th~~ the box needs lid. If you do get them on 1st March I can pay £10, £11, £12, £13 or £14.

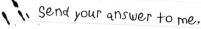
Send your answer to me,

Love from Anthony,

London, NW11

WRITE

Now proof-read and rewrite Anthony's letter. Do not change his sentences. Only correct his spelling errors.

CREATE

Imagine that you are on the *Blue Peter* team. Talk to the person beside you about what you think you should say in a letter in reply to Anthony. Then write the letter between you (about 150 words).

The boy who wrote the letter is now a Professor of Tissue Engineering. He was part of a medical team that used stem cells to grow an artificial windpipe and implant it in a patient, saving her life. This was a great surgical breakthrough that made world headlines. Recently, talking about the letter and Biddy Baxter's reply to him, Anthony said that if they had 'failed to reply, or had treated my letter as a joke (as perhaps others might have done) it could well have altered the course of my life.'

Blue Peter's reply to Anthony (we've turned it upside down so that you can't see it when you write your own letter!)

Dear Anthony,

Thank you very much for your letter. It was nice to hear from you again after such a long time and we are sorry we have been delayed replying.

We are receiving over 4,000 letters every week and are having difficulty answering them as quickly as we would like.

We were interested to hear that you think you know how to make living people – and your list of necessary items intrigued us!

We are sorry we can't help you at all, but we wondered if you had thought of talking to your family doctor – he might be glad to help you with some diagrams and other information.

We are sending you a photograph of the Blue Peter team – it has been signed specially for you.

With best wishes from Valerie, John, Peter, Lesley and all of us on the programme.

Yours sincerely,

B (Biddy Baxter)

Editor

Blue Peter

A Film Clip

What I will learn:

vocabulary for writing about a drama either in a play or a film

WATCH

Life is Beautiful (Roberto Benigni, dir.)

You will now watch a clip from the 1997 Oscar-winning Italian film, *Life is Beautiful*. In this scene, a Nazi camp officer comes into the hut, bellowing orders at the inmates. When he asks for a translator, the father volunteers and 'translates' the orders into a funny game so that his son will not be frightened. As the little boy listens to his father's 'translation', the camera moves from face to face. The boy is silent, but his eyes and his facial expressions show that his father is protecting him from fear and making it seem that the camp officers and the prisoners are all playing a funny game.

Complete the grid below. Fill it with words that describe the clothes, voices, eyes and facial expressions you see and hear with these three characters.

Characters	Costume	Voice (tone, volume)	Eyes and facial expressions
The camp officer			
Guido (the father)			
The little boy			

Using the **CCMC** approach, describe the setting in this scene. For 'Message', ask the question, 'Why did the director leave the door behind the soldiers slightly open?'

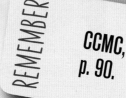

REMEMBER

CCMC, p. 90.

CREATE

Write the speech that you think the camp officer really made to the prisoners. Perform this speech as if you are acting the part of the camp officer in the film clip.

Performance Tips

- Imitate the camp officer's posture. This means the way he stands, how he holds his hands, his arm movements, the way his eyes survey the room, the way he leaves abruptly

- Imitate his eye movements, facial expressions, volume and tone of voice

Drama – A Musical

What I will learn:

script-writing and stage directions; the role of a dramatic narrator

READ

Blood Brothers is a musical by Willy Russell. A musical is a play or a film in which singing and dancing play a crucial part. In the following scene, Mrs Johnstone, a woman who has been abandoned by her husband, has just been told at the hospital that she is expecting twins. Mrs Lyons, the wealthy woman whose house Mrs Johnstone cleans, has no children of her own. On hearing the news about twins, Mrs Lyons has an idea.

TOP TIP

In *Blood Brothers*, a man in a dark suit – the narrator – steps forward in the opening scene and asks the audience, 'So did y' hear the story of the Johnstone twins?' He appears on the side of the stage throughout the performance, sometimes singing, sometimes talking; watching the characters, giving warnings and commenting on what is happening until the last scene.

Extract from *Blood Brothers* by Willy Russell

On stage, there are two characters; a narrator enters midway through the scene.

Mrs Lyons: Hello, Mrs. J. How are you?

There is no reply.
(*Registering the silence*). Mrs. J. Anything wrong?

Mrs Johnstone: I had it all worked out.

Mrs Lyons: What's the matter?

Mrs Johnstone: We were just getting straight.

Mrs Lyons: Why don't you sit down.

Mrs Johnstone: With one more baby we could have managed. But not with two. The welfare have already been on to me. They say I'm incapable of controllin' the kids I've already got. They say I should put some of them into care. But I won't. I love the bones of every one of them. I'll even love these two when they come along. But like they say at the welfare, kids can't live on love alone.

Mrs Lyons: Twins? You're expecting twins?

*The **Narrator** enters.*

Narrator   How quickly an idea, planted, can
           Take root and grow into a plan.
           The thought conceived in this very room
           Grew as surely as a seed, in a mother's womb.

*The **Narrator** exits.*

Mrs Lyons: (*almost inaudibly*) Give one to me.

Mrs Johnstone: What?

Mrs Lyons: (*containing her excitement*) Give one of them to me.

Mrs Johnstone: Give one to you?

Mrs Lyons: Yes … yes.

Mrs Johnstone: (*taking it almost as a joke*) But y' can't just …

Mrs Lyons: When are you due?

Mrs Johnstone: Erm, well about … Oh, but Mrs …

Mrs Lyons: Quickly, quickly tell me … when are you due?

Mrs Johnstone: July, he said, the beginning of …

Mrs Lyons: July … And my husband doesn't get back until the middle of July. He need never guess …

The device of the 'narrator' is a very old idea in a play. It was even used by the ancient Greeks. The narrator speaks directly to the audience, commenting on the action and explaining what is happening.

Think about performing the dialogue. At this point, should the lines be spoken quickly or slowly?

Mrs Johnstone: (*amused*) Oh, it's mad.

Mrs Lyons: I know, it is. It's mad, but it's wonderful, it's perfect. Look, you're what, four months pregnant, but you're only just beginning to show … so, so I'm four months pregnant and I'm just beginning to show. (*She grabs a cushion and arranges it beneath her dress.*)

Look, look, I could have got pregnant just before he went away. But I didn't tell him in case I miscarried, I didn't want to worry him whilst he was away. But when he arrives home I tell him we were wrong, the doctors were wrong. I have a baby, our baby. Mrs Johnstone, it will work, it will if only you'll …

Mrs Johnstone: Oh, Mrs Lyons, you can't be serious.

Mrs Lyons: You said yourself, you said you had too many children already.

Mrs Johnstone: Yeh, but I don't know if I wanna give one away.

Mrs Lyons: Already you're being threatened by the welfare people, Mrs Johnstone, with two more children how can you possibly avoid one of them being taken into care? Surely it's better to give one child to me. Look, at least if the child was with me you'd be able to see him every day as you came to work.

*Mrs Lyons stares at **Mrs Johnstone**, willing her to agree.*

Mrs Lyons: Please, Mrs Johnstone. Please.

At this point, the stage designer would have made sure there was a cushion on stage to be used as a prop.

REMEMBER
A prop is a moveable, portable object needed in a stage play.

EXPLORE

1. What problems does Mrs Johnstone have in her life?

2. What problems does Mrs Lyons have?

3. What does 'almost inaudibly' mean? Why do you think Mrs Lyons speaks almost inaudibly at that moment? **P I E**

4. How does Mrs Lyons plan to explain this baby to her husband?

5. What arguments does she give Mrs Johnstone to persuade her to give the baby away?

CREATE

1. What do you think Mrs Johnstone says next? Continue the dialogue between the two women until Mrs Johnstone either agrees or disagrees to give one of the babies to Mrs Lyons.

2. If you were the stage designer for this scene, how would you decorate the room in which this conversation happens? Decide on colours, furniture, items around the room, props, backdrop, etc.

Peer Assessment

Read your partner's work and then write down two things you think he/she did well and one thing he/she could improve on.

Backdrop n.

Definition: a large painted piece of material that is hung at the back of a stage in a theatre as part of the scenery

Extract from a Memoir

What I will learn:

descriptive vocabulary for storytelling

Match these words – which appear in the extract you are about to read – with their definitions. Use your **dictionary** to help you if you need to.

tutu	material for making clothes or curtains
mutt	piece of skin fixed to damaged part of body
wiener	ballerina's short, stiff skirt
tentatively	metal press with drawers or shelves
fabric	hesitantly, unsure
cabinets	German or Austrian sausage
graft	a small dog of nondescript breed

In this chapter from her memoir, *The Glass Castle*, Jeannette Walls remembers being in hospital when she was three years old. She had been cooking for herself at the stove when her dress caught fire. Her mother didn't like cooking or cleaning, saying that she 'would rather paint a painting that would last forever than cook a family meal'.

'I Was On Fire' from *The Glass Castle* by Jeannette Walls

Notice the short, simple sentence to start the story: 'It's my earliest memory'

It's my earliest memory. I was three years old, and we were living in a trailer park in a southern Arizona town whose name I never knew. I was standing on a chair in front of the stove, wearing a pink dress my grandmother had bought for me. Pink was my favourite colour. The dress's skirt stuck out like a tutu, and I liked to spin around in front of the mirror, thinking I looked like a ballerina. But at that moment, I was wearing the dress to cook hot dogs, watching them swell and bob in the boiling water as the late morning sunlight filtered in through the trailer's small kitchenette window.

I could hear Mom in the next room singing while she worked on one of her paintings. Juju, our black mutt, was watching me. I stabbed

one of the hot dogs with a fork and bent over and offered it to him. The wiener was hot, so Juju licked at it tentatively, but when I stood up and started stirring the hot dogs again, I felt a blaze of heat on my right side. I turned to see where it was coming from and realised my dress was on fire. Frozen with fear, I watched the yellow white flames make a ragged brown line up the pink fabric of my skirt and climb my stomach. Then the flames leaped up, reaching my face.

I screamed. I smelled the burning and heard a horrible crackling as the fire singed my hair and eyelashes. Juju was barking. I screamed again.

Mom ran into the room.

'Mommy, help me!' I shrieked. I was still standing on the chair, swatting at the fire with the fork I had been using to stir the hot dogs.

Mom ran out of the room and came back with one of the army-surplus blankets I hated because the wool was so scratchy. She threw the blanket around me to smother the flames. Dad had gone off in the car, so Mom grabbed me and my younger brother, Brian, and hurried over to the trailer next to ours. The woman who lived there was hanging her laundry on the clothesline. She had clothespins in her mouth. Mom, in an unnaturally calm voice, explained what had happened and asked if we could please have a ride to the hospital. The woman dropped her clothespins and laundry right there in the dirt and, without saying anything, ran for her car.

* * *

When we got to the hospital, nurses put me on a stretcher. They talked in loud, worried whispers while they cut off what was left of my fancy pink dress with a pair of shiny scissors. Then they picked me up, laid me flat on a big metal bed piled with ice cubes, and spread some of the ice over my body. A doctor with silver hair and black rimmed glasses led my mother out of the room. As they left, I heard him telling her that it was very serious. The nurses remained behind, hovering over me. I could tell I was causing a big fuss, and I stayed quiet. One of them squeezed my hand and told me I was going to be okay.

'I know,' I said, 'but if I'm not, that's okay, too.'

The nurse squeezed my hand again and bit her lower lip.

The room was small and white, with bright lights and metal cabinets. I stared for a while at the rows of tiny dots in the ceiling panels. Ice cubes covered my stomach and ribs and pressed up against my cheeks. Out of the corner of my eye, I saw a small, grimy hand reach up a few inches from my face and grab a handful of cubes. I heard a loud crunching sound and looked down. It was Brian, eating the ice.

* * *

The doctors said I was lucky to be alive. They took patches of skin from my upper thigh and put them over the most badly burned parts of my stomach, ribs and chest. They said it was called a skin graft. When they were finished, they wrapped my entire right side in bandages.

'Look, I'm a half mummy,' I said to one of the nurses. She smiled and put my right arm in a sling and attached it to the headboard so I couldn't move it.

The nurses and doctors kept asking me questions: How did you get burned? Have your parents ever hurt you? Why do you have all these bruises and cuts? My parents never hurt me, I said. I got the cuts and bruises playing outside and the burns from cooking hot dogs. They asked what I was doing cooking hot dogs by myself at the age of three. It was easy, I said. You just put the hot dogs in the water and boil them. It wasn't like there was some complicated recipe that you had to be old enough to follow. The pan was too heavy for me to lift when it was full of water, so I'd put a chair next to the sink, climb up and fill a glass, then stand on a chair by the stove and pour the water into the pan. I did that over and over again until the pan held enough water. Then I'd turn on the stove, and when the water was boiling, I'd drop in the hot dogs. 'Mom says I'm mature for my age,' I told them, 'and she lets me cook for myself a lot.'

Two nurses looked at each other, and one of them wrote something down on a clipboard. I asked what was wrong. Nothing, they said, nothing.

1. Where and in what kind of accommodation does this family live?

2. Explain how the accident happens.

3. How do you know that the neighbour understands how serious the situation is?

4. Write the note that you think the nurse wrote on her clipboard.

RESEARCH ZONE

Consulting an atlas or the internet, find out where Arizona is. Then, list the four American states beginning with 'A' and the eight states beginning with 'M' in alphabetical order.

EXPLORE

Jeannette tells the nurses: 'Mom says I'm mature for my age, and she lets me cook for myself a lot.' Bearing that in mind, read the following statement:

Parents nowadays are too protective of their children.

Do you agree or disagree with this opinion?
Discuss your opinion with the person beside you.
Now write your opinion down, giving clear evidence for it.

CREATE

Look at these photographs of girls swinging on a lamp post and boys peering down a drain in 1960s England. What differences are there between how children spent their time then and how children spend their time nowadays?

A Short Story

What I will learn:

to write dialogue and develop a storyline

READ

In this story, a small boy is starting kindergarten. It is the first time he has been away from his parents. The story is told from the mother's perspective. She and his father want him to tell them all about his experiences in school. You will see that they are quite protective of him, and that their eldest child going off to school is as important an event for them as it is for him.

'Charles' by Shirley Jackson

The day my son Laurie started kindergarten he renounced corduroy overalls with bibs and began wearing blue jeans with a belt; I watched him go off the first morning with the older girl next door, seeing clearly that an era of my life was ended, my sweet-voiced nursery-school tot replaced by a long-trousered, swaggering character who forgot to stop at the corner and wave good-bye to me.

He came home the same way, the front door slamming open, his cap on the floor, and the voice suddenly became raucous shouting, 'Isn't anybody here?'

At lunch he spoke insolently to his father, spilled his baby sister's milk, and remarked that his teacher said we were not to take the name of the Lord in vain.

'How was school today?' I asked, elaborately casual.

'All right,' he said.

'Did you learn anything?' his father asked.

Laurie regarded his father coldly. 'I didn't learn nothing,' he said.

'Anything,' I said. 'Didn't learn anything.'

'The teacher spanked a boy, though,' Laurie said, addressing his bread and butter. 'For being fresh,*' he added, with his mouth full.

'What did he do?' I asked. 'Who was it?'

Laurie thought. 'It was Charles,' he said. 'He was fresh. The teacher spanked him and made him stand in a corner. He was awfully fresh.'

'What did he do?' I asked again, but Laurie slid off his chair, took a cookie, and left, while his father was still saying, 'See here, young man.'

The next day Laurie remarked at lunch, as soon as he sat down, 'Well, Charles was bad again today.' He grinned enormously and said, 'Today Charles hit the teacher.'

'Good heavens,' I said, mindful of the Lord's name, 'I suppose he got spanked again?'

'He sure did,' Laurie said. 'Look up,' he said to his father.

'What?' his father said, looking up.

'Look down,' Laurie said. 'Look at my thumb. Gee, you're dumb.' He began to laugh insanely.

'Why did Charles hit the teacher?' I asked quickly.

'Because she tried to make him colour with red crayons,' Laurie said. 'Charles wanted to colour with green crayons so he hit the teacher and she spanked him and said nobody play with Charles but everybody did.'

The third day – it was Wednesday of the first week – Charles bounced a see-saw on to the head of a little girl and made her bleed, and the teacher made him stay inside all during recess. Thursday Charles had to stand in a corner during storytime because he kept pounding his feet on the floor. Friday Charles was deprived of blackboard privileges because he threw chalk.

---

*   *fresh: in this context, an American saying for a child being naughty or cheeky*

On Saturday I remarked to my husband, 'Do you think kindergarten is too unsettling for Laurie? All this toughness, and bad grammar, and this Charles boy sounds like such a bad influence.'

'It'll be all right,' my husband said reassuringly. 'Bound to be people like Charles in the world. Might as well meet them now as later.'

On Monday Laurie came home late, full of news. 'Charles,' he shouted as he came up the hill; I was waiting anxiously on the front steps. 'Charles,' Laurie yelled all the way up the hill, 'Charles was bad again.'

'Come right in,' I said, as soon as he came close enough. 'Lunch is waiting.'

'You know what Charles did?' he demanded, following me through the door. 'Charles yelled so in school they sent a boy in from first grade to tell the teacher she had to make Charles keep quiet, and so Charles had to stay after school. And so all the children stayed to watch him.'

'What did he do?' I asked.

'He just sat there,' Laurie said, climbing into his chair at the table. 'Hi, pop, y'old dust mop.'

'Charles had to stay after school today,' I told my husband. 'Everyone stayed with him.'

'What does this Charles look like?' my husband asked Laurie. 'What's his other name?'

'He's bigger than me,' Laurie said. 'And he doesn't ever wear a jacket.'

✳ STOP AND THINK ✳

At this point in the story, write a few sentences stating what you now know about Laurie; about his mother; his father; his experience at school. Quietly, speak what you have written to your partner. *Now read on …*

Monday night was the first Parent-Teacher meeting, and only the fact that the baby had a cold kept me from going; I wanted passionately to meet Charles's mother. On Tuesday Laurie remarked suddenly, 'Our teacher had a friend come to see her in school today.'

'Charles's mother?' my husband and I asked simultaneously.

'Naaah,' Laurie said scornfully. 'It was a man who came and made us do exercises, we had to touch our toes. Look.' He climbed down from his chair and squatted down and touched his toes. 'Like this,' he said. He got solemnly back into his chair and said, picking up his fork, 'Charles didn't even do exercises.'

'That's fine,' I said heartily. 'Didn't Charles want to do exercises?'

'Naaah,' Laurie said. 'Charles was so fresh to the teacher's friend he wasn't let do exercises.'

'Fresh again?' I said.

'He kicked the teacher's friend,' Laurie said. 'The teacher's friend told Charles to touch his toes like I just did and Charles kicked him.'

'What are they going to do about Charles, do you suppose?' Laurie's father asked him.

Laurie shrugged elaborately. 'Throw him out of school, I guess,' he said.

Wednesday and Thursday were routine; Charles yelled during story hour and hit a boy in the stomach and made him cry. On Friday Charles stayed after school again and so did all the other children.

With the third week of kindergarten Charles was an institution in our family; the baby was being a Charles when she cried all afternoon; Laurie did a Charles when he filled his wagon full of mud and pulled it through the kitchen; even my husband, when he caught his elbow in the telephone cord and pulled telephone, ashtray and a bowl of flowers off the table, said, after the first minute, 'Looks like Charles.'

During the third and fourth weeks it looked like a reformation in Charles; Laurie reported grimly at lunch on Thursday of the third week, 'Charles was so good today the teacher gave him an apple.'

'What?' I said, and my husband added warily, 'You mean Charles?'

'Charles,' Laurie said. 'He gave the crayons around and he picked up the books afterward and the teacher said he was her helper.'

'What happened?' I asked incredulously.

'He was her helper, that's all,' Laurie said, and shrugged.

'Can this be true, about Charles?' I asked my husband that night. 'Can something like this happen?'

'Wait and see,' my husband said cynically. 'When you've got a Charles to deal with, this may mean he's only plotting.'

He seemed to be wrong. For over a week Charles was the teacher's helper; each day he handed things out and he picked things up; no one had to stay after school.

'The PTA** meeting's next week again,' I told my husband one evening. 'I'm going to find Charles's mother there.'

'Ask her what happened to Charles,' my husband said. 'I'd like to know.'

'I'd like to know myself,' I said.

On Friday of that week things were back to normal. 'You know what Charles did today?' Laurie demanded at the lunch table, in a voice slightly awed. 'He told a little girl to say a word and she said it and the teacher washed her mouth out with soap and Charles laughed.'

'What word?' his father asked unwisely, and Laurie said, 'I'll have to whisper it to you, it's so bad.' He got down off his chair and went around to his father. His father bent his head down and Laurie whispered joyfully. His father's eyes widened.

'Did Charles tell the little girl to say that?' he asked respectfully.

** *PTA: an abbreviation, standing for Parent-Teacher Association*

'She said it twice,' Laurie said. 'Charles told her to say it twice.'

'What happened to Charles?' my husband asked. 'Nothing,' Laurie said. 'He was passing out the crayons.'

Monday morning Charles abandoned the little girl and said the evil word himself three or four times, getting his mouth washed out with soap each time. He also threw chalk.

My husband came to the door with me that evening as I set out for the PTA meeting. 'Invite her over for a cup of tea after the meeting,' he said. 'I want to get a look at her.'

'If only she's there,' I said prayerfully.

'She'll be there,' my husband said. 'I don't see how they could hold a PTA meeting without Charles's mother.'

At the meeting I sat restlessly, scanning each comfortable matronly face, trying to determine which one hid the secret of Charles. None of them looked to me haggard enough. No one stood up in the meeting and apologised for the way her son had been acting. No one mentioned Charles.

After the meeting I identified and sought out Laurie's kindergarten teacher. She had a plate with a cup of tea and a piece of chocolate cake; I had a plate with a cup of tea and a piece of marshmallow cake. We manoeuvred up to one another cautiously, and smiled.

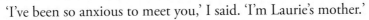

'I've been so anxious to meet you,' I said. 'I'm Laurie's mother.'

'We're all so interested in Laurie,' she said.

'Well, he certainly likes kindergarten,' I said. 'He talks about it all the time.'

'We had a little trouble adjusting, the first week or so,' she said primly, 'but now he's a fine little helper. With occasional lapses, of course.'

'Laurie usually adjusts very quickly,' I said. 'I suppose this time it's Charles's influence.'

'Charles?'

'Yes,' I said, laughing, 'you must have your hands full in that kindergarten, with Charles.'

'Charles?' she said. 'We don't have any Charles in the kindergarten.'

EXPLORE

1. Which character in this story is the narrator (the one who tells the story)?

2. What changes did the narrator notice in Laurie when he started kindergarten?

3. Why was Laurie late home from school on Monday?

4. Laurie's mother says she's worried that kindergarten is 'too unsettling' for her son. What is she worried about?

5. Why did Laurie's parents take so long to find out the truth about Charles?

6. What clues are there in the story regarding Charles's real identity?

WRITE **W8.5**

Find, remember or write a poem on the theme of parents and children.
Choose or write a poem that you can recite for a small group or for the class.

SHOW WHAT YOU KNOW

You have learned many writing and speaking skills throughout this collection. Now it's time to *Show What You Know!*

My Portfolio Task

Write a scene for a film or a play in which you show a parent (or parents) and a child (or children) in a happy, sad or dramatic situation. It can be set either now or at some time in the past.

Write **two introductory paragraphs** before your characters begin to speak.

- Paragraph 1 – Describe the **setting** (time, place, surroundings). The filmmaker or stage manager needs this information to create the place in which the scene will occur.
- Paragraph 2 – Name the **characters** and describe what they look like and what they are wearing.

Now write the **dialogue** they speak in the play or film. Remember to include **stage directions** like you saw in *Blood Brothers*.

SUCCESS CRITERIA

I must
- Name the characters in the scene
- Write a short description of the setting before I start the dialogue
- Read what I've written to check for punctuation marks (, . ! ?) or missing words
- Use a **dictionary** to check any spellings I'm not sure of

I should
- Give the actors directions about gestures and tones of voice
- List some furniture or props to be put on stage for the scene
- Give directions for what the actors should wear

I could
- Get ideas for characters from the short extracts or stories in this collection
- Add music or sound effects in the background
- Have a narrator speaking to the audience about what is going on, like in *Blood Brothers*
- Give my characters unusual names or names that say something about their personalities

Self-Assessment
Re-read what you have written and then write down two things you think you did well and one thing you could improve on.

Redrafting
Review the success criteria again to make sure you have met all the requirements. Taking into account your own self-assessment notes, now revise your scene to create a second draft. When you are happy with it, you can put it in your **portfolio**.

Reflection Question

Which moment in my scene would an audience really enjoy? For example, something a character says or does, the costume they wear or the name I gave them? Maybe a dramatic sound effect or a piece of music?

Oral Communication

Write and then speak three paragraphs for or against the following statement:

'A child born in the twenty-first century has a greater chance of happiness than a child of the past.'

Writing Tips

Each paragraph must have a **leader sentence** which makes a clear point, e.g.

'Children in past centuries might have worked on farms, in factories or down mines instead of going to school ...'

Then, in the rest of the paragraph, you have to argue your case and give evidence for the point you are making. When you have finished writing, highlight or circle your key words.

Peer Assessment

Reflect on your classmate's oral communication task and write down two things that he/she did well and one thing he/she could improve on.

SUCCESS CRITERIA

I must

- Write a clear opening sentence that says which side of the argument I am on
- Speak in a strong, clear, confident voice
- Make eye contact with listeners as I speak
- Pause at my full stops, not rushing on, but giving the listeners time to understand my points
- Rehearse on my own before I speak to an audience

I should

- Use what I know from history or from facts or stories I learned in reading this collection
- Use points I hear in the news at the moment as evidence for my arguments
- Slow down as I speak my last line

I could

- Imitate a good speaker, broadcaster, politician or public figure whose way of speaking I admire
- Vary my volume, sometimes soft, sometimes loud, to keep listeners' attention
- Use flash cards with key words so that I don't have to look down at my script to read what I wrote

Places

As I explore this collection I will learn about:

- Persuasive writing
- Product research
- Buzzwords and typography
- Apostrophes
- Speaking persuasively
- Imaginative writing
- Flyers
- Metaphor and rhyme
- Visuals
- Characterisation
- Interview skills
- Performance skills

SHOW WHAT YOU KNOW

The skills you learn in this collection will enable you to **show what you know** in your final tasks at the end of this collection.

For my portfolio task I will:
Create a print advertisement

For oral communication I will:
Record or perform an audio/visual advertisement

Learning Outcomes
OL2, OL5, OL7, R3, R8, W3, W4

Exploring the Theme – Places

When we think of 'place', the first thing we might think of is a locality that is familiar to us, whether it is home, school, county or country. Where are you at this very moment? Where will you be in three hours' time? When deciding what they're going to write about, writers often begin with setting their story in a special place. For example, it might be a lonesome story near the jagged and wild cliffs of Moher or an adventure story in the tropical growth of the Amazon. Poets may write about their beloved home or a country in conflict. Film studios spend huge amounts of money getting the right location for their blockbusters.

1. List the capital city for each of the countries below. You might need to consult an atlas or the internet to do this.

England	L _____
France	P _____
Poland	W _____
Pakistan	I _____
China	B _____
Philippines	M _____
Brazil	B _____
Romania	B _____

2. Now, can you identify some of these places made famous in books and films?

Many of the scenes from the *Jurassic Park* film series were filmed in a popular tropical island in the Pacific Ocean called H_____i.

The film and book *The Lord of the Rings* is set in the fictional land of M_____ E _____ .

Peter Pan lives in N_____d.

You would find the Simpson Family in the town of S_____.

Roald Dahl's character Charlie finds a golden ticket and gets to visit the famous C_____ F_____.

3. List your five favourite places in order of preference (your favourite being number one). Discuss your choices with your classmate, explaining why you like them. You might think about how the place made you feel, whether you associate it with a particular person, or whether you had a memorable moment there.

Advertising

to explore buzzwords and typography; practise persuasive writing

While we are usually very familiar with our homes, travel allows us to visit and explore places we have only imagined in the past. If we get the chance to holiday abroad, foreign places can make a great impression on us. The travel industry is big business, with travel companies and countries spending millions every year on promoting their services or locations.

Have you taken a trip recently? Was it local or far away? Do you know why your family decided to go to this particular location?

We will now look at how advertising works and later investigate how the travel industry uses it effectively.

Advertising is Everywhere!

Really … where? Make a list of all the different places in which you have seen advertising. Go!

Now read the following short article on advertising.

Advertising is Everywhere!

It is hard to deny the power of advertising and its presence in our society – on TV and radio, in newspapers and magazines, on billboards and website banners, on the clothes sport stars wear, on the drinks pop stars hold. Adverts are presented in all these different forms to try and persuade people that they want and have to have certain products and services, and so need to buy them.

Products and services are presented in a variety of ways – serious, aspirational, humorous, with catchy jingles – but all are designed to convince you, the consumer, that you need the product. Jingles – those short, catchy tunes designed to stick in your head – have a very prominent place in advertising, be it on radio or television. The first jingle was broadcast on radio in the United States in 1926.

Advertising is a powerful tool for businesses to attract potential customers. Companies know the power of advertising and realise the importance of getting their products and services into the public sphere. It is estimated that €500 billion is spent every year on advertising worldwide. It is also estimated that by the time a person in the United States is sixty-five years old, they will have seen approximately two million television commercials!

There are so many creative advertisements out there. Choose your current favourite advertisement and give three reasons why you think it is successful.

REMEMBER

Advertisements appeal to different groups called target audiences, p. 141.

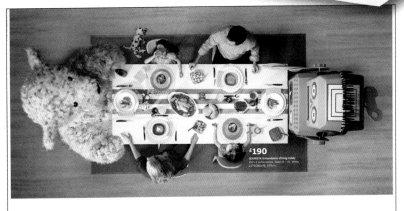

Extend your guest list

It's nice to get everyone together during party season. That's why we've designed our BJURSTA extending dining table. So no matter who turns up, the only thing you need to worry about is finding space for that extra piece of cake.

IKEA

£190

Evian, Cadburys and IKEA have released very popular advertisements over the past few years. Can you call them to mind? This shows you how effective advertising can be.

Advertisements about Place

1. **'South Africa – Inspiring New Ways'**

EXPLORE

1. TRUE OR FALSE?

Examine this print ad, advertising South Africa as a holiday destination. Your teacher will call out statements about the advert one by one. In pairs, decide if the statement is true or false. Show the teacher your answer by holding up a **TRUE** or **FALSE** sign between you.

We saw the horizon for miles and miles and had a feeling of being open and free, a feeling that we've never had before
Go to www.southafrica.net

South Africa

Inspiring new ways

Buzzword n.

Definition: a word or phrase to make the product seem attractive/desirable, e.g. ice-cream advertising might use the buzzwords 'creamy', 'smooth', 'heavenly'
Synonyms: catchwords, lingo

Statements

- The slogan of this advertisement is 'Go to www.southafrica.net'

- The logo is 'We saw the horizon for miles and miles'

- The advertisement uses repetition

- The typography doesn't change throughout the advertisement

- Examples of **BUZZWORDS** are 'open' and 'free'

- The advertisement has used a personal touch to persuade potential customers

- The target audience is young people looking for vibrant night life

- The advert uses many different visuals to advertise the country

Typography n.

Definition: the style, arrangement or appearance of printed letters on a page

REMEMBER

Slogan, p. 143.
Logo, p. 143.
Visual, p. 141.

2. Carefully read this design brief for the South African advertisement.

Design Brief for South Africa Tourist Board Advertisement

We would like to see an image(s) that shows the natural beauty and the vast landscape of South Africa. We would like to have a simple, effective slogan that people can easily and quickly read. The slogan must reflect what is happening in the image. We want a logo that shows the identity of South Africa. We don't want to see a lot of writing but we want vocabulary that reflects the idea of adventure and unlimited possibilities. This advert should be aimed at young couples who like adventure but wish to stay away from the hustle and bustle of a city.

Design brief n.

Definition: a written plan for a design project, outlining what it is hoped the finished product (advert, poster) will look like, giving the designer a clear idea of what they need to do

3. Having read the design brief, do you think the designers did a good job? In other words, did they meet the brief given to them by the South African Tourist Board?

4. Find another print advertisement and write a design brief suitable for the designer. You can use phrases or words from the sample design brief to help you.

Your class has just won a local competition. The prize is a once-in-a-lifetime trip to New York with luxury accommodation and €10,000 to spend, but alas, there are only tickets for four representatives from your class. Who will go?

Your job is to persuade a committee made up of three judges – one of whom is your teacher, the other two chosen from amongst your classmates – as to why you should be chosen. Before you speak, you must write our your presentation. You should try to have at least three strong reasons supported by evidence as to why you should go on the trip. Persuasive words and phrases (such as those below) will help you build your persuasive speech. There are speaking tips on the next page to help you give your speech and win the prize!

Personally, I feel …	I fully believe …
Absolutely	Furthermore …
In comparison to …	Definitely
It would be foolish to believe …	I strongly recommend …
It's important …	More than …
My greatest attributes/qualities are …	For example …

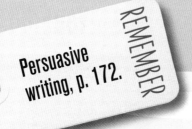

Persuasive writing, p. 172. REMEMBER

Speaking Tips

In your oral presentation, you must pay attention to the following elements:

- Address your audience: make good eye contact but don't stare them down!

- Use hand gestures to highlight your points.

- Talk about your strengths, e.g. 'I'm fun-loving but responsible'.

- Use positive language about yourself, e.g. 'I'm very pleasant and easy to travel with'.

- State what this trip would mean to you, e.g. 'Going on this trip would be the greatest moment of my life'.

You have between one and two minutes to convince the judges. You will be marked out of ten based on your powers of persuasion. The judges will then announce the winners and give oral feedback on the strengths and weaknesses of each proposal. Good luck!

Peer Assessment

Reflect on your classmate's oral communication task and write down two things that he/she did well and one thing he/she could improve on.

Imagine that Discover Ireland has sent a representative to your school looking for ideas for a new advertisement campaign. Working in pairs, you must come up with a two-minute pitch (idea) for a new video advertisement about Ireland that you will deliver to the representative.

Consider the following items in devising your pitch:

* Theme of the video
* Music
* Buzzwords
* On-screen text
* Will your advertisement tell a story?
* Will you need to think about setting?
* Will you need to use actors?

TOP TIP

Go to http://www.discoverireland.ie to see their various campaigns advertising Ireland as a holiday destination. Also look up these two advertisements, which use powerful stories to get their message across:

Duracell: Derrick Coleman commercial

Google Chrome: Dear Sophie

REMEMBER **Setting, p. 188.**

Advertisements about Place

2. 'The Lions Have Arrived'

THE LIONS
HAVE
ARRIVED.

Examine this print ad, advertising a zoo, and answer these questions.

1. Write down two words to describe your first reaction to the advertisement.

2. What is happening in the advert?

3. Who is the target audience?

4. Based on this advertisement, would you like to visit this zoo?

5. If you had to make one change to this advertisement, what would it be and why?

6. Do you think the slogan is appropriate?

1. Now that you have revised what a slogan is, study this one carefully:

No self-respecting monkey would live anywhere else but here.

Draw or design the print advertisement that you would use to accompany this slogan, which has been written to advertise another zoo. Consider the following when designing your advertisement:

→

* What is the name of my product?

* Who is my target audience?

* Will the print be light-hearted or serious?

* What image best represents this slogan?

* Will there be any other text (buzzwords, important information)?

2. Looking back on the two print advertisements you have just studied, write a paragraph on which one you think is more successful in its aims and why. You may take the following into account to help you evaluate which one is best:

* Does it have a catchy slogan?

* Are the visuals and colour attractive and interesting?

* Does it provide enough information?

* How does the typography complement the product?

* Is it memorable?

* Is it appropriate for its target audience?

* Would it convince that target audience to purchase the product?

A Travel Article

What I will learn:

how to create a flyer; to research facts about a product (place); to effectively use visuals, typography and slogans

Persuasive writing is also used by travel writers – those lucky journalists who get to travel and report back on the places they have visited. They combine facts with opinion to convince you that you must go to a particular place if you ever get the chance. Travel writers review hundreds of different locations, from the USA to Romania, from Siberia to Patagonia.

Make a quick list of some of the famous tourist attractions in the world that you would like to visit. Once you have completed your list, share these ideas with your partner. You must then come up with a combined wish list of five places that you and your partner would most like to visit.

READ This article is about an extraordinary natural occurrence that people travel great distances to see.

The Northern Lights – An Awe-Inspiring Spectacle

High above the Arctic Circle, in the cold and isolated darkness, occurs one of nature's most spectacular shows – the Northern Lights. Thousands flock each year to witness this wonder of nature, when enchanting colours are made manifest by particles from solar explosions making contact with the earth's magnetic field. This curtain of lights or swirls of rolling smoke ensures that the phenomenon, properly known as Aurora Borealis, is most certainly a sight to behold.

Known in Finnish folktales by a term literally translating as 'fire fox', lore has it that a magical beast swept his tail across the land, spraying the snow up to the sky. Many believe that, if sighted, good luck will be granted to the viewer. Most who are fortunate enough to visit will agree that merely seeing the spectacle is good fortune in itself.

The Northern Lights are visible throughout Norway, but there are particular spots which allow for the maximum opportunity to see them at their best. From the Lofoten Islands all the way to the North Cape, the skies along this geographical path enjoy more regular occurrences of the lights than the rest of the country. The best time to visit is early autumn or late winter/early spring, but these are peak times and so booking is essential.

If you are lucky enough to stay at Kakslauttanen Arctic Resort, you will enjoy a unique experience. This resort boasts an igloo village where guests can sleep under glass covering, enjoying the Aurora Borealis as they lie in their warm beds. It also includes the world's largest snow restaurant, an ice bar, an ice chapel and an ice gallery.

If you want to experience more of Norway's landscape, you can indulge in a wide range of activities such as sledding or a husky safari. You might even spot reindeer or Arctic foxes, reminding you that you are in a very special place.

EXPLORE

1. What is the proper name for the Northern Lights?

2. What legend have people told about the Northern Lights?

3. Apart from viewing the Northern Lights, what other activities can people enjoy when visiting this part of the world?

4. Would you like to visit the Northern Lights?

5. The author wishes to show the magnificence of the Northern Lights. Do you think they have done this well?

CREATE

Investigate the Northern Lights phenomenon a little more using an encyclopaedia or the internet. Then create a flyer for a tour company that will bring people to see the Northern Lights. You must include:

* An image(s) that will highlight the attraction

* A sentence that will grab people's attention

* Some basic information on pricing and times

* Contact information for the company

TOP TIP

Colour and variation in font size and style will add to the attractiveness of your flyer.

Peer Assessment

Read your classmate's work and then write down two things you think he/she did well and one thing he/she could improve on.

RESEARCH ZONE

These three words are associated with the Arctic Circle and Norway:

* Fjords

* Arctic foxes

* Lofoten Islands

RESEARCH ZONE

Create your own encyclopaedia entry for each word. To do this you must:

* Research as much information as possible on each topic

* Examine other encyclopaedia entries to discover the layout and see what type of headings are used

* In your own words, write at least two short paragraphs (between four and six sentences) on each topic, including some key facts

* Include an image and a description of the animal/place

A Short Story

What I will learn:

to use my imagination to create a short story

Whether the place we read about is being described from reality or from the author's imagination, we as the reader still have to use our imagination to picture it (especially if there are no photographs or illustrations with the text). The following story is all about a place that is very difficult to imagine – the future.

In primary school, did you have a favourite teacher? Why did you like this teacher?

Read the following story to yourself, keeping in mind a part you would like to read afterwards. When you have read the story to yourself, your teacher will ask for volunteers to read it again, with each volunteer choosing a particular part. →

Characters: The narrator, Margie, Tommy, the Inspector, Mrs Jones and the computer

Setting: Margie's bedroom

Props: An old-looking book

'The Fun They Had' by Isaac Asimov

Margie even wrote about it that night in her diary. On the page headed May 17, 2155, she wrote, 'Today Tommy found a real book!'

It was a very old book. Margie's grandfather once said that when he was a little boy his grandfather told him that there was a time when all stories were printed on paper.

They turned the pages, which were yellow and crinkly, and it was awfully funny to read words that stood still instead of moving the way they were supposed to – on a screen, you know. And then, when they turned back to the page before, it had the same words on it that it had had when they read it the first time.

'Gee,' said Tommy, 'what a waste. When you're through with the book, you just throw it away, I guess. Our television screen must have had a million books on it and it's good for plenty more. I wouldn't throw it away.'

'Same with mine,' said Margie. She was eleven and hadn't seen as many telebooks as Tommy had. He was thirteen.

She said, 'Where did you find it?'

'In my house.' He pointed without looking, because he was busy reading. 'In the attic.'

'What's it about?'

'School.'

Margie was scornful. 'School? What's there to write about school? I hate school.' Margie always hated school, but now she hated it more than ever. The mechanical teacher had been giving her test after test in geography and she had been doing worse and worse until her mother had shaken her head sorrowfully and sent for the County Inspector.

He was a round little man with a red face and a whole box of tools with dials and wires. He smiled at her and gave her an apple, then took the teacher apart. Margie had hoped he wouldn't know how to put it together again, but he knew how all right and, after an hour or so, there it was again, large and black and ugly with a big screen on which all the lessons were shown and the questions were asked. That wasn't so bad. The part she hated most was the slot where she had to put homework and test papers. She always had to write them out in a punch code they made her learn when she was six years old, and the mechanical teacher calculated the mark in no time.

The inspector had smiled after he was finished and patted her head. He said to her mother, 'It's not the little girl's fault, Mrs. Jones. I think the geography sector was geared a little too quick. Those things happen sometimes. I've slowed it up to an average ten-year level. Actually, the overall pattern of her progress is quite satisfactory.' And he patted Margie's head again.

Margie was disappointed. She had been hoping they would take the teacher away altogether. They had once taken Tommy's teacher away for nearly a month because the history sector had blanked out completely.

So she said to Tommy, 'Why would anyone write about school?'

Tommy looked at her with very superior eyes. 'Because it's not our kind of school, stupid. This is the old kind of school that they had hundreds and hundreds of years ago.' He added loftily, pronouncing the word carefully, 'Centuries ago.'

Margie was hurt. 'Well, I don't know what kind of school they had all that time ago.' She read the book over his shoulder for a while, then said, 'Anyway, they had a teacher.'

'Sure they had a teacher, but it wasn't a regular teacher. It was a man.'

'A man? How could a man be a teacher?'

'Well, he just told the boys and girls things and gave them homework and asked them questions.'

'A man isn't smart enough.'

'Sure he is. My father knows as much as my teacher.'

'He can't. A man can't know as much as a teacher.'

'He knows almost as much, I betcha.'

Margie wasn't prepared to dispute that. She said, 'I wouldn't want a strange man in my house to teach me.'

Tommy screamed with laughter, 'You don't know much, Margie. The teachers didn't live in the house. They had a special building and all the kids went there.'

'And all the kids learned the same thing?'

'Sure, if they were the same age.'

'But my mother says a teacher has to be adjusted to fit the mind of each boy and girl it teaches and that each kid has to be taught differently.'

'Just the same, they didn't do it that way then. If you don't like it, you don't have to read the book.'

'I didn't say I didn't like it,' Margie said quickly. She wanted to read about those funny schools.

They weren't even half finished when Margie's mother called, 'Margie! School!'

Margie looked up. 'Not yet, Mamma.'

'Now,' said Mrs Jones. 'And it's probably time for Tommy, too.'

Margie said to Tommy, 'Can I read the book some more with you after school?'

'Maybe,' he said, nonchalantly. He walked away whistling, the dusty old book tucked beneath his arm.

Margie went into the schoolroom. It was right next to her bedroom, and the mechanical teacher was on and waiting for her. It was always on at the same time every day except Saturday and Sunday, because her mother said little girls learned better if they learned at regular hours.

The screen was lit up, and it said: 'Today's arithmetic lesson is on the addition of proper fractions. Please insert yesterday's homework in the proper slot.'

Margie did so with a sigh. She was thinking about the old schools they had when her grandfather's grandfather was a little boy. All the kids from the whole neighbourhood came, laughing and shouting in the schoolyard, sitting together in the schoolroom, going home together at the end of the day. They learned the same things so they could help one another on the homework and talk about it.

And the teachers were people …

The mechanical teacher was flashing on the screen: 'When we add the fractions ½ and ¼ …'

Margie was thinking about how the kids must have loved school in the old days. She was thinking about the fun they had.

EXPLORE

1. Based on your reading of the text, did you like the idea of having a computer as a teacher?

2. Pick your favourite description from the story and explain why you like it.

3. List some of the differences between the 'old' school and the 'new' school.

CREATE

'The Fun They Had' is set in a futuristic place where school is no longer as we know it. Imagine you live in the future and the world is different to what you know now. Write a short story describing how things have changed. You could use https://bubbl.us/mindmap.com or www.storybird.com to help you plan your short story.

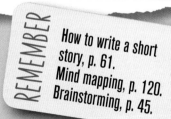

REMEMBER
How to write a short story, p. 61.
Mind mapping, p. 120.
Brainstorming, p. 45.

Poetry [1]

What I will learn:

to recognise metaphor and rhyme

While it is exciting to dive into the unknown as we did with 'The Fun They Had', sometimes the most wonderful places are in our very own area. Familiarity is a powerful tool because we feel comfortable with, and have love for, particular places.

PREPARE

2 MIN

The poem you are about to read is about a place that is very special and familiar to the poet. Before you dive in, quickly scan the poem and ask yourself these questions:

* What is the title?
* Who is the poet?
* Have you ever heard of this poet before?
* When was it written?
* Does it have stanzas?

READ

This poem is known as a sonnet. A sonnet is a fourteen-line poem of eight lines and six lines. Read the poem quietly once, and then listen to it being recited.

Composed upon Westminster Bridge, September 3, 1802

by William Wordsworth

Earth has not anything to show more fair:
Dull would he be of soul who could pass by
A sight so touching in its majesty:
This City now doth, like a garment, wear
The beauty of the morning; silent, bare,
Ships, towers, domes, theatres, and temples lie
Open unto the fields, and to the sky;
All bright and glittering in the smokeless air.

Never did sun more beautifully steep
In his first splendour, valley, rock, or hill;
Ne'er saw I, never felt, a calm so deep!
The river glideth at his own sweet will:
Dear God! the very houses seem asleep;
And all that mighty heart is lying still!

EXPLORE

1. Having read the poem yourself, and having listened to it, come up with one thing that you noticed about the poem. For example: 'I noticed that there are no stanzas in this poem.'

2. William Wordsworth wrote his poetry during the 'Romantic Period', 1790–1850. Based on your reading of the poem, the Romantic Period was a time when …

   * Everybody fell in love really easily

   * Writers showed a great appreciation of nature and its beauty

3. Where was the poet standing when he wrote this poem?

4. Make a list of the buildings that he notices.

5. At what time of the day was this poem written?

6. Wordsworth is using a metaphor in the final line when he refers to the 'mighty heart'. What do you think the 'mighty heart' is?

Metaphor n.
Definition: a figure of speech to compare two things that share a common characteristic. A stronger image than a simile that allows the reader to see or feel something in order for them to understand it better.

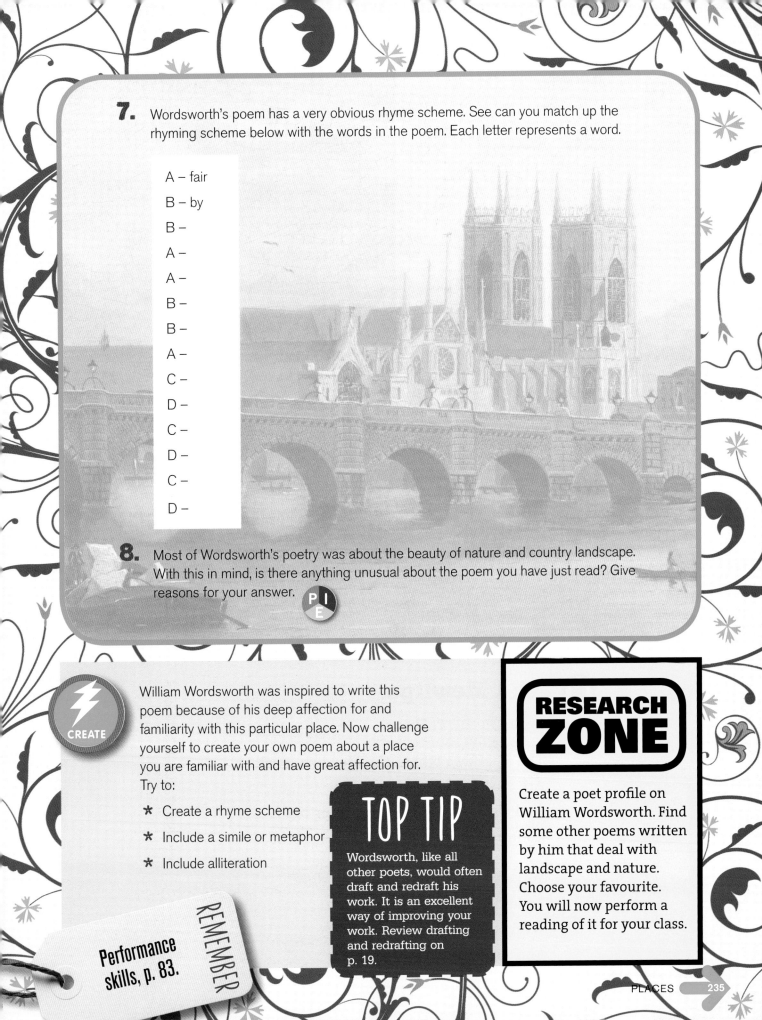

7. Wordsworth's poem has a very obvious rhyme scheme. See can you match up the rhyming scheme below with the words in the poem. Each letter represents a word.

A – fair
B – by
B –
A –
A –
B –
B –
A –
C –
D –
C –
D –
C –
D –

8. Most of Wordsworth's poetry was about the beauty of nature and country landscape. With this in mind, is there anything unusual about the poem you have just read? Give reasons for your answer. **P I E**

William Wordsworth was inspired to write this poem because of his deep affection for and familiarity with this particular place. Now challenge yourself to create your own poem about a place you are familiar with and have great affection for.
Try to:

* Create a rhyme scheme

* Include a simile or metaphor

* Include alliteration

CREATE

TOP TIP

Wordsworth, like all other poets, would often draft and redraft his work. It is an excellent way of improving your work. Review drafting and redrafting on p. 19.

RESEARCH ZONE

Create a poet profile on William Wordsworth. Find some other poems written by him that deal with landscape and nature. Choose your favourite. You will now perform a reading of it for your class.

Performance skills, p. 83. **REMEMBER**

Poetry [2]

to speak persuasively

In 'Composed upon Westminster Bridge', we saw how a poet who is familiar with a place can create beautiful images and bring that place to life for us. Wordsworth was describing something he could see, but many writers have a great talent for bringing fantastical places to life in great detail.

Working with a partner, look carefully at these adjectives and see if you can come up with places to associate with each one:

dark	**gloomy**
wet	mouldy
slimy	dank
noisy	cold
rotting	**miserable**

This poem, by the author of *The Hobbit* and *The Lord of the Rings*, brings you to a strange and dangerous place.

 The Mewlips

by J. R. R. Tolkien

The Shadows where the Mewlips dwell
Are dark and wet as ink,
And slow and softly rings their bell,
As in the slime you sink.

You sink into the slime, who dare
To knock upon their door,
While down the grinning gargoyles stare
And noisome waters pour.

Beside the rotting river-strand
The drooping willows weep,
And gloomily the gorcrows stand
Croaking in their sleep.

Over the Merlock Mountains a long and weary way,
In a mouldy valley where the trees are grey,
By a dark pool's borders without wind or tide,
Moonless and sunless, the Mewlips hide.

The cellars where the Mewlips sit
Are deep and dank and cold
With single sickly candle lit;
And there they count their gold.

Their walls are wet, their ceilings drip;
Their feet upon the floor
Go softly with a squish-flap-flip,
As they sidle to the door.

They peep out slyly; through a crack
Their feeling fingers creep,
And when they've finished, in a sack
Your bones they take to keep.

Beyond the Merlock Mountains, a long and lonely road,
Through the spider-shadows and the marsh of Tode,
And through the wood of hanging trees and gallows-weed,
You go to find the Mewlips – and the Mewlips feed.

Fill in the blanks using these words:

alliteration   **Merlock Mountains**   **atmosphere**   **moonless**   **J. R. R. Tolkien**

eerie   **slimy**   **onomatopoeia**   **ventures** (*dares to go*)   **slyly** (*secretly*)

gruesome (*horrifying*)   **lair** (*hideout*)

This poem is written by _____ who also wrote *The Hobbit* and *The Lord of the Rings.* The Mewlips are a secretive but _____ group of creatures that live far over the _____ _____. They live in a dark and _____ place where nobody really _____. The Mewlips are like something out of your nightmares because they creep _____ around and catch you by surprise. If you are unlucky enough to stumble upon their _____, they will capture you and keep your bones in a sack. They don't mind living in their _____ and sunless place of nothing because they keep their gold hidden away. The _____ created in this poem is _____ and uncomfortable. There is nothing attractive about the Mewlips' home and it seems like a terrible place to die. The poet uses lots of _____ such as 'dark and damp' and 'walls are wet' to create the mood of this frightening poem. The poet also uses _____, for example 'squish-flap-flip', to make us imagine the horrible sounds coming from the Mewlips' dwelling.

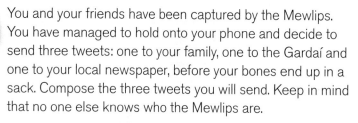

You and your friends have been captured by the Mewlips. You have managed to hold onto your phone and decide to send three tweets: one to your family, one to the Gardaí and one to your local newspaper, before your bones end up in a sack. Compose the three tweets you will send. Keep in mind that no one else knows who the Mewlips are.

REMEMBER A tweet is currently 140 characters long.

The tweets didn't help – you and your friends are still being held by the Mewlips. Work in groups of five. One person will act as the judge (the Mewlip). The other four group members need to make a one-minute improvised persuasive speech about why they should be allowed to live. The Mewlip must ensure that everyone speaks for at least thirty seconds.

RESEARCH ZONE

Look up information about the poet J. R. R. Tolkien and create a profile on him. (You might like to use prezi.com or slides.com to create your profile.)

Drama – A Play Script

What I will learn:

*to explain and give examples of characterisation;
practise my performance skills*

Private Peaceful tells the story of Private Thomas Peaceful, a World War I soldier. The book, written by Michael Morpurgo in 2003, was adapted into a play in 2004 by Simon Reade. Private Peaceful looks back on his life from the trenches of World War I. The trenches were horrific places for the soldiers who fought in World War I. They were filthy and disease-infested, while the battleground above meant certain death for many.

If you were going into battle, what two things would you miss the most?

In this extract, Private Peaceful recalls a critical moment in his life and the life of his brother, Charlie, as they face the horrors of World War I. Although both brothers have been injured, their commanding officer, Sergeant Hanley, expects them to fight on with the rest of the troops.

Extract from the stage adaptation of *Private Peaceful*

Setting: Ypres, France, 24th June 1916, No-man's-land

Tommo *(as narrator)*: I waked to the muffled sound of machine-gun fire, to the distant blast of the shells. The earth quivers and trembles about me. It must be night and I am lying wounded in no-man's-land, looking up into the black of the sky but then I try to move my head a little and the blackness begins to crumble and fall in on me, filling my mouth, my eyes, my ears. It is not the sky I am looking at, but earth. I am buried, buried alive – they must have thought I was dead and buried me. But I am not dead. I am not! My fingers scrabble, clawing frantically at the earth – and then I feel something. Another body. And I hear a voice:

Charlie: Thought we'd lost you, Tommo. The same shell that buried you killed half a dozen of the others. You were lucky. Your head looks a bit of a mess, though. Me, I can't feel my legs. I think I've lost a lot of blood.

Tommo: Where are we, Charlie?

Charlie: Middle of bloody no-man's-land, that's where, some old German dug-out.

Tommo: We'd best stay here for a while, hadn't we, Charlie?

Sergeant Hanley: Stay put? Stay put? You're worse than your brother, Peaceful. Our orders are to press home the attack and then hold our ground. Only fifty yards or so to the German trenches. On your feet, all of you. (*No one moves*)

Sergeant Hanley: What in hell's name is the matter with you lot? On your feet, damn you! On your feet!

Tommo: I think we are all thinking the same thing, Sergeant. You take us out there now and the machine guns will mow us down. Maybe we should stay here and then go back later when it gets dark? No point in going out there and getting ourselves killed for nothing, is there Sergeant?

Sergeant Hanley: Are you disobeying my order, Private Peaceful?

Tommo: No, I'm just letting you know what I think. What we all think.

Sergeant Hanley: And I'm telling you, Peaceful, that if you don't come with us when we go, it'll be a court martial for you. It'll be the firing squad. Do you hear me, Peaceful? Do you hear me?

Tommo: Yes, Sergeant. I hear you. But the thing is, Sergeant, even if I wanted to, I can't go with you because I'd have to leave Charlie behind, and I can't do that. He's wounded. I don't think he can walk, let alone run. I'm not leaving him.

Sergeant Hanley: You miserable little worm, Peaceful. I should shoot you right where you are and save the firing squad the trouble. The rest of you, on your feet. I want you men out there. It's a court martial for anyone who stays. *(Screaming)* Let's go! Let's go!

(Sound: the German machine guns open fire)

Charlie: I'm not sure I'll make it, Tommo. I want you to have this. *(Charlie takes off his watch)* It's a wonderful watch. It will never let you down. If you wind it regular, time will never stop and when you get back home, my little Tommo can have it. He's got all the time in the world.

Tommo (as narrator): Then Charlie spoke no more and I must have slept, because when I open my eyes, there was Sergeant Hanley, staring at me from under his helmet, cold hate in his eyes. We waited, but by nightfall there was no sign of the others who had joined the Sergeant on that futile charge.

EXPLORE

1. Do you think that Tommo and Charlie get on well?

2. Do you think Sergeant Hanley is a forceful character?

In groups of three, give a dramatic performance of this extract. Remember there are some stage directions that you must try and act out. Think carefully about how you will act your part.

Based on your reading and performance of *Private Peaceful*, explain how you would bring one of the characters to life (characterisation). Use the following headings to help you explain your ideas.

* Facial expressions, e.g. *frowning*

* Movements, e.g. *crawling*

* Costume, e.g. *helmet*

* Make-up, e.g. *facial hair*

* Voice and accent, e.g. *squeaky*

* Physical build, e.g. *thin*

Thought-Tracking and the Freeze-Frame Technique

Have you ever put on a brave face but really felt awful inside? Have you ever felt embarrassed but pretended you didn't care? What a character says doesn't always reflect what they are thinking. When we try to follow a character's thoughts, we are using **thought-tracking**. In drama, an actor will often speak aloud his or her thoughts, giving the audience more information, as we saw with Tommo in *Private Peaceful*.

The **freeze-frame technique** is used in drama when actors freeze at a certain point in the action to enhance a certain scene or to show an important moment.

 In groups of four, create a freeze-frame based on one of the scenes below. One person in the group will be the director. If your director taps you on the shoulder you must speak your character's thoughts aloud.

Possible scenes:

* Bank robbery

* Circus

* Fun fair

* Family trip

* School

Song Lyrics

What I will learn:

to understand and use apostrophes; to conduct an interview

In both 'The Mewlips' and *Private Peaceful*, the authors described places that trap people, with little hope of escape: the lair in the Mewlips and the trenches of World War I. The following text deals with a place no one would ever want to find themselves in.

Before you read the text, however, you will have to learn about apostrophes.

APOSTROPHES

An apostrophe, as you'll remember from primary school, is a punctuation mark used to indicate ownership and possession, or to mark the spot of missing letters.

Rules for the Use of Apostrophes

Indicating Ownership – Singular Words

When you are indicating **ownership** or **possession**, you must use **'s**.

Examples:

Harry's book (the book belonging to Harry)

The tree's branch was bending in the breeze (the branch belonging to the tree was bending in the wind)

Some people think that you can't add an apostrophe and an 's' to a noun already ending in an 's'. However, as long as it sounds natural, it's perfectly fine.

Examples:

Agnes's pencil case (the pencil case belonging to Agnes)

Charles's coffee is cold (the coffee belonging to Charles is cold)

However! If the noun that follows begins with an 's', you should just use an apostrophe.

Example:

Charles' socks were making his feet itch

Indicating Ownership – Plural Words

When you have a plural word and you want to indicate ownership, you must use an apostrophe *after the 's'* **if the possessive noun ends in 's'.**

Examples:

The teachers' staffroom is enormous (the staffroom belonging to the teachers)

The girls' lockers are closer to the social area (the lockers belonging to the girls)

However! If the plural of the noun does not end in 's' (e.g. sheep, women, men, children), you add **'s**.

Example:

The children's playground was flooded

Missing letters

Sometimes you are allowed to omit (leave out) letters, but you must use an apostrophe to replace them, and close up the space either side of the missing letter(s).

Examples:

I'm (I am)

Don't (Do not)

We weren't (We were not)

An Important Exception to the Rule!

It's and Its

We encounter the words 'it's' and 'its' in our speaking and writing, but many people often don't know which is the right one to use when writing. There is **only one way** to use them:

> *It's (with an apostrophe) is the shortened form of 'it is'.*
>
> *Its (without the apostrophe) indicates possession.*

Usually you add an apostrophe to indicate possession, **but this is not the case *with 'its'*.** Do not use an apostrophe with the word 'its' when it relates to possession:

The dog stayed in its kennel all night (The dog stayed in the kennel belonging to it all night)

The chair is not in its proper position (The chair is not in the proper position belonging to it)

Only use an apostrophe when you are writing the shortened form of 'it is' – 'it's':

It's a fine day today (It is a fine day today)

TOP TIP

To know exactly whether you should use 'it's' or 'its' in your writing, try saying the sentence in your head using 'it is'. If it makes sense, you use 'it's'; otherwise you use 'its':

'The dog stayed in it's kennel all night' The dog stayed in it is kennel all night

'The dog stayed in its kennel all night.'

  In the song lyrics on the next page, certain words are missing. These words all use an apostrophe. Listen to this song and while you do, write down the missing words, making sure to place the apostrophe in the correct position.

Folsom Prison Blues

by Johnny Cash

I hear the train a comin'
_____ rollin' _____ the bend,
And I _____ seen the sunshine
Since, I _____ know when
I'm stuck in Folsom Prison
And time keeps _____ on
But that train keeps a-_____
On down to San Antone

When I was just a baby
My Mama told me, 'Son
Always be a good boy
_____ ever play with guns,'
But I shot a man in Reno
Just to watch him die
When I hear that whistle _____
I hang my head and cry

I bet _____ rich folks _____
In a fancy dining car
_____ probably drinkin' coffee
And smokin' big cigars
Well I know I had it _____
I know I can't be free
But those people keep a-_____
And that's what tortures me

Well, if they freed me from this prison
If that railroad train was mine
I bet _____ move it on a little
Farther down the line
Far from Folsom Prison
_____ where I want to stay
And I'd let that lonesome whistle
Blow my blues away

True or False

TRUE OR FALSE?

Your teacher will call out these statements one by one. In pairs, decide if the statement is true or false. Show the teacher your answer by holding up a **TRUE** or **FALSE** sign between you.

Statements

- This song features some elements of rhyme.
- The song is written in the first-person narrative.
- It describes a pleasant and safe place.
- The narrator is happy where he is.
- The narrator has killed a person.
- The narrator regrets his past actions.
- The narrator comes from a wealthy background.
- The train reminds the narrator of his freedom.

CREATE

Johnny Cash performed this song in Folsom Prison for the inmates. Write an informal letter to Johnny Cash where you talk about another place that restricts the freedom of people; for example, in *Private Peaceful*, Tommy's freedom is restricted because of war and his duty to fight.

REMEMBER

How to write an informal letter, p. 10.

SPEAK

W9.9

You have been given the opportunity to interview a prison inmate. Work in pairs and decide who will be the interviewer and the interviewee (person being interviewed).

Then, with your partner, create a set of questions that you would ask the inmate and imagine what their answers might be. What do you imagine their life in prison is like? How did they end up in prison? Have they a chance of being released?

Pay attention to the types of questions you decide to ask and answer. They will either be open questions (a question which allows for more information) or closed questions (questions that only require one-word answers). For example: 'What is your name?' (closed); 'What is your typical day like?' (open).

SHOW WHAT YOU KNOW

You have learned many writing and speaking skills throughout this collection. Now it's time to *Show What You Know!*

My Portfolio Task

Imagine you work for an advertisement agency and you have been asked to create an advertisement for one of the following places:

- A local place of historical significance, e.g. Blarney Castle
- A city, e.g. Paris
- An exotic location, e.g. Antarctica
- A new theme park, e.g. Harry Potter Land
- A trip to an unusual place, e.g. the moon

You must create a print advertisement for one of these places. You will be expected to use advertising techniques effectively and respond imaginatively to the task in your design.

SUCCESS CRITERIA

Self-Assessment

Re-read what you have written and then note two things you think you did well and one thing that could be improved on.

Redrafting

Reviewing the success criteria again to make sure you have met all the requirements, and taking into account your own self-assessment notes, you can now revise your advertisement to create a second draft. When you are happy with it, you can put it in your **portfolio**.

I could

- Link the copy with the visuals

I should

- Create a logo
- Experiment with typography
- Be original in my design
- Research facts about the product

I must

- Highlight the placename
- Create a catchy slogan
- Create copy (text) that provides details of the place
- Use buzzwords
- Include visuals
- Read what I've written to check for punctuation marks (, . ! ?) or missing words
- Use a **dictionary** to check any spellings I'm not sure of

Oral Communication

You must record or perform a radio or television advertisement for the place you chose in your portfolio task. You will be expected to use advertising techniques effectively and respond imaginatively to the task in your presentation.

SUCCESS CRITERIA

Peer Assessment

Reflect on your classmate's work and then write down two things you think you/they did well and one thing you/they could improve on.

Reflection Question

Discuss why a person would continue to listen/watch your advertisement if it was on a major television/radio station.

I must

- Highlight the placename
- Create a catchy slogan
- Provide important details about the place
- Create effective narration/dialogue
- Speak clearly and confidently

I could

- Create a logo (television only)
- Experiment with camera shots (television only)

I should

- Include music and/or sound effects
- Interview people to promote the place
- Edit my piece effectively
- Create a series of visuals (television only)
- Use persuasive language
- Research facts about the place

Acknowledgments

Yu Ming is Anim Dom, directed by Daniel O'Hara; 'Clonehenge' from RTÉ Radio 1's *Documentary on One*; 'Great White Shark Attack' from BBC's *Planet Earth*; 'Gale Force Winds Sweep Scotland' from BBC Scotland; 'A New Planet' from NASA; AIB/GAA All-Ireland Club Championships Advertisement, Rothco Agency; *Rockmount*, directed by Dave Tynan; 'Lumps of Coal' from RTÉ Radio 1's *Documentary on One*; 'Mary's Retelling of the Story of John the Baptist' from *Give Up Yer Aul Sins*, directed by Cathal Gaffney; *Life is Beautiful*, directed by Roberto Benigni; IKEA 'Playin with my Friends'. 'The New Boy' by John Walsh, copyright © John Walsh, 2016. Extract from the novel *See If I Care* by Judi Curtin and Roisin Meaney, published by The O'Brien Press Ltd, Dublin, copyright © Judi Curtin and Roisin Meaney, used with permission. 'whatspunctuation' copyright © John Foster, from *The Poetry Chest* (Oxford University Press, 2007), used with permission. 'Suddenly Autumn' copyright © Ulick O'Connor, from *The Kiss: New and Selected Poems and Translations* (Salmon Poetry, 2008), used with permission. 'Blackberry-Picking' by Seamus Heaney, from *Opened Ground* (Faber and Faber, 1998), used with permission. Samuel Beckett's letter to John Hughes, used by permission of The Little Museum of Dublin. Extract from *Losing My Virginity* by Richard Branson, published by Virgin Books, reprinted by permission of The Random House Group Limited. 'The Visitor' by Ian Serraillier © Estate of Ian Serraillier, used with permission. Extracts from *The Thornthwaite Inheritance* © Gareth P. Jones 2009, Bloomsbury Publishing Plc., used with permission. Extract from *The Birds* by Daphne Du Maurier © 1952. 'When Katie's Arm Went Up We All Went Ballistic' by Brian Byrne, used with permission. 'Happy Birthday, Squirt', copyright © Deirdre Murphy and Tomás Seale, 2016. 'Danitra's Family Reunion' by Nikki Grimes, from *Danitra Brown Leaves Town*, copyright © Nikki Grimes, 2002. 'Blessing' by Imtiaz Dharker, from *Postcards from god* (Bloodaxe Books, 1997), used with permission. 'You Tell Me' by Michael Rosen from *You Tell Me* (© Michael Rosen and Roger McGough, 1979), printed by permission of United Artists Agents (www.unitedagents.co.uk) on behalf of the Author. Extracts from *The Glass Castle* copyright © Jeannette Walls, 2005, published by Virago, an imprint of Little, Brown Book Group, used with permission. 'f for fox' copyright © Carol Ann Duffy, reproduced by permission of the author c/o Rogers, Coleridge & White Ltd., 20 Powis Mews, London W11 1JN. 'She – is like a bubble' by Elaine George, copyright © Elaine George, 2016. 'Going Steady' by Ian Serraillier © Estate of Ian Serraillier, used with permission. 'A Crow and a Scarecrow' copyright © Carol Ann Duffy, reproduced by permission of the author c/o Rogers, Coleridge & White Ltd., 20 Powis Mews, London W11 1JN. 'Paul the Conkerer' copyright © Deirdre Murphy and Tomás Seale, 2016. *Romeo and Juliet* modern English translation copyright © Mary Ellen Snodgrass (Scribner, 2006). 'The White Wolfhound' from *Best-Loved Irish Legends* by Eithne Massey, published by The O'Brien Press Ltd, Dublin, copyright © Eithne Massey. 'The Hitch-hiker' © copyright Roald Dahl, from *The Wonderful Story of Henry Sugar and Six More*, published by Jonathan Cape Ltd & Penguin Books Ltd, used with permission. Extract from *Blood Brothers* by Willy Russell, used with permission of Negus-Fancey Agents Ltd, on behalf of the Author. 'Charles' by Shirley Jackson, used with permission of the Jackson Estate. 'The Fun They Had' copyright © Isaac Asimov from *The Best of Isaac Asimov* (Doubleday, 1974). 'The Mewlips' by J. R. R. Tolkien. Reprinted by permission of HarperCollins Publishers Ltd ©The Tolkien Estate Limited, 1962. Extract from the stage adaptation of *Private Peaceful*, by Michael Morpurgo (stage adaptation by Simon Reade) copyright © Simon Reade. 'Folsom Prison Blues' words and music by JOHN R. CASH © 1955 HI-LO MUSIC, INC. (BMI) Copyright Renewed 1984 and assigned to HOUSE OF CASH, INC. (BMI) (Administered by BUG MUSIC) in the USA. All Rights outside the USA Administered by UNICHAPPELL MUSIC INC. All Rights Reserved. Used by Permission of Carlin Music Corp., London, NW1 8BD. 'Fire and Ice' by Robert Frost from *The Poetry of Robert Frost*, edited by Edward Connery Lathem. Copyright © 1969, the estate of Robert Frost/Random House/Jonathan Cape.

For permission to reproduce photographs, the authors and publisher gratefully acknowledge the following:

© Advertising Archive: 141TR, 221TL, 221CL, 221TR, 221B; AIB / ROTHCO / Mount Leinster Rangers: 143T; © Alamy: 69BL, 71, 82CR, 87T, 88, 94, 104TR, 104TL, 108BL, 110, 132L, 132R, 133BL, 133TR, 133TC, 133BC, 133BR, 145T, 153BR, 154TC, 153BR, 163TR, 167TR, 171T, 173BC, 173BR, 174TR, 188, 195TL, 195TC, 195TR, 197CL, 197BR, 198TR, 198CL, 198BL, 203, 206, 228, 238, 240, 241; © AMVBBDO; Illustrator: Greg Abbott, Creatives: Diccon Driver & Alan Wilson, Photographer: Lydia Whitmore: 141BR; © BLACK / TED2013: 152T; © Bloomsbury: 62T; © Brown Bag Films: 190; © Colin Willoughby / ArenaPAL / Topfoto: 204; © Corbis: 91CTL; © Dough Productions: 23T; © Facebook : 144C; © Getty Images: 36, 37TR, 53T, 56, 75TL, 75BL, 82BL, 82TR, 82CL, 91T, 91CL, 97BL, 108BR, 121B, 133TR, 163BL, 165TL, 173BL, 174TL, 174TC; © Gill Books: 112; © Inpho: 78, 107B, 108T, 108CL; © Instagram: 144TL; © IRFU: 144CR; © Linda Mc Nulty: 46; Little Museum of Dublin: 37L; © Love Agency: 141BL; © Mary Evans Picture Library: 210L, 210R; © MDV: 154B; © Microsoft: 144TC; © Miramax, LLC / Visual Icon: 202; © NASA Ames / SETI Institute / JPL-Caltech: 105; © Nike: 144CL; © The O'Brien Press Ltd.: cover design and illustration by Mandy Norman: 13TR, illustration by Lisa Jackson: 169T; © Penguin Ireland: 144BC; © Photocall Ireland: 82BR; © Picture-Desk / Kobal: 156T; © Press Association: 247T; © The Random House Group Ltd.: 41; © Rex Shutterstock: 108CR, 109, 111, 197TR; © Richard Svensson: 236; © Spotify: 144TR; © Twitter: 44, 80, 81, 144BR; © UK Government Art Collection: 233; Wikipedia: 229; © Zoological Society of San Diego: 225.

Additional images supplied by iStock and Shutterstock.

The authors and publisher have made every effort to trace all copyright holders, but if any have been inadvertently overlooked we would be pleased to make the necessary arrangement at the first opportunity.